The Island Pilgrimage ·

The Island Pilgrimage

Fay Sampson

ROBERT HALE · LONDON

ISBN 0 7090 7660 6

Robert Hale Limited
Clerkenwell House
Clerkenwell Green
London EC1R 0HT

2 4 6 8 10 9 7 5 3 1

Typeset in 10¾/14 Souvenir
Derek Doyle & Associates, Liverpool.
Printed in Great Britain by
St Edmundsbury Press, Bury St Edmunds, Suffolk.
Bound by Woolnough Bookbinding Limited.

AUTHOR'S NOTE

All the characters in this story are fictitious. So is the Fellowship of Columba. Hy was the ancient Celtic name for Iona in Columba's time. I have used these names to emphasize the distinction between my fiction and present-day reality. There is a real Iona Community, for which I have the warmest admiration. No one portrayed in this book is based on any member of their staff, past or present.

1

The doorbell pealed. Its travesty of monastery bells summoned her mind back from the Dark Ages. She did a time-check on the computer screen, and annoyance was converted into a slow warm smile: 15.55. No one else knew her well enough, or was so thoughtful of her needs, to time his visit with such precision, on Wednesday afternoon when she worked at home, and just when he knew she would have surfaced into the present anyway and put the kettle on.

Margaret hesitated a moment, torn between the prudent need to save her afternoon's work and eagerness to run downstairs. She clicked the 'Save' icon and released herself from her desk.

Frosted glass fogged his face. But the outline was clear enough. That ridiculous blue knitted bobble-cap, which made him look like a rather-too-tall garden gnome. It brought an exasperated smile to Margaret's face. When she opened the door, he was rubbing his gloved hands together against the chill of the February afternoon, his feet, below the bicycle clips, doing a little dance on the porch that was also joy.

He came over the threshold quickly, sure of his welcome. Swift too was his kiss on her cheek, but strong. Margaret was not quite sure about this current effusiveness of Christian love, the hugs and kisses. It had not been part of her chapel background. Had it been Brian's? He was only a little younger than herself. She would have liked to think this was a mark of his special friendship with her, but he kissed all his congregation. At least, the women. Some Methodist men might hug each other, a little awkwardly, but they did not yet kiss.

'Would you like tea?'

'That's what I came for.' The little-boy grin teased her.

She knew it was not. He would have been sipping tea all afternoon on a round of calls. Bright old ladies in retirement homes. Gaunt convalescents, moved out of hospital beds two days after surgery. Harassed young mothers, trying to talk over the insistent attention-seeking of their children and the television cartoon they dared not turn off.

It was not tea Brian wanted, but the peace of the cushioned settee in front of the French windows, the last gleam of winter light on the still pond, their shared comfortable silences.

He stirred his cup. He was the only friend she knew who still took sugar.

'Would you like to come to Hy?'

His eyes danced. He knew he had caught her off-guard and he enjoyed that. The directness of his blue-grey eyes made it seem like an invitation just for her. Of course, it could not be. Brian was a minister. It was part of his professional skill to make everyone he talked to feel uniquely loved and valued.

At least . . . the shrewder part of her brain reminded her that he did not succeed with everyone. Rather too often, she had to mollify the property stewards when the youth club had scarred the walls of the church hall or Maurice had to ring the manse to remind Brian he should be with them chairing a finance meeting.

'Why?' she asked, playing for time.

He set down his cup, rattling on the coffee table, the better to smack his hand on his knee in exasperation.

'Why? That's a *sensible* question, Margaret.' He made it sound like an accusation. 'You're supposed to say, "Fantastic! I've always wanted to go! When can we start?" We're writing a musical about Saint Columba. We *need* to be on Hy. It's his holy island.'

'*You're* writing a musical about Columba. I'm only your historical adviser. And I *am* a sensible person.'

'Are you, Margaret?' He leaned back in the cushions and watched her, with laughing eyes.

'When?' she said. 'And who else with?'

'All of us. The whole caboodle. Kids, musicians, the club leaders. Anybody who's involved in *The Exile*. This could change their whole lives, working on the island together, planning it there, where it happened.'

'But we're staging it in May!' Margaret laughed too, shaking her head. 'You can't possibly plan a trip like that in just three months. You wouldn't get a booking on Hy in the first place. There's only limited accommodation. I'm sure you need to book a year or more in advance.'

'The third week in April.' The grin was wider, prouder. 'They've got a cancellation. I've made a provisional booking on the phone. They'll hold it for a week.'

'A week! And who's going to plan it, cost it, get all the details typed and duplicated, circulated to everyone you want to invite and get replies back? . . . Oh, no. No! You're not seriously asking . . .'

The laughter was still in his eyes, but steadier now, willing her.

'Oh, come on, Margaret. You're not *that* sensible, are you? You couldn't be a little mad, for Columba?'

'For you, you mean.' She couldn't help being cross with him. She knew she was being manipulated. But she was cross with herself, too. She wanted to please him, to see the delight flash across his face, more perhaps than a middle-aged married woman should. The rational side of her brain told her Brian traded on his charm. That did not make his charm less powerful.

They got busy with paper and plans. The long train journey north to Glasgow, then through the Highlands. The ferry to Oban, the bus across Mull.

'Then you stand on the beach and shout for the monks to row over and fetch you,' he teased her.

'There aren't any monks there now. There'll be another ferry.'

She took the leaflet he gave her and went away to make phone calls and establish prices, with group discounts. She came back with her calculator and added the accommodation costs.

'Macbeth Lodge,' he explained. 'Bunk beds. Everybody helps in the kitchen and cleans the loos.'

'Very appropriate. I'm sure Columba's monks had to – well, the kitchen anyway. The loo was probably a plank over a hole. If I have the letters duplicated by tomorrow, how do you propose to deliver them?'

'It'll be about fifty, with all the adults involved. But some are from the same family. I'll do half.'

'No,' she said, catching his hopeful look. 'You know I don't like town driving. And I have a mountain of essays to mark.'

'I suppose I could ask Don,' he said, visibly disappointed that he must now try his persuasion on the youth club leader.

'And I am *not* taking responsibility for collecting the deposits,' she said, gaining courage from her own resolution.

Brian's face fell further. 'Don'll do it,' he said optimistically. 'He's a good man.'

His cup was still three-quarters full of tea, gone cold. She knew he had not wanted it. It was a convention of politeness, hostess and guest, the church member and the minister. An excuse for something more real, the communication between them, the help only she could offer him.

But today had been different, sweeping aside her expectations. Was it inappropriate to raise it now?

'Did you bring any poems?'

'I thought you'd never ask.' His smile was affectionate now, genuinely grateful.

He reached into the inner pocket of his jacket and drew out a folded sheaf of paper. Shyer now, more vulnerable.

'It's some I wrote in Wales, when Ruth and I went walking there, after Christmas. Pennant Melangell. Have you ever been there? You must go. It's holy ground. Like Hy. What the Celts call "a thin place". Where the screen between the physical and the spiritual world is only a curtain of gossamer, and you can easily step from one into the other.'

'Delightful, and dangerous. I know about Celtic fairylands.'

'I'm not talking about fairyland. This is reality.'

He laid the folded papers on the coffee table, looked at his watch and stood up.

'I'll see Don tonight, after he gets in from work.'

Margaret checked the clock on the mantelpiece. Half-past four. Astonishing that they had achieved so much this quickly. Yet she felt a sharp disappointment that Brian would not, after all, stay to hear her read his poetry aloud, tasting the newness of his words and rhythms on her lips, then read it back to her with the poet's own conviction, before they settled down for a critical discussion. It was a special, private understanding between them, which had neither the public responsibility of their church roles nor the physical intimacy of a man with a woman. The meeting of two minds that delighted in the same things.

But the half-hour was up. Brian always jumped to his feet with the same decisive finality. Did they teach all students in ministerial training colleges to do this, to ration their pastoral time, or to inhibit the relationship which might develop if someone licensed to talk of the deepest personal things lingered too long alone with a member of the opposite sex?

She knew the rules. She would not detain him.

In the hall he kissed her suddenly, surprisingly, on the mouth. Swift, but warm, like everything about him. Then he was gone.

She closed the door behind him, and found herself blushing and confused, like a young girl. He had never done that before. Was that a reward for her help today? A compensation for the pleasure of poetry lost?

2

'You've got to be joking. An uninhabited island? In *Scotland*?'
'It's not uninhabited. There's a village, with shops and fishing boats and a hotel. It's not just the Fellowship of Columba at the monastery.'

'Mum, do I look the fisherman type to you?'

Margaret had to admit that Laurie did not. She eyed her youngest child with an increasing sense of disbelief. He was leaning his dark head over the breakfast table with the early-morning weariness of one for whom life begins when night falls. The red school tie was askew, not, she knew, from carelessness, but deliberately calculated to reveal that the top shirt-button was unfastened. The white shirt itself, which she had conscientiously ironed, had wilted languorously on contact with his body. Laurie and his friends could make even the correct school uniform look like a gesture of rebellion.

'The others will be going. Jon and Zak and Ben.' She didn't know that yet. She should be crossing her fingers.

'Unh, unh. Not me.'

'But we need the band. You could have a whole week playing your drums.'

'What did you tell us yesterday? Two trains, two boats and a bus ride across Mull? With a full drum-kit? Get real, Mum.'

'You don't want to let Brian down, do you? He was thrilled to bits when you said you'd play. He says there's no one else to touch you on the drums.'

She was pushing her luck. She knew she should stop. It was

amazing enough that Laurie was still playing for a church youth group at seventeen. It had nothing to do with Maurice and her, she knew that, and probably not love for God, either. It was not only middle-aged history lecturers Brian could charm.

'Yeah, well. Brian's a good laugh. His music's not bad, either – for a Methodist minister.'

'Then you'll come?'

'Unh, unh.'

She had reached the end of the road. Every push she made would strengthen his resistance. She was aware of the danger, but her logical mind hated to admit that emotions could not be changed by reasoned argument.

Maurice spoke apologetically into the silence of defeat, as though Laurie had left open a convenient door for his father.

'You'll have to count me out too, I'm afraid. Shame. I've always fancied a run on that Highland Railway. But you know what it's like with admin. There's always twice the mountain of work on my desk when we open the office again after Easter. I can't take another week off, especially at such short notice.'

'Three months.'

'In the finance department, we work to a much longer time-schedule than that. Brian's a lovely chap, but I'm afraid he wouldn't last five minutes in the real world.'

'He's creative. You have to make allowances.'

She wanted to say, 'He *does* make things happen in the real world. Look what he's doing with kids like Laurie.' But she could not argue this in front of their son.

She watched the first sunbeams back-light the golden catkins beyond the garden pond. An unexpected sense of peace and pleasure dawned slowly over her. It caught her by surprise as she realized what their refusal meant. She was being offered a week of freedom, a time when she would be herself. Not Laurie's mother, not Maurice's wife. Just Margaret, on an island she had longed to see, working on a story she loved, with someone whose company she enjoyed.

'You don't need to go, do you?'

13

Maurice's question startled her. She had not for a moment considered that she might stay behind with them.

'But Brian's relying on me!' She snatched at a virtuous form of words. The shock of protest she felt had been for herself, not for Brian. She had not realized just how much she wanted this week, until she saw herself in danger of losing it.

'You're only his historical consultant. The script's all written now, isn't it?'

That was the convenient fiction. Only Margaret and Brian knew how much more it was than that, how much he still depended on her. He was poet, dramatist, composer; she was his sounding-board, scene by scene, and line by line. She was by nature an editor, not a creator. She could never have written those singing lines, called up those images. But she could put her finger unerringly on the word that rang false, on the reason a scene failed to work its intended magic. Yet it was Brian, not she, who could find a way to write it better. That was the respect, the trust between them, a private understanding. They would be working together right up to the dress rehearsal.

History was safer with Maurice. 'That's the point. Brian wants me to do an input on the background each day. You know, bringing the history to life: Columba and Hy and the Celtic Church and the Druids. All the things *The Exile* is about. It's going to make such a difference to the kids. Being *there*. Living it.'

'Well, I suppose I can't stop you, if you're that keen.'

An expression of alarm was growing on Laurie's face. He mauled the cornflake packet nervously as he looked from one to the other.

'You're leaving me with *him*?'

'It's your decision,' she said, with the crisply heartless tone she should have adopted from the beginning. 'You didn't want to come. And I offered to pay.'

'Yeah, but . . . Should have known you wouldn't trust me in the house on my own.'

'Could we?' asked Maurice. 'Trust you not to invite your friends in and trash the place?'

Laurie looked accusingly at his mother. 'Are you sure Zak's going?'

14

'No. They only delivered the letters last night.' She found herself treacherously wishing he would not change his mind now. She felt guilty that she did not enjoy the company of her youngest child, as she had that of Ros and Jake when they were at home. He sometimes seemed to her like an alien from another planet.

And Maurice? Was it safe to examine the lift in her spirits when she found he was staying at home? There was surely nothing uneasy in their relationship. They were long used to each other. They slept side by side in the double bed. They kissed dutifully when they met after work. Occasionally, rather briefly, they had sex. She had been caught unawares by the surge of pleasure when she realized that on Hy she could be just herself. Just Margaret. Like a pruning of overhead branches, which will let the plant beneath lift its head to receive the sun and rain.

And the wind? Hy lay in the track of the gales. What would she be exposed to there, without them both?

So Columba had made himself vulnerable, a disgraced abbot, leaving his beloved Ireland, with the guilt of that terrible battle and the thousands slain. Landing almost alone on that Hebridean island. Just a handful of companions and his painful self-knowledge.

This is ridiculous, she told herself. For you, Hy is just a holiday. All right, a working holiday. You'll share responsibility for the teenagers. Very well, you may call it a pilgrimage.

But Celtic pilgrimage is unlike any other sort. You do not follow the steps worn by thousands of other feet. You do not go to visit the past at some well-loved famous site. You do not return home.

The pilgrimage of the Celts is a one-way voyage into the unknown. In the legends of their saints, you may launch out on a leaf or a millstone. You may have a sail, but no oar. You must trust to the wind of God to blow you where it will. And there, in the place of the stranger, you serve until you die. The end of your pilgrimage is the place of your grave and your resurrection.

This is all nonsense, she scolded herself. There's no analogy. Of course I'm coming back. I rang the train company myself to negotiate a discount for our return tickets.

15

3

Noise assaulted her. She censored the word 'noise' and replaced it with 'music'. But she was not convinced. It seemed impossible to use the same word for this and Mozart. Margaret's objective, academic mind stood back and accused her emotions of prejudice. Yet she still felt as though someone had slipped a drug into the thin orange squash she was sipping from a plastic beaker. The room rocked.

The kids were rocking with it. The round tight bottoms of the girls gyrated. The locks of the boys' hair jumped on their foreheads. Her son was one of them. Laurie was bent forward over his drums with a zest that made him a different animal from the one who slouched over the breakfast table at home. His eyes were intent on Brian, following his beat, trusting him.

It was a miracle, the truthful part of Margaret conceded. It was a marvel to her how a man who wrote poems so shy and sensitive he dared show them to no one but her could draw a generation so different under the spell of his music, his drama.

Yes, Brian really did call this music. She had to come to terms with the fact that he genuinely liked it. How else could he write it and convince the kids?

'How can you stand this every week?' she almost shouted to Ruth beside her. 'I feel as if someone's pounding on my head.'

'You get used to it,' Ruth mouthed back. 'It's just part of the job.' The number ended and the taut, concentrated dancers swayed and relaxed into self-conscious teenagers. Ruth's voice dropped to normal 'Your Laurie's going at it like a pile-driver tonight . . . Great shoes, Annie! Have you taken out an insurance policy, in case you fall off them?'

The girl passing with a tray of drinks giggled and twitched the beaded twists of her black hair. 'No, but they just lost me a date, didn't they? Jon says he's not going out with me if I wear them, because they make me taller than him.'

'Have you noticed,' said Margaret, watching Annie clunk her way up on to the stage, 'that girl's got a profile like Nefertiti? That wonderful backward slope from nose to forehead.'

'You should tell her. It might make her day.'

'I don't imagine she's heard of Nefertiti.'

Ruth swung slowly round to level her cool grey-blue eyes at Margaret. 'That's remarkably snobbish. Why shouldn't she have heard about the most beautiful queen in Ancient Egypt? How much do you know about Annie?'

'Nothing,' admitted Margaret. 'Except that she's endangering a very pretty pair of ankles with those platform soles.'

She sipped at the orange squash to hide her face. She often managed to feel guilty, faced with Ruth. There were many reasons to be. The combined income Margaret and Maurice enjoyed as university staff did not amount to a fortune, but must far outweigh a Methodist minister's stipend. It was for the church of which Margaret was a member that Brian and Ruth accepted this financial sacrifice.

Margaret had children, even if the last of them, clowning now on the stage with Zak and Jon, was almost beyond her comprehension. Ruth had none, and the round, stolid face that stared at Margaret in accusation, lit up with ready laughter for other people's children, from the toddler crying for its mother in the crèche on Sunday morning, to the elegant Annie at the Friday club.

Most problematic of all, of course: Ruth was Brian's wife.

With a twang of warning, Margaret pulled up short at the thought, as though she had tried to go beyond what a tether of circumspection would allow. She was just a friend of Brian's, a supportive member of his congregation. She was only here to help him make this musical happen. Why should there be anything about their relationship to make her feel uneasy in the presence of Ruth?

17

The poetry? Brian showed his poems to Ruth, too. Some were about her. Love for his childhood sweetheart, his life's companion, sang in their lines. Ruth was part of the woven fabric of his life. But it was Margaret's judgement he trusted. It was with her, not Ruth, that he wanted to discuss them, not merely metre and metaphor, but drawing aside for her the curtain to the moment of inspiration, the experience that mattered to him so much that he could not keep silent, but must strive for the perfect distillation of words to express it. She could help him.

It was a fragile, private thing, those Wednesday afternoons. Asexual, Margaret was confident about that. Delightful, yet in a sublimated way, and only metaphorically as a lover might delight in a tryst with her beloved. She stopped herself in the act of comparing the mystical language Mother Julian of Norwich had used about her beloved, Christ.

What is he indeed that is maker and lover and keeper? I cannot find words to tell. For until I am one with him I can never have true rest nor peace. I can never know it until I am held so close to him that there is nothing between us.

That *was* erotic, but it stood for something else, since human experience can supply no higher language than this for religious ecstasy.

Or was the boundary between the religious experience and the sexual only in the mind? Could the body know the difference?

Brian is not Christ, she scolded herself. This is not a religious experience we are talking about, just a meeting of minds for which religion is a field of delight. Over a cup of tea.

The beat began again. To her relief, the number they were rehearsing now was more lyrical. Columba, exiled on Hy, was yearning for the lost shores of Erin. Soon, thought Margaret, unconsciously swaying to Brian's music like the teenage girls, I shall be there, on that beach on Hy where Columba landed. I shall see the western sea, as he did, search the horizon and find no mountains of home, only the limitless horizon and the gull's wail.

18

4

Margaret watched Faith across the dining-room table. A glimmer of the paper-clipped chapters of the student's dissertation was reflected faintly white in the glossy oak. Margaret suppressed a sigh. They were so painstakingly typed. It seemed a cruel severity to ring grammatical mistakes or make marginal suggestions about more felicitous English. But it was what she had volunteered to do. This was what Faith wanted of her. English was, after all, her third language.

Margaret tried to imagine herself writing a master's dissertation in Latin. Her imagination quailed. Yet generations like Faith had made such a step from their vernacular into the lingua franca of current scholarship. Columba, in his time, had been one of them. They called him Crimthann, the Fox, in Irish; Columba, the Dove, in Latin. Could the switch of culture change your personality so much?

Again and again, she had tried to persuade Faith to word-process her work on a library computer, explaining how much easier it would be to make changes, to avoid retyping whole chapters. But Faith clung proudly to the electronic typewriter her husband had given her as a leaving present when she boarded the plane from Nigeria. There was a prim obstinacy in the way she folded her hands in her lap and lowered her eyes as she said, 'Thank you, madam. My typewriter is very good. Perhaps I will use the computer when my dissertation can be printed.'

'How are the children? Have you had a letter lately?'

Faith's head went up. Her doe-dark eyes shone. Suddenly she was radiant. 'Simeon has drawn me a picture of his baby sister. And my husband says she is starting to walk. Look.'

She drew from her large shiny black handbag a folded square of grey sugar paper. Margaret admired the orange-crayoned straggle of lines. One small child's conception of an even smaller one.

'You'll see a big difference in them when you get back.'

'Simeon is so clever,' said Faith proudly. 'Perhaps he will be a great artist.'

'It's lovely,' said Margaret diplomatically. 'You must miss them.'

The glow of Faith's smile clouded. She seemed to shrink, a slight, lonely young woman in a strange country, when at home she had been the mother of a son and daughter.

'I will finish my work soon and go home to them. They will be so proud of their mother, the Master of Education.'

Margaret bit back the acerbic comment she would have made to an English student. There was much work to be done yet to knock this dissertation into shape. That was not her job; she was not Faith's academic supervisor. She had only offered to help with the language problem. Yet she longed to volunteer advice about structure and argument. Faith had interesting evidence of how African infants carried everywhere on their mothers' backs may acquire language differently from those European babies left from an early age in a nursery environment. Yet her tutor seemed less sharp about the methodology than he needed to be. There was still a long way to go before the thesis stood up.

'Are you sure you are looking after yourself properly?' This was a more legitimate concern. 'You're getting yourself proper meals? Remember, you're coming to lunch with us on Sunday.'

'Thank you, madam. I am doing very well.'

It was hard to know whether her pride was offended. Margaret looked with a surprised envy at the slight but dignified figure opposite her. Other West African women students wore their traditional dress on high days and holidays. Faith, from the rural interior, kept to it always. There was a shy pride in the way she carried those flamboyant puffed sleeves high above her shoulders, the swathed turban of blue and orange. They spoke of a cultural inheritance visibly stronger than the small meek face between this exuberance of figured cloth. Modest lips occasionally parted in a swift smile, like curtains twitched aside on a glimpse of brilliant sunshine.

She rose to go, the easy swaying of her hips accentuated by the wrapping of the colourful skirt. Margaret felt the prosaic understatement of her own tweed skirt and limp cardigan. She regretted that English national dress was confined to morris dancers.

But how traditional was it? What had West African women worn before the advent of European missionaries? Perhaps when Margaret sat in the car outside a disco, watching for Laurie among the tumbling bright-lit crowd emerging, she was indeed seeing the festival dress of English culture. Visible markers changed, whether she wanted them to or not.

The gorgeously stiff cloth was crushed under a dark, somewhat shabby, overcoat. Faith looked more small and pinched than ever. Margaret's pang of anxiety was sharper now. Was she really all right? Of course she would feel lonely and alienated, far from country and husband and children. Anxious about her work, like any student. Enduring the English winter. There were multiple reasons why she should look so vulnerable. With an uncharacteristic impulse, Margaret hugged the younger woman, surprising herself.

'Take care,' she said. 'We'll see you on Sunday.'

'Thank you. You are very good.'

Faith never complained. It was impossible to tell if this contact with an English family really helped, beyond the formal language work. Margaret had to believe it did, that the offer of friendship was something she could do, however self-consciously. She worried a little, in case it was tainted with an inverse racism, a particular wish to be kind to Faith because she was African.

As she opened the front door for Faith, she met Brian on the threshold. For a startled moment, she thought it must be Wednesday, not Saturday.

'Ah, two of my favourite people in one go,' he beamed. 'How are you doing, Faith? Heard from the family?'

Again the folded drawing came out, the crayon beginning to be smudged now. Brian exclaimed with delight over it.

They're both putting a brave show on it, Margaret thought, watching them. Faith, hundreds of miles from her children. Brian with none of his own. And I can't wait for Laurie to leave home.

Brian had a sheaf of papers in his hand, plucked from the pocket of his anorak as Margaret took it from him. But his mind was on something other than administration, his eyes eager as a robin's as he followed her into the sitting-room. In the less formal atmosphere than the dining-room she felt herself already laughing at him tolerantly, beginning to relax after her anxiety about Faith.

'Was it all right?' Brian would not sit down yet. 'Last night. It's working, isn't it?'

'Of course it is. You can't start getting cold feet at this stage. I hate the music – well, the noisy bits, anyway – but the kids love it.'

'There wasn't anything. . . ?'

'Well, since you press me. That scene where Columba goes storming off to the King of the Picts, but the Druids bar the door against him. Lots of nasty discords for them. That's fine. But when Jon sings Columba's part and commands the door to fly open, it's a bit too . . . well . . . holy. It's more like that bit in the Old Testament, where the still, small voice of God speaks to Elijah, after the wind and the storm have passed by.'

'But it's *supposed* to be holy. Columba's bringing them the word of God.'

'Only that's not what the primary sources say he sounded like. He had a voice so loud you could hear him shout from miles away.'

There was a critical pause. 'Margaret. You're a scholar. I'm a poet. Never mind accuracy. Jon's song is the poetic truth.'

'But aren't you denying Columba's humanity? The whole point of his story is that he *wasn't* a plaster saint, he wasn't a dove. He was a red-blooded Irish prince with a temper, who was used to getting what he wanted. That's why he made that secret copy of a manuscript he wasn't allowed to have. That's why he wouldn't hand it back when the High King ordered him to. Why he roused the Ulstermen for that terrible battle. All right, he's repented now and gone into exile. But he's the same man. Just as Saint Paul was the same man after he stopped putting the Christians to death and started rooting for Christ instead. He's got the same energy, the same loud mouth, but he's putting it to a different use.'

Brian rubbed his chin. 'Ye-es, I hear what you're saying. And Laurie will love it if I let him hammer those drums some more. But is that really going to get through to the audience? The two sides shouting at each other. Christians and Druids? I wanted to show the difference between them.'

'You wanted Columba to be like you.'

'He was a poet, wasn't he?'

'Yes. And you can have your poetic bits. When he's on the seashore, remembering Ireland. Or saying goodbye to the old white horse before he dies. Are you sure about that horse, by the way? You don't think it's too like a pantomime?'

'So what if it is? The old mystery plays had plenty of pantomime.'

'*And the kids love it!*' they chorused, and sank into the cane armchairs, laughing.

'Twenty,' Brian said, suddenly recalling the papers in his hand. 'That's all right, isn't it?'

Margaret frowned. 'It's more than enough for a block booking . . . the dormitories in the hostel and the travel tickets. But it's not as many as you hoped for, is it? Have you got the people that really matter?'

'Well, we've got Columba; Jon's coming. And Annie to sing the narration.'

'She's got a voice like an angel.'

'She's *meant* to be an angel. We've done better on the cast than on the band. What about Laurie?'

'No. He's dug his heels in. A Hebridean island isn't his idea of where it's at.'

'He'll be sorry afterwards, when the other kids come back saying what a fantastic time they've had.'

'You're sure about that, are you? Even if it rains the whole time?'

'Trust me.'

I do, she thought, looking into his dancing eyes. Hy will be unforgettable. Brian will make sure of that. If I do the organization, he'll weave the magic. For me too.

'I'll put the kettle on,' she said.

23

5

Oddly enough, the church acquired a greater beauty for the solemn season of Lent than it offered for most of the year. Its modern design was functional rather than adventurous, furnished by a committee whose imagination soared no higher than a suburban sitting-room. Honey-coloured wood, rows of chairs thinly upholstered in green mock-leather, a yellow tufted carpet before the communion rail. Without this softening, the framework of the space might have served for a bus garage.

But Brian had a taste for the symbolic, even the theatrical. Tall purple candles surrounded the central white one. Each Sunday in Lent, one more of these purple ones took fire, while the white waited for Easter. At the back of the sanctuary was propped the cross, which they would carry through the streets on Good Friday. It was fashioned with heartrending simplicity. One by one, this congregation had chopped the branches from the Christmas tree which had stood at the front of the church in a dazzle of decorations only a few weeks before. Everyone had taken a share in shearing it, with axe, or saw, or secateurs. The largest bough now formed the cross-piece, lashed to the bare, wounded trunk. A crown of barbed wire girdled it.

Margaret felt unexpected tears prick behind her eyes. This was not her style. She had been brought up in the severity of Victorian chapels, suspicious of anything that smacked of Rome. It was still slightly shocking to her to see candles in a Methodist church, Brian in a long cassock of unbleached white, with a stole embroidered in

24

purple and black hung round his neck.

And yet this cross moved her. The wounds of the severed branches were darkening with exposure, but they would always be there, like the nail prints in Christ's hands after he had risen. She had been responsible for one of those scars. Every one of them in this church had shared that experience, down to the youngest child. Without words, Brian had taught them the price of love, more surely than any sermon on atonement or hellfire. Sin was not breaking the Ten Commandments; it was taking the Christmas child and hanging him on his own tree.

After the service ended, the congregation dissolved into a sea of colourful, chatting friends. Coffee was being poured at the back of the church, a Traidcraft stall offered ethically marketed cereals and dried fruit, Brian was shaking hands at the door, cheerfully trying to remember everyone's personal news. Margaret accepted the mug of coffee Maurice handed her and tried to focus on finding Faith and her fellow student Naomi in the crush. She felt disorientated, the noise of so many competing conversations numbing her ability to concentrate. She wanted to listen to the Bach chorale which Tony was pealing out on the organ now, almost unnoticed.

'Good morning,' a shy giggle at her elbow. Maurice had found the two women.

Margaret turned, with a smile almost too dutifully ready. She had acknowledged long ago that she was not instinctively sociable, still less gregarious. It was something of an effort of will on Sundays to identify the stranger, or the person standing alone, and make conversation that sounded bright, welcoming, interested. But it was not insincere. Caring was a matter of the will, as much as instinctive emotion.

Her conventional greeting faded in mid-sentence. For a moment she thought she was addressing the wrong person. Was this young woman really Faith? Her eyes took in the slim green skirt, the slender stockinged legs below, that neatly moulded, brass-buttoned jacket, the hair scooped back and coiled behind her ears to reveal the smooth sculpture of her bare head.

Beside her friend, Naomi smiled triumphantly.

'Doesn't she look like she ought to be on the front cover of *Vogue*? I told her, I'm not going to be seen with her any more till she gets herself some proper clothes.'

'You look stunning,' Margaret said truthfully. 'I mean, I loved your national dress, Faith. I used to be really envious every time I saw you wearing it. But now you look . . . like a different person. Naomi's right. Has anyone told you you're really beautiful?'

Faith's smile was less shy than Margaret might have expected. She had looked so small, so vulnerable, beneath her more flamboyant African dress, wanting it to shield her from the eyes of strangers, but only attracting their stares. Now, when Margaret might have supposed her to feel exposed, the shape of her body so much more visible in figure-tight European clothes, she carried herself with surprising poise, almost enjoyment.

'It cost a lot of money,' she laughed. 'I hope my husband won't be cross with me.'

'What will he say when he sees you? Does everyone at home wear African dress?'

'Oh, no. I am sure he will like it.'

'We'll give him a preview. I'm going to take pictures of you all after lunch,' Maurice said. 'Especially you, Faith. I don't know that I can get you in *Vogue*, but I'll let you have a photograph to send home, so that he can see what a credit you are to him.'

Faith grinned more broadly. 'Thank you, Mr Maurice. But you see, I have brought my own camera.'

Sunday lunch, which Margaret had expected to be uphill work, drawing conversation out of the reticent Faith, proved instead to be a feast of gaiety. Naomi effervesced over the sparkling white wine, while Faith leaned back in her chair laughing spontaneously, more relaxed than Margaret had ever seen her before.

As she carved roast beef and ladled out Yorkshire puddings – she always served the most traditional English food to foreign visitors – Margaret wrestled to decide what had made such a difference. It must be the clothes. Just as a fancy dress party or a masked ball allowed people to try out another persona, so Faith had shed her inhibitions with her customary dress. And yet . . . Margaret paused, knife hovering over the dwindling joint . . . a carnival mask was a concealment. It promised anonymity. Behind its shield the wearer could do or say things they would normally feel restrained from, for fear of the consequences.

Faith wore no disguise. These western clothes revealed far more of her to the curious world than before. Her face looked naked without its turban, set off by the careful braids of black hair. Her bone structure was more petite and frail than Naomi's, making her seem like a small neat bird. A starling perhaps, shades of green and purple shimmering over its black plumage.

'Chop, chop. It's a shame to let the gravy go cold.' Maurice broke into her thoughts, holding up his plate.

Margaret was suddenly aware that she had become the reticent one, her knife poised over the rolled ribs.

'Sorry! I was daydreaming.' The knife descended and the circulation of plates, vegetable dishes, gravy boat, resumed its hospitable flow, like the kitchens of Sleeping Beauty's palace when the spell was broken. Or, Margaret wondered, as she sat down to eat her own plateful, was it more like Rip Van Winkle, returning after a hundred years to see the world changed?

'No. I don't think I can go to that dance.' Faith shook her head vigorously, endangering the neatly pinned coils. 'I am an old married mama, without my husband! It would not be proper.'

'You're twenty-five,' said Naomi. 'You need a life. This is your one chance for freedom. You know what will happen when you go back. More babies. You will go to work, come home, cook, put the children to bed, tidy the house, then do whatever your husband wants you to.' Faith covered her mouth to hide her embarrassed laughter. 'You'll be old by thirty. Come on, girl. You have to live a little. Give yourself something to remember.'

Faith shook her head more gently, smiling and confused. 'I have so much work to do. Mama Margaret knows. I am a bad student. I must write my essay many times.'

'There's nothing wrong with your brain,' Margaret protested. 'It's just that you're not used to writing in English. If they'd let you submit in French, you'd probably be finished by now. And an academic essay needs a very special sort of English of its own. Even some English students complain it's as hard as learning a foreign language.'

'Can't get away with "know-wharra-mean?"' Maurice chuckled. 'And most of them don't seem capable of completing a sentence without it.'

'Isn't that what we're here for?' Margaret heard the note of indignation harden her voice. 'I thought the point of a city university like ours was that we take local kids from schools where they haven't been polished and drilled to Oxbridge standards. I think it's much more exciting to find talent that might have been thrown on the scrapheap. We change people's lives.'

'Rough diamonds, eh?'

It was a fair summary of what she had been saying, even if a clichéd metaphor. Yet Margaret felt a flash of irritation with Maurice as he reached for the last of the gravy. His had been the laughter of condescension, when she stood in awe of some of her students, particularly the mature students, married women who blossomed so unexpectedly against all the odds. Women like Faith. Faith would get there, despite her inadequate tutor. Margaret would see to it.

'We're going to have to raid the shops again,' Naomi was saying. 'You look great for church, or a job interview, but I can't take you to a disco wearing that suit. You need a dress. Something slinky with a very short skirt. You've got the hips for it. Not like me. I'm as broad as a baobab tree. Or maybe some silvery leather trousers and a spangled top.'

Faith pushed her away laughing. 'No, no! I've spent all my money.'

'What do you think, Mrs Jenkins?'

'Well, steady on. Faith's not seventeen. What's she supposed to do with a teenager's wardrobe when she gets home? Stop bullying her.'

'Call me an old fogey,' said Maurice, 'but I wouldn't let my daughter out at night looking as if she'd put her dress together from two dishcloths and a safety pin. I think you look very nice as you are, Faith.'

'Pudding?' said Margaret, feeling that he was again overstating her argument. 'Bread and butter pudding, or sherry trifle? Then we'd better take those photos before it starts to rain.'

In her blue and orange printed cloth, Faith would have blazed like a summer flower under the lowering March sky. Now she stood on the patio between Maurice and Naomi, in her slim dark-green suit with the brass buttons. Margaret squinted through the unfamiliar viewfinder of Faith's camera, worrying whether the flash would come on and be reflected in the French windows.

A strange country was another carnival mask, separating you from the expectations of friends and family. Would the voice that spoke from behind this mask reveal the true self, free from inhibitions, or something more dangerously transgressive?

6

Was Hy a strange country? Margaret sorted through the rail of her wardrobe. What did one wear for a pilgrimage? Think Scottish island, she told herself. Trousers. Sweaters. Strong shoes. But the Hebrides were lapped by the Gulf Stream and it would be after Easter. Perhaps a silk shirt? And would there be occasions when she would be glad of a skirt or a dress? There might be Scottish dancing, mightn't there? And what did one wear to church there?

It would have been simpler once, to be a pilgrim. You wore what you had. She laid a tentative selection of clothes out on the bed. Too much choice. And yet . . .

She was aware, scanning the pile, of dissatisfaction. All duns, muted greens, understated blues. Nothing sang vibrantly or called attention to itself. The reaction surprised her. She had always thought this restraint of colour evidenced good taste. Today it seemed like cowardice. A mouse-like scuttling away from the announcement of her own personality.

Or is this me, she thought in sudden alarm? Beige and olive green? Is that my personality? Is this how the rest of the world sees me?

Unbidden, a more particular thought forced itself into her consciousness. Is this how Brian sees me? Dull, safe.

'What's this for? You're not packing already, are you? You're not off for another ten days.' Maurice came into the bedroom and eyed the heaped double bed with tolerant amusement.

'I know. But I want to check I've got the right things, in case I need to go out and buy anything extra. What do you think I need?'

'A good raincoat.'

'I've got my walking-gear. There's a whole-day pilgrimage on the Wednesday. They'll take us right round the island to all the special places. The beach where Columba landed. His hermitage.'

'I hope it keeps fine for you. But don't bank on it.'

'Bad weather will make it more authentic. I bet Columba got rained on. Don't you wish you were coming?'

'I'd have enjoyed the train journey through the Highlands. And maybe the boat, if the weather's good. But I don't think I could stand a week of that music, even without Laurie on the drums.'

'But you're going to get the drums, and without a Hebridean island. You'll be all right with him? I'm not sure about leaving the two of you together.'

'We hardly communicate. He's barely awake in the mornings, and in the evening he's tied to his computer, or out. It minimizes the potential for aggravation.'

'Maybe you should talk.'

'About what, exactly? One of us would need to learn another language.'

He was gone, leaving Margaret with the unsolved problem of what to take.

Brian knows that other language. It's nothing self-conscious or false, like copying the latest slang. How does he do it? Just by listening, as though he's really interested in what they're saying, the things they like, what makes them angry.

Will they talk to me? Would I want them to? She tried to imagine an island of misty mornings. Walking on the beach with the moisture beading her jacket. If she came across a teenager, hunched and lonely on a rock, would she know what to say, how to listen?

Don't be daft. The only people walking on the beach in the early morning will be us oldies. Ruth, Brian, Don. Don was another wizard, who oversaw the stage sets and the electronics, giving the kids access to equipment they had only dreamed of.

Maybe that's what I'll be good for. To counsel the counsellors.

31

When someone gives himself as generously as Brian, there must be a price. She adjusted her daydream. The slim hunched figure on the rock was a grown man, gazing out to sea. He did not hear her at first, making her way over the soft sand. She was quite close before the slurred swish of her boots made him turn his head. It was Brian.

Her mind shied away from the expression her imagination glimpsed in his eyes. She had no right to attribute to him something more than she had seen in real life. And there *was* nothing more, surely? Theirs was an innocent friendship. Shared laughter. Joy in poetry and story. Arguing over history and the way it should be told. An enthusiasm for the wandering Celtic saints.

Ruth will be there. She'll keep us firmly on the ground.

She began to make a definitive pile of the unadventurous clothes. Well, I suppose it's appropriate. The modern equivalent of Columba's monks in their undyed sheep's wool. And there's bound to be a monastery gift shop. I can treat myself to a sweatshirt with a Celtic motif. Margaret Jenkins, who had never worn a logo emblazoned on her bosom before.

Next day, she went to Marks & Spencer and, for the first time in her life, bought herself a pair of stretch jeans. They were a more vivid shade of blue than she had been looking for. They hugged her hips in a way that was surprisingly flattering for someone her age.

7

The snowdrops had given way to daffodils, trumpeting the approach of Palm Sunday and Easter. Margaret dug down under the thick green of the snowdrop clumps to lift and thin them before they withered. The seed heads hung like pearls, though the petals had vanished. She hollowed new beds for them in the soft loam and leaf mould under the lilac tree, laying them to rest for their summer sleep.

'Is it true you should always transplant snowdrops in the green?'

His voice made her jump. At eye-level, the bicycle clips were instantly identifiable. Still on her knees, she looked up the length of fraying jeans and baggy sweater to find Brian's face laughing down at her.

'I met Maurice on his way out. He told me I'd find you round here. Didn't you hear the garden gate?'

'No.' She wiped her hands on her worn brown corduroys, juggling the trowel from one to the other. She felt at a disadvantage, squinting up at him with the morning sun over his shoulder. 'You don't usually call at this hour.' It was almost an accusation. 'Has something gone wrong?' Her mind fast-checked the state of their plans. They had had to be made swiftly, but everything had fallen into place: accommodation, travel, insurance, the week's programme, lists of what to take . . .

'No. No problem,' he laughed, cutting short her anxious inventory. His hand shot out to help her as she struggled to rise a little awkwardly. She felt herself hauled up by the strength of his grip before she could assure him she didn't need it.

'I'm not as nimble as I was.' The self-deprecation was a defence against her growing awareness that his hand was still around hers.

'Still in the green, and about to be transplanted. You'll flower all the better for it.'

He bent forward, removed a speck of dirt from her nose, smiled and kissed her. There was a teasing formality about the sequence of movements, like an Elizabethan dance. Margaret found she was blushing. Brian always did greet her with a kiss, swift but enthusiastic, as though he had nerved himself to make a provocative statement of something he deeply believed in. Yet now, because it had taken her time to get to her feet, this kiss seemed slower, more deliberate. She was not normally a kissing person. The sun dazzled her. She was strangely conscious, not just of his lips on hers, the warmth of his skin, the tickling of his sideburns, but of her own body, stirring against barriers of cloth.

It was Brian who ended it, separating his face from hers, laughing gently at her. She felt confused, frightened even. Her reaction had lasted only a few seconds. Had he felt it? Had some barrier been crossed? His hand was still holding hers.

'I've had this great idea. We could build a bonfire on the beach. Only there's hardly any wood on the island, so we'll have to tell everybody to bring a log. We can sing songs round it, and you can tell us a story. You've got such a wonderful voice. Especially when you forget about being a history lecturer and get carried away with your own enthusiasm. It's the Welsh *hwyl* in you. I can hear you, spinning a Celtic tale out of the darkness, with the firelight playing on everyone's faces. I thought I'd better warn you.'

And make sure I chivvy them all to remember to bring firewood, a small sensible part of her mind protested. But she did not say it aloud, as he probably expected her to. The rational history teacher, the literary critic: that was her role in their friendship. He was the poet, the charismatic bard to whom the faces turned, the weaver of dreams. This was some other Margaret he was describing, who could weave spells of her own.

A wonderful voice . . .

Belatedly, she freed her hand from his, and bent to retrieve her tools. She was disturbingly conscious of his eyes watching her. She hardly knew what she was doing, or why. The job was only half-finished. She would go back to it when he was gone.

'Don't let me stop you. I'd like to watch you work.'

'Would you like some coffee?' Coffee was safe. Coffee was what female members of the congregation offered the minister when he called.

'Would you stop for one yourself now?'

She pushed back the sleeve of her sweater to check her watch, but she had not put it on. Her confusion deepened. She was over-whelmed by a helpless uncertainty about whether this was morning or evening, what season of the year it was.

'Half-past nine.' Brian's voice was reassuring, amused.

'I'd like a coffee.' She needed the shock of hot caffeine. And an escape into the kitchen.

'Could you make mine tea?' The undercurrent of laughter.

Three years, they had been friends. She knew he never drank coffee. But this morning she had forgotten. The givens on which she had based the hypothesis of their relationship were still rocking.

They sat on garden chairs, braving the cool spring air for the sake of its soft sunshine.

'Do you think Faith's all right?' she asked. It was not just concern. She needed a topic that was objective, safe.

'Why shouldn't she be? She looks fine to me. She seems to have got a whole new wardrobe.'

'That's partly what I mean. She's changed. Do you think Naomi's a good influence on her? She seems determined that Faith shall have what she calls "a good time".'

'Maybe that's what we all need. A change of scenery. Let our hair down. Try coming on stage as somebody else.'

'What about integrity? Aren't we supposed to be the same, through and through?'

'Only if we've got it right in the first place. Look at Columba. Ambitious scholar. Insulted prince. And then Hy. He becomes

Columba the Dove. His monks are so in love with him, they feel him carrying their burdens when the going gets tough.'

'You're a romantic. Columba was a politician, even on Hy. He was staking out territory for the Irish Scots. To get the Picts to admit their claim to the Hebrides, he needed to make the King of the Picts a Christian and do down the nationalist Druids.'

'Margaret, Margaret. If I'm a romantic, you're a cynic. But I have high hopes. I'm going to enjoy watching Hy put its spell on you. The thin place, where the boundaries are so fragile you can step right through them. I promise you, nobody comes away unchanged.'

8

Margaret released the tailgate of the estate car. Laurie loomed suddenly dark across the street lights as he bent forward to unload his precious drums. She unfolded herself from the driving-seat and locked the side doors. A growing family of instruments had ranged itself across the tarmac around Laurie. Names flickered uncertainly across her mind: floor-tom, hi-tom, snare. Cymbals gleaming faintly golden.

Margaret picked up the hi-hat, with the awkward apprehension of a grandmother who doubts her ability to relate to the infant offspring of her own children. As they crossed to the lit windows of the church hall, Margaret was glad of Laurie's presence. It was not because the car park was only dimly illuminated by the street lamps beyond the hedge. Tonight, she wanted a chaperon as they entered the hall.

The knowledge brought a stab of disappointment. Something precious had been taken away from her, that innocent eagerness with which she had come to any encounter with Brian. Now she was nervous. It was foolish exaggeration. There had been nothing to suggest that that moment in the garden had been, for him, more than their usual greeting, a pastoral kiss made warmer by the genuine friendship between them, deeper than professional, but still blameless. He had sat by the plastic table on the patio afterwards, chatting and laughing as though nothing had happened.

Nothing *had* happened. Nothing could happen. Whatever her middle-aged body had felt, like the unexpected tremor of a long-dormant volcano, it had not been, and must not be, repeated. The relationship she had with Brian was too precious to be endangered by the interference of her rebellious body. She would not allow it.

'Watch out, Mum!' Laurie's anguished yell warned her just in time that the swing doors were about to crash back on the hi-hat.

'Put it down before you turn it into a concertina.' He deposited his own load inside and came charging back to relieve her. 'That cost fifty quid.'

'It's all right. I can manage it if you hold the door open.'

She needed this shield of helping Laurie with his gear. She did not want to walk unprotected into the wide bright space of the hall, to see Brian turn and feel her face naked under the neon lights. For once she was glad to be cast as Laurie's inept, middle-aged mother. There was no danger in that.

It was Ruth who turned, with that slow wide smile that was nevertheless watchful. Margaret returned it briefly and struggled across the floor to the stage. Dutifully, she passed the drums to Laurie, as he indicated them. Still she lingered, untypically, snapping the legs of his music stand into position. He was too busy shouting news to Zak and Emma to notice.

She had her back to Brian. He had not appeared to notice her as she crossed the hall. He was surrounded, as usual, by a press of eager teenagers. Annie, more stunning than ever in a red leather skirt, was competing for his attention.

'Bri-an! Listen, will you? I've got this great idea. Like, when I'm singing about Columba crossing the sea, we could have this dry ice, see? Like it's this sea fog, and my face is sort of rising up out of it. Get the picture?'

She heard Brian's laughter, but not his answer. She would not turn round.

'You don't think the band should be in the wings, and not in front of the stage?' she asked Laurie. She twitched at the heavy red curtain, to see how far back it would go.

'You still here, Mum? Quit fussing. The kids are going to want to see us playing. You stick to the history.'

A strange tolerance had developed between them over

rehearsals. In the last few weeks, against all the odds, their very different worlds had come together. Listening to Laurie shouting unnecessarily loudly to his friends, watching him slide into his seat, pick up the drumsticks and roll an ostentatious riff, finishing with a clash on the loudest cymbal which made Annie stop with a shriek, she knew that he felt proud of what he was doing, and that she, his mother, was helping to make this possible. Even Laurie, whom she so little understood, could express an obscurely felt gratitude.

It could have happened without me, but not without Brian. How long will he be with us? What's the longest Methodist ministers can stay in one church? Seven years? He's been here two. Five more will be enough for Laurie. He'll be almost through university by then, if we can make him concentrate on his A-levels first. Miraculously, a man. But he'll never forget his teenage years. He won't forget Brian.

'We'll make a groupie of you yet.' The laughter was shockingly warm and close, just behind her shoulder.

He had given her the excuse to laugh – to blush, even – before she turned to face him. It was part of the grace of him to put people at their ease, to make it easy and natural for them to be themselves. By the time she faced him she had become the self-deprecating older woman, at sea amongst this teenage culture, but determinedly doing her bit to help the minister.

'That's more or less what Columba said to King Bruide, when the saints were bellowing out Christian psalms to drown his Druid bards.'

'You think Laurie's drums are on the side of the angels?'

'Laurie didn't write this music. You did.'

'But you don't like it.'

'I like what it's doing.'

She looked at him straight. It was all right. The pounding in her blood had been needless apprehension. She had it under control. As soon as they began to talk, it was the old friendship, the meeting of minds, the gentle teasing, the acknowledgement of the things they loved, another world from what they were doing here.

This is his world, too. He doesn't talk down to these kids. He's not pretending.

He didn't kiss me. The sudden irrational thought inserted itself. He had stood so close before he spoke, he could have hugged her before she realized it. He was still close. He needed to be, to talk to her above the clatter of Laurie's drums, the yells of the cast. But he was turning to go already. There were other people claiming his attention.

Perhaps he thought it would embarrass me, in front of Laurie. But that was nonsense. Brian had kissed her at church, in front of the family, many times. It was an innocent greeting, the kiss of peace.

Did that mean he had felt it too, that morning in the garden? A loss of innocence? A step on to trembling ground? He had shown no sign of it.

She left the band and went, uncharacteristically, to the kitchen. She was not good at institutional domesticity. She left it to others to organize coffee and tea urns, to calculate pints of milk and packets of biscuits. But this evening she busied herself, setting out plastic tumblers on trays, filling kettles. She didn't need to do this.

Ruth found her there. 'So this is where you've got to. Are you all right?'

'Yes, why?'

'You're not normally here.' It was never easy to tell if Ruth was making an accusation. There was a touch of Yorkshire bluntness in her voice that bordered on the belligerent.

'I don't know what use I am in the hall. The script's written. Well, more or less. They do say plays are not so much written as rewritten. But the kids seem to be telling Brian what it needs from now on, better than I can.'

'But you still came.'

Margaret hesitated. She did not know how much Brian discussed their relationship with Ruth. The delicate delight of those teatimes, when they sat in the cane armchairs, discussing his poetry. She did not repeat those conversations to Maurice, or even tell of their substance. It was not guilt. There was nothing wrong in their friendship, everything right. If she could help so creative, so loving, a person, it must surely be good, not only for him, but for the whole church.

And for me. When Brian moves on, this will be a precious part of my life to look back on.

When he moves on.

With a searing pain, she realized she had never faced that eventuality for herself, only for Laurie. And it must come. In a few years' time, he would go. Brian and Ruth would go away, and she must stay. With a blinding jealousy she saw that stolid, unpoetic Ruth would have, always and undisputed, what she, Margaret, who had so much to give him, must lose.

Brian would feel that loss, wouldn't he? He would constantly remember. He would long to be back, sitting by the French windows overlooking the pond, nursing a cup of tea he didn't really want. Venturing shyly a new poem. Wanting and fearing her reaction.

'I feel responsible.' For the way they were telling the story of Columba. For Brian.

'Then shouldn't you be watching it?'

'I can hear them from here.'

It was an understatement. The band was playing the passionate anger of the Druids. The pagan priests had lost their hold on the king's heart. The certain faith of the Irish newcomer had swept all before him, the Celtic lays twining now with the song of the angels. But the Druids were bitter. They wanted revenge on the usurper. They were raising a storm over the loch.

'It sounds as if they're going to need this orange squash in a minute.' She took hold of the tray and carried it to the hatch, as the drums thundered to the climax and rolled away, leaving only the celestial soaring of Annie's voice.

9

'I wish you were coming.' Margaret surprised herself with this unplanned acknowledgement of need.

Maurice loomed reassuringly large and masculine in the narrow kitchen. He seemed not quite at home there. His shoulders were hunched forward, his hands in his pockets, as though he felt he were too big for that domestic space and his hands, if he used them here, likely to cause trouble. Margaret, by contrast, felt small and womanly, her academic credentials smothered under a pile of Sainsbury's carrier bags.

'I'm putting the fish in the freezer, and there are chops and sausages. I didn't buy ready-made meals because I know you hate them and the price is robbery compared with cooking your own. But the stuff I've got you should be quick and easy.'

'Laurie can do his own thing, then. I'll probably drop in to the pub for a meal most evenings.'

Margaret restrained an outburst of irritation. Undomesticated though she felt herself, she had always done the cooking, though Maurice proved perfectly capable in the kitchen when she was ill. It was perhaps her fault. She liked to be in control, to know just what was in the cupboards. If Maurice took a turn at getting meals, he would forget to tell her what he had used up and she would find too late that there was no more sugar. But now that he could have undisputed use of the kitchen for a week, without her critical oversight, he backed away. It irked her housewife's thrift that he would spend money for someone else to cook a meal he could easily have made himself.

He did not want to spend time alone with Laurie.

Or did the pub attract him more than as a means of escape? Not for the pint of shandy, which was probably all he would drink, but for the chance of other company. Neighbourhood friends who might be dropping in, like him. Margaret, whose judgements were so sharp, whose listening so sympathetic, with students and, yes, with Brian, found herself tongue-tied in casual company. She found such unplanned socializing difficult.

Did she limit his freedom when she was at home? Was he wishing he could drop into the pub more often? It was a shock to realize Maurice might be glad she was going alone, just when she had discovered she wanted his solid presence with her.

She reached behind him to put away the olive oil in the wall cupboard and then surprised herself again by hugging him. Guilt? It was something she had not done spontaneously for a long time. He stirred slightly, like a sleepy dog being stroked, but did not reciprocate.

'What's that for?'

'Oh, just stocking you up with enough hugs for the week, I suppose, like baked beans.'

They did not normally hug each other in the kitchen, but neither of them said so.

That night, she lay in bed with Maurice's large warm body close beside hers. They had not made love since Christmas. It had not seemed necessary. It was enough to feel each other's reassuring presence.

Made love? Had sex? Were they really synonymous? Surely not.

There had been a time, when they were students, when she would moan, with what she realized now was frustration, at her unfulfilled closeness to Maurice. Sexual liberation had passed them by. There were things her old-fashioned non-conformist conscience would not allow her to do. Was that all it had been about? An animal need?

The hormones had done their work and she had produced three children. Was this a reason for the end of physical love?

It needn't be. If it was an expression of genuine love. If we still needed each other in every way.

Or was it just reticence on Maurice's part, finding it as difficult to communicate his need of her as she did to chat with friends in the pub?

She moved her hand tentatively. It was ridiculous to be so inhibited, to feel that, in spite of decades of equal opportunities, she still could not take the initiative in lovemaking.

She put her hand over his. Gently she tried to move it to where she was beginning now to realize she needed satisfaction urgently. He stirred, and her body leaped with delight to meet him. Maurice rolled over with a heavy sigh and settled to sleep again.

She wriggled closer, shaping her body against his back. Her hand rested now over his thigh. She let her fingers move softly, insistently, trying to insinuate her physical presence into his dreams. He slumbered on.

Why was she doing this? What had suddenly woken this urgent desire in her?

Exquisitely, painfully, she felt again the treacherous surge that had overtaken her body standing in Brian's arms among the snowdrops. Was it a kind of adultery to be trying to satisfy her need with her own husband, when what she really wanted was someone else?

Her mind recoiled from the thought. It was too explicit. It was what she had been trying not to think.

She rolled away.

I'm a married woman. And Brian has Ruth. He writes poems about her.

10

Maurice set down her bag on the station concourse.
'I won't wait. It's only twenty minutes free parking.'

He bent and kissed her on the cheek, a little awkwardly. He did not hug her. She was aware of the formality of this kiss. With a shock of tenderness, she realized how shy he was of expressing emotion in front of other people. She hugged him hard, trying to strain more warmth into the kiss she was returning.

Guilt?

They were already separating. Maurice was retreating, to the security of home inland, leaving her on the edge of a sea of excited young people.

It was too late to change her mind. She was committed. She looked around and saw the rocks that would be her stability for the next week. Don, burly, shouting for order. His dark head moved from left to right as he checked faces against his list.

Ruth and Brian. They seemed small and distant, as though through the viewfinder of a camera. She found she was as much conscious of Ruth's presence as of Brian's. It was better so.

It would not have been easy to struggle through the crowd towards them. She smiled and waved, then turned conscientiously to the group around her.

'Are you all good travellers?' She smiled gamely at Annie and Emma and their friends. 'I've got some tablets, if anyone wants them.'

They looked round at her in mild curiosity, as though she had spoken in a foreign language. I'm in the wrong place, the wrong person, she thought in panic. Why did I ever think I could take a horde of teenagers on holiday? Male and female adolescents, away from their families, perhaps for the first time, and their parents looking to me to be responsible for them. What if one of the girls comes back pregnant? Or the boys' bravado ends up with one of them falling off a rock and drowning? We're insured for public liability, Don's seen to that, but you can't insure against a lifetime's guilt.

'Did anybody hear a weather forecast?' Emma asked. 'I had this rotten dream last night about how we were on this ferry and it was really rough and I dropped my sax overboard. My dad'd kill me.'

'Force 5 in the Hebrides,' Margaret heard herself saying. 'They call that a fresh breeze. But it's a big steamer from Oban to Mull, and the little ferry across to Hy only takes a few minutes. You'll be OK.'

As though lock gates had opened, the tide of people flowed out through the barriers, drawing her with them. She was almost the last. She tried to be helpful, looking round for stragglers, for forgotten luggage.

There was nothing left. The space where they had been was beginning to fill with strangers. She was committed now. She hurried to catch up with the others on the platform.

Ruth and Brian were still together, shepherding the party on to the train. The quintessential minister and his wife. They even wore identical hiking boots. Ruth saw her looking at them.

'We always wear them for travelling. Less weight in the rucksacks. Trust Brian to think of bringing logs for a bonfire!' There was a bulky cylinder, wrapped in a plastic bag, strapped under each of their backpacks.

The couple were already dressed for the Hebrides. Gaberdine knickerbockers, looped wool stockings, warm checked shirts, sweaters and anoraks. Margaret felt her own attempt at casual holiday-wear too sedate, suburban. The polyester slacks, the new laced shoes. At least her waterproof jacket showed signs of wear.

'How are you, anyway? I haven't said good morning.' Ruth moved forward to hug her.

46

'I must be mad,' said Margaret. 'I've no idea how to talk to these kids. They make me feel a hundred and fifty years old.'

'But you've had teenagers of your own.' Ruth, childless, looked shocked.

'I'm not sure Jake and Ros ever were teenagers, in the accepted sense of the word. They were quite civilized. And I've never pretended to understand Laurie.'

The disapproving expression left Ruth's face. She punched Margaret's arm in a gesture of friendliness. 'Go on with you. Laurie's proud of his mum. He's chuffed you're helping to get this show off the ground.'

'Is he?' She felt herself grow pink with pleasure. 'You see! You know more about him than I do.'

'Margaret! You made it. I was beginning to think you'd got cold feet and run out on us.'

It was the moment she had known must happen, though she had been delaying it. Brian pushed his way forward to hug her in his turn. It was warm, genuine. His kiss barely brushed her cheek, but the arms reassured her he wanted her presence and would be there for her. It was over in seconds. It felt no more than their old friendship. She felt both relieved and disconcerted.

They boarded the train, and the four adults sat around a table, from where they could watch the group in both directions. The train pulled out from the overhanging canopy into the thin spring sunlight. They chatted lightly. Brian unfolded the *Guardian* and settled down to read.

Margaret had brought a book for the long journey, but today, untypically, she reverted to the childish pleasure of looking out of a train window. She felt obscurely that if she turned her eyes to the printed page she might miss some unrepeatable moment, an epiphany offered only in the instant of her passing, a treasure that was hers because she had watched for it.

She was rewarded with hares bounding through a field of young wheat, the level shafts of early morning sun illuminating dried reed beds round a reservoir. A mural on a house, on which a purple hand reached round as if to open a bedroom window.

'Look at that fox!' It was standing in full view beside the railway line, unconcernedly waiting for the chance to cross.

Ruth had been staring out of the window too, but as if preoccupied.

'Where?'

She had missed it.

The mood was wearier by the time they reached Glasgow. Heads sprawled over tables littered with drinks cans. They had ceased to jig to the music relayed through their headphones, drugged with sound. It was an effort to gather up coats and luggage, herd them all on to the grey streets and find another station.

Now everyone was looking out of the window. After the midlands, there was a grandeur of mountains plunging precipitously down to the grey waterline of the loch, and surely deep below.

'This is Loch Lomond,' Margaret informed the company round her.

'So?' said Emma.

'You know. *The bonny, bonny banks of Loch Lomond.*'

They stared at her, uncomprehending.

'I wonder if they've factored that into their tourist trade projections,' said Don. 'You get thousands of people coming here to be photographed on the banks of this loch, just because they've heard about it in a song. There's nothing else special about it. No story like the Loch Ness monster. So if the next generation doesn't know the song, why will they want to go on coming here?'

'Because it's beautiful,' Margaret defended it. 'There are still daffodils round Derwentwater, even if you've never read Wordsworth.'

The braes were darker than she had expected as they pulled through the Highlands. She had pictured in her mind the glory of purple heather. Silly, she told herself, it's only April. You'll have to come back in the autumn.

With Maurice next time. He was the railway enthusiast. For him, this train ride would have been the high point of the week.

She felt now the pull of nervous excitement. They were surely all making this expedition for different reasons, with different hopes

48

and expectations. For her, it was a pilgrimage to a sacred place, Hy. The name itself spelt enchantment to her. The place of Columba's exile. An island poignant with personal grief. The powerhouse of a community of monks who had changed history.

Oban smelt, prosaically, of fish. They sat on the quay in the fresh wind, eating sandwiches. As the herring gulls advanced over the cobblestones, Margaret noticed how much larger and more menacing they looked at close quarters, their yellow eyes fixed on the food in her lap.

The steamer was exhilarating. Margaret stayed on deck throughout, imagining she could feel the spray on her face.

They bumped in a bus over Mull, always expecting the end of the ride would be over the next hillock. At last the sea swished dark lines of seaweed beside stony beaches. It was not a soft land. As strangers in it, they were already drawing closer to each other.

'How much further?' grumbled Emma. 'It's not exactly Disneyland, is it?'

'You wait,' said Brian. 'You'll be crying your eyes out this time next week, when you have to leave it.'

Then the road dipped and they were at the little cluster of houses that was Fionnphort. Margaret drew in a deep breath as she got her first sight of Hy. She stifled an instinct of anticlimax. Of course, she had known there were no mountains like the Cuillins of Skye. That was the point. Columba had climbed its highest hill, as he had done on other islands he passed, and found that here at last he was out of sight of his beloved Ireland. The wind of God had blown him to the place of his death and resurrection.

Her scholarly mind reminded her that on a clearer day he might have reached a different decision.

Across the sound, the island lay low, like a grey seal basking. She tried to remember. Three and a half miles long, a mile and a half wide? So small a compass to contain so large a soul.

But, of course, it had not. This was only the reservoir, from which the stream of Celtic Christianity flowed out to change the life of Scotland. From the court of the Irish colonists on the western coast, through the Great Glen to the Picts at Inverness. And smaller leats had nourished the cottagers on the mainland, the freed slaves.

'So, you think if we call, a monk will row across from Hy to fetch us?'

'No, but the ferry's on its way.'

They watched it grow towards them, seeming to magnify rather than move. Returning day-tourists disembarked, and then it was ready for them.

The ferry, like Fionnphort, was small and spartan. Margaret sat on a wooden bench out of the wind and watched the crewman taking money for tickets.

'Did you notice?' Brian laughed after they had paid. 'He didn't ask us whether we wanted a return. He just assumed nobody would want a single.'

'That's not authentic,' Margaret told him. 'The point of Celtic pilgrimage is that you don't go back.'

'But the point of today's Fellowship of Columba is that you must. One base on Hy, the other on Clydeside. The spiritual is the practical. If you meet God here, and it doesn't make you want to go and change the world, you haven't been listening. Don't say I didn't warn you, Margaret. Hy is dangerous.'

'Did it change you?'

'Yes.'

'I'm sorry. That was intrusive. You don't need to tell me your spiritual autobiography.'

'Maybe I should. Maybe we all should. It might make sense to the kids, if I told them here.'

'Is that it? The monastery?'

A sudden urgency made her turn from him. A grey haze near the shoreline solidified into the bulk of a squat tower, a broad-backed church, a range of stone buildings, hunching their shoulders low against the wind.

'Yes. Not your Columba's, of course, but the same site.'

She watched it hungrily, though the buildings were restored Benedictine, until it was hidden from view as they came into the fishing port. There were people running down to the slipway to greet them, pulling a handcart with them.

'Welcome!'

'Quick, your supper's waiting.'

They all looked young, little older than the youth club, who were standing now a little forlornly by their luggage.

'Is this the station bus?' asked Zak.

'Put your bags on the cart. Does anyone have trouble walking? Good, then the rest of you just follow us. It's only ten minutes.'

Pete was looking round in astonishment at the handful of little shops selling basic groceries or tourist gifts, the lobster pots on the quay, the half-dozen short streets. He stared back at the dark hills of Mull, Fionnphort tiny across the water.

'Is this really it? People *live* here? I mean, year in, year out?'

He kept twisting round, as if another revolution might prove he was mistaken. There would, after all, be buses, takeaways, record shops, a football stadium.

'Some people like it,' she said.

But all round Britain, every island community must wonder how long it could keep its young people.

It was not the bright lights but the Vikings who had swept the Celtic monks from Hy. Brian was right. Hy was a dangerous island. She might have been wrong to see it as a sanctuary of peace.

They walked up the village street, and along the lane that wound through the fields. Margaret's eye leapt ahead to the first ruins.

'An Augustinian nunnery,' said Ruth, seeing her head turn. 'That'll be after Columba, I suppose?'

As they drew level, Margaret ran a knowledgeable eye over the stonework. The stones were warm, almost fleshy in colour. Not chiselled with military precision, like Roman ashlars. The haphazard spaces between them were packed with slabs of slate. There was an eroded carving over one of the hollow windows. She took out her glasses to inspect it more closely.

The image shocked her. It was not the subject itself. She had seen similar photographs in textbooks of Celtic iconography. But here, on a nunnery wall?

'That's a Sheela-na-gig!'

'If you say so.'

Ruth had stopped politely, while the caravan of travellers moved on ahead.

Margaret still stared. The carving was worn, but unmistakable. A naked crone, with large staring eyes, squatted with her knees wide apart. Her hands pulled aside her labia to bare her genitals. Her eyes stared defiance.

'On a nunnery?'

'You get gargoyles outside churches, don't you?'

'Yes! Yes, that's brilliant, Ruth. That's got to be it. The nuns inside want to guard their virtue. So what can they think of that will scare men off? An ugly old woman who wants to have sex with them. A vagina that will eat them up.'

'I wasn't going to put it quite like that.' Ruth's usually generous mouth was pursed.

'I'm sorry. Have I shocked you?'

'I was brought up in a Primitive Methodist manse. We didn't talk about things like that.'

'Did any of us?'

'But you just did. Is that what a university doctorate does for you?'

'Lets you say the unspeakable? No, I don't think it does. Academia has its own taboos. You're not supposed to give weight to the emotions. They'd rather you talked about knowledge than wisdom. But this is about emotion, isn't it? It touches you to the core. It does me, anyway. The nuns may have made an intellectual decision that this was a clever strategy, but they knew the emotional effect it was going to produce. They knew a lot about men.'

'About putting them off.'

They walked slowly on up the lane. Two married women, one barren, one fertile. Ruth, here with her husband, though they would not be sleeping together in the hostel. Margaret, more widely separated from hers.

'A lot of nuns were married women,' Margaret said. 'Or had been.'

'Is that a reason to hate men?'

'For some of them, it could be. But they just rated chastity higher than sex. Being a nun was like having sex with God.'

History was a fiction, which might or might not be true. How could you tell how anyone thought or felt, a thousand years ago? They were not 'just like us'. That was the liberal humanist fallacy.

How could she tell how anyone else felt and thought, even Ruth beside her?

The monastery was swinging into view again, larger and more complex from this approach. With keen regret Margaret saw that they were passing it by. She had known, of course, that they were staying at the youth centre. She had booked it herself. But it would have meant something more to her to have slept where Columba's people slept, even if in a newer, grander building.

You're a Methodist, she scolded herself. You don't really believe in sacred places. It's what people do there that makes them holy. Without the right people, they're nothing. But she looked with hunger at both the ruins and the modern restoration. A hostel anywhere else would not have attracted her.

Brian was touched by physical places, more than she was. She heard that in his poetry. Hy was holy to him, and he wanted her to feel it. It seemed to matter to him to share with her what they both loved. It was dangerous to think that, walking beside Ruth.

Macbeth Lodge was barrack-like on the outside, though reflected in a marsh pool ringed with yellow iris.

'Why Macbeth?' queried Zak. 'What's a murderer got to do with a religious bloke like Columba?'

Brian's eyes sparkled with fun. 'Don't believe everything you read in Shakespeare! The real Macbeth had a good claim to the crown. He killed Duncan in fair battle, not in bed. And he and his wife were good friends to hermits on an island in Loch Leven. He's buried in the royal graveyard here on Hy.'

'Macbeth? No kidding!'

They were impressed.

It was cosier inside. An Argentinian girl, with a Scottish brogue, showed them where to sleep. Margaret was sharing with Annie, Emma, and the sisters Lucy and Ceri. There were three pairs of bunk beds. By common consent, the four girls left Margaret with the empty place above her. She felt uncomfortably shy, unpacking her Marks & Spencer underwear in front of them. But they were all hungry. The long journey had brought them here after the hostel's usual suppertime. A meal was waiting downstairs.

The food was almost stereotypically wholesome, chunky vegetable soup, home-made bread.

She stood on the porch in the cool night air. People were coming back from the monastery church, specks of torchlight on the darkened path. Their own group had arrived too late for evening prayers. Don and Brian joined her, indistinct, quiet.

'Mercifully, even the kids seem ready for the early night,' Don said, lighting a cigarette.

'Blow that match out and look at the stars,' said Brian. 'You won't see this in the Black Country.'

' "*Proud and sudden, the stars came out for me . . . like hailstones of the brilliant sun, the mirrors, the half-pennies of great God, lovely as red gold under the hoarfrost, the saddle-jewels of the hosts of Heaven.*" Dafydd ap Gwilym, fourteenth century,' Margaret added apologetically.

'It was magnificent.'

'Yes, but he was actually on his way to commit adultery one dark night, when he fell in a bog. This is his hymn of praise when the cloud cleared and he saw his way out.'

'God can use anything,' Brian said softly. 'Even our sin.'

11

Margaret woke early. It was tempting to lie under the blankets in the grey half-light and shut out the thought of the coming day. She should not have come. Her dream of a Celtic holy island had not included sharing a dormitory with four adolescent girls she hardly knew.

Yet we are related. The same humanity, the same church family, most of all this week related by a shared drama.

Still, uprooted and breakfastless, she was scared. She had ventured out of her depth.

She tweaked the curtain aside. The sky was pale. She might have thought it was greyed over, had there not been little puffs of rosy wool which must be clouds. The pallor beyond was waiting to become blue.

Fumbling for her clothes as quietly as she could, she tiptoed to the bathroom to dress. Lucy groaned as she passed. Emma was humped deep under the bedclothes. She could see little of the higher bunks. She crept back for her jacket and left them sleeping.

The narrow road stretched on north, low walls and thin fences. It was better than retracing her steps to the village. Between her and the Channel of Hy the monastery loomed, its stonework dark with morning damp. She was longing to enter its little cathedral, or find Columba's oratory, but she was nervous of disturbing other people so early.

Where would Columba have made his early morning prayers? Before he even left his cell, her brain answered. She stood at the hostel gate, testing the Trinitarian pattern of Celtic prayer.

'With this jacket, I put on the protection of the Father. With these shoes, I walk in the service of the Son. With these glasses, I ask for the clear sight of the Spirit. In the name of the blessed Trinity. Amen.'

Something like that.

She started to walk towards the north of the island. The sea was still distant, across bullrushed fields on her right, hidden by low hills to her left. But as she went, the sky grew luminous ahead with the coming morning and the reflection of light from a wider expanse of water. The promontory was narrowing, the rocks starkly black against silver sand. The fences had ended. She could walk down at any point now to the beach. But she followed the little road on until it gave out and only sandy tracks led forward or bent round the coast to the south.

Here she left it. It seemed important, this first choosing of a place of solitude. She knew she was investing it with an importance, a hope, it might not be able to satisfy.

Like a first date.

The beach was lightly littered with the flotsam of storms. Some was natural, the yellowed bones of peeled branches. She turned them over, studying the beauty of sea-carved driftwood. Tangled in the bladder-wrack there was less lovely detritus, plastic bottles, polystyrene, a broken trainer.

It was not the desire for beachcombing which had drawn her out before sunrise.

The rocks were damp. If she laid her jacket over one to sit on, she would soon be cold. If she did not, she would need to change her trousers when she got back. It would be inconvenient to stain them on the first day.

Celtic monks would stand waist deep in freezing water to sing their psalms alone to God. Reckless enthusiasm. Why should she, sensible Margaret Jenkins, be drawn to them? She removed her coat and sat down on it.

The sea rolled out its silk before her. A pearly grey shot with pink. It whispered to her. She was beguiled by the scenery. It had been in her mind to come and pray. But now she was here, she did not know how to begin. She was only doing this because it was Hy. She did not normally go out before breakfast to pray in the garden. Perhaps she should have sought out a prayer manual to tell her how to do it.

But prayer, surely, was not an intellectual exercise, requiring an approved curriculum and a certificate. It should be meeting with God like a friend. Chatting, or keeping silence together.

Was God an equal? Or should she be falling flat on her face, her arms spread-eagled like a cross, hiding her face from the King of kings, the Almighty Judge? Or, and this gave her some relief, was the Holy Spirit so close within that there was no need to picture, or even gender, God? A voice, an inner dwelling, closer than a heartbeat.

And all the while my mind is busy with this, I am evading the meeting.

She lifted her eyes again to the seascape, trying to empty her mind of expectations. Be where you are. Experience this. God is here; that will be part of the experience.

It is the whole of the experience.

Do not name it, do not define it, do not analyse it.

Shouldn't I be praying for somebody? The youth club, Brian, Ruth, Don. All the things we've come to do this week. For myself, and all the responsibilities I'm frightened of. For Maurice at home. And Laurie . . .

She checked herself. That was what prayer usually meant. A recital of categories. It was supposed to be a balance of adoration, confession, thanksgiving, intercession, petition. Mostly it was just lists of people who needed praying for. On a good day, you remembered to start with praise, to focus your thoughts on God. But it quickly declined into the mundane, the self-centred. My sins, my needs, the people I love, the causes I support. You could not look into the face of God for more than a moment. Your eyes were soon back to the floor of the world, sweeping up the dust.

And all the time, God was there watching. With a wry smile? With tears in his eyes? Waiting.

You're analysing again. Trying to pin it down in clever words. You've forgotten the colour of the waves. You haven't noticed how the sky has turned to blue and the water is jade green over sand, purple above the weed-hung rocks.

Naming the world by parts. There are no words for God. All the language we have was formed to tell of human experience.

She looked at her watch, astonished at her purpled hand. She had not noticed how cold she had grown. It was ten to eight. She struggled to her feet, relieved of the impossibility of the task of real prayer. There had been no numinous moment. Only fleetingly a sense of peace. It had been impossible to get her mind out of the way.

Perhaps it had been the twentieth-century heresy to believe that all we needed was to do our own spiritual thing. That the mystical experience would just happen. In reality, it took years of discipline. Celtic monks and nuns worshipped every three hours with the community. They read the scriptures and the commentaries, meditating even while they did manual work. Only the most mature Christians, steeped in liturgy, were allowed to launch out on the lone spiritual expedition of the hermit. The experience could be terrifying.

She started to walk fast, back to the hostel. She was in charge of one of the three teams for domestic chores. But their first duty was to wash up after breakfast. Somebody else would be laying the tables now, making toast.

She had not been the only one lured out by solitude and sanctity. Black pen-strokes on the line of the road showed where others were coming back, too. She turned. She was not the last.

It had been only a glance, too swift to identify. She hurried on.

There were steps close behind her as she reached the gate. A hand reached over to open it for her.

'Boy, I'm ready for that porridge!'

Brian grinned at her, that little-boy mischief dancing in his eyes.

12

Margaret's terror of institutional domesticity proved unnecessary, though the staff of the Fellowship still filled her with helpless awe. Young women and men, vigorous and competent, who looked as if they had backpacked from Norway or New Zealand. Older Scotsmen, whose handsome ruggedness might have been daunting, had not their kindness made it reassuring. She was shown what her team must do in the kitchen and the dining-room, and felt, to her surprise, that she could manage it. This week might yet prove an enjoyable holiday.

'What do I do with leftover marmalade?'

The voice undid her.

Brian traded shamelessly on the helplessness Margaret struggled to disguise.

'You're not in my team.' It came out like an accusation.

'Yes, I am. Look.'

He showed her Don's print-out. Three lists of names. She ran her eye down the second one.

'Your name's not here. I knew I wouldn't have missed it.'

He pointed to the top of the page. '*Leaders: 1, Ruth. 2, Margaret and Brian. 3, Don.*' She had been so nervous about which half-dozen youngsters she was responsible for, she had not even read that line properly.

'If you're the co-leader, why weren't you here when we started washing up?' She gestured to Jon and Emma, drying milk jugs, Lucy and little Tim stacking cereals and washing table-tops.

'Well, since I am here, what do I do with the marmalade?'

'We were given the briefing when we began this shift. You'll find a shelf in the larder.'

'Brian, Brian, what are we going to do today? Can we practise that battle again? Did you bring the swords and everything? *Yah! Gotcher! Aaargh!'* Tim, who was thirteen, but only looked eleven, was barricading Brian in the larder with the rush of his enthusiasm.

'We've got more important business first. Sunday service in the monastery.'

'We don't have to go to *church*, do we? I thought we were on holiday.'

'I won't force anyone to a date with God. But you might be missing out if you don't come with the rest of us.'

Tim's pale blue eyes under the sandy lashes swivelled to the eastern window. The sky was busy with fast moving clouds, bright-edged over the hills of Mull and the dancing channel. People were already thickening on the paths to the monastery church. The more glamorous of the older teenagers, Zak and Annie and Pete, with the impossibly blond hair, were going through the gate in a group, following Don. They were chatting easily, as if going to church were the most natural thing in the world.

Margaret saw the struggle in Tim's thin face. The wish to be with them, to be like them. The fear that something might happen there for the others and he would be left out. Unlike Margaret, nothing about this historic church building drew him. The symbolic ecclesiastical message of tower and arched windows rather repelled him. But he must be with his peers.

'Will these jeans be OK? I didn't bring my best ones. Never thought about Sunday or anything.'

'You look fine. I don't think anybody dresses up much here.'

'I'm wearing trousers and a sweatshirt. It's not like home, is it?' Margaret reassured him. She felt oddly pleased as Tim walked beside her across the road and down to the waiting church. The others of her team were coming behind them, keeping close to Brian. It was astonishing, the thread by which he drew them. You could forgive him a great deal.

And she was in control of herself. Able to scold him as well as admire him. It was going to be all right.

The church was cool and dim. She stepped down into it with a sense of relief and refreshment, like finding a shaded pool after the end of a dusty walk. The nave was already filling up, not only with the young people from the hostel, but also older guests coming along the cloisters from the restored monastery. There were faces she recognized from the Fellowship staff, and less familiar ones from the direction of the village. Some of the youth group looked nervous, unsure about doing the wrong thing in a strange place. Ruth and Don were already there, shepherding them into seats.

Once the service began, Margaret was beguiled by the Hy liturgy, simple but arresting, marrying Celtic forms to contemporary concerns.

> When our eyes have been dazzled by riches
> and blind to the poor,
> when our unfeeling strides
> have trampled creation,
> when we have thought ourselves lonely
> yet missed the love in your eyes,
> forgive us.

Even the hymns made use of Scottish folk tunes. She found herself envying this confident celebration of Celtic identity.

We English hardly know who we are. Only the St George's cross painted on a football fan's face shows any such pride.

She tried to still herself again, to stop herself looking around with the eye of a tourist or a student of history. She could explore the church building later. Just now, it was what was being done in it which mattered.

One small part of her being was conscious of the odd and unusual pleasure of having Brian sitting in the congregation at the other end of the same row. It was strange not to see him at the front, conducting worship. This must be even more of a refreshment for him, not only to be here on Hy on this Sunday morning, but to become, for a little while, just like the rest of us.

She should not be speculating about someone else's spirituality. She must concentrate on her own.

As they left, they were each given an oatcake to share with someone else. There was tea in the cloisters, around a green lawn with a statue at its centre. Margaret sipped her tea, making polite conversation with a couple from Ohio. Fellow pilgrims, she supposed. Everybody came to Hy with great expectations. The morning communion had heightened her sense that Hy might have its own expectations of her. She found that both exciting and threatening. The sensible monitor in her mind urged caution. She must beware of making some rash commitment she would regret when she got home.

The homely couple in their plaid shirts and snow-white trainers showed no such awareness of danger.

'Don't you feel this place is just steeped in sacred history?'

'When you think of Columba praying right here . . .' The husband looked respectfully round at the cloistered quadrangle, the modern sculpture.

'Well, it wasn't exactly like this, of course,' Margaret said gently. 'In his time, it would have been a bit more rough and ready.'

'Oh, sure. I guess they've had to repair the roof a few times since then.'

'Might even have been thatch,' his wife added. 'Did they do that here?'

Margaret forbore the academic's instinct to sweep away the Benedictine monastery entirely and leave them with a scatter of huts, just big enough to sleep one or two, a tiny oratory, a separate library, a guesthouse. This more imposing edifice was, for the moment, a far enough staging-post in their journey back towards the truth. We cannot bear too much reality.

Her eyes were drawn over their shoulders to the sculpture standing out in the quadrangle, where the sun could strike it. Rain had fallen on it earlier and left its polished surface dark and slick.

A dove descending. That much was easy. The traditional symbolism of the Holy Spirit. Below its beak, a pear-shaped hollow, defined by ribbons of curving bronze. And something at its heart she could not quite identify.

As the Americans moved on, with good wishes for their week, she stepped out on to the damp turf to inspect it more closely. The hollow enclosed a primitive human figure. Yes, female.

'God made man,' Ruth's voice came rather loud and harsh beside her. 'And I use the exclusive language intentionally. Do you see? Mary's been split in two. So God can come straight in at one end as the Holy Spirit, and out the other as the incarnate Lamb, without soiling himself with the female body. She's just a channel.'

'And I thought you were shocked by my Sheela-na-gig.'

'I'm afraid the founders of the Fellowship of Columba may well have approved. When they came to Hy, they brought men from Clydeside to rebuild this place, and they really were all men. They wouldn't allow a woman in the monastery.'

'Nor did Columba. That was the Island of Women we passed on the ferry.'

'Quite right, too.' Don had suddenly joined them. 'Dangerous distraction, women. How's a bloke supposed to meditate on the higher things of the spirit with stunners like Annie in a three-inch leather skirt?'

'So that's why you didn't bring Joan with you.'

'I'm beginning to think I should have made her come.'

They moved companionably out into the monastery precincts. Brian had disappeared. So had most of the youth club.

They found them gathered round a rough mound, just inside the boundary bank. A small ring of stones showed among the tufts of grass perched on its summit.

'Any guesses?' Brian was asking.

'There was a building there?' said Emma cautiously.

'Oh, brilliant!' crowed Zak. 'Take a Smartie and go to the top of the class.'

'A watchtower?' tried Pete. 'It's narrow and round.'

Brian shook his head.

'A little house,' said Ceri shyly.

'Don't be silly,' her sister Lucy corrected her. 'It's not big enough.'

'It could be. For just one person.'

'Wonderful, Ceri.' Brian's smile must have illuminated her day. 'You've got it. But which person?'

They stared at him, with the one name they all knew hovering on their lips.

'Columba?'

'But it's tiny. I thought he was the boss man. Didn't you say he was a prince?'

'Try it. I think our Columba should go first.'

Jon straightened up. His square face, pockmarked with acne, looked self-conscious, yet pleased and proud.

'Is it really OK to climb up on it?'

'Go on. Everyone else does.'

Jon clambered up the low hillock, no higher than their heads. They saw him circle the little ruined wall, serious-faced, then find the entrance and bend down to examine something inside. He sat down, chin in his hands, seeming now to forget they were watching him. His head turned slowly, looking out beyond the island to where the sea ran south towards the far-off peaks of Jura and on to an invisible Ireland.

'Well?' said Brian, as he came down again.

'It's so small.'

'And the sea is so big,' suggested Brian softly.

'There's a stone up there. With a sort of groove in it.'

'His pillow.'

'Columba really slept there?'

'Almost certainly. And read the Bible there. And wrote poetry. And talked to any monk who wanted his advice.'

Jon almost shivered. 'It makes it different. Singing his part. Like he's real. It's not just a good plot for a musical.'

The shiver communicated itself to Margaret. This is the magic. This is what Brian meant to happen. He knew he could get through to them, here.

She watched them, one by one, ascend the mound. Some of

them were serious, trying to imagine themselves into the experience of living here. Annie stood, tall and striking, the wind stirring her black hair. She threw her arms wide and sang of the wind that carried the monks' boat. When Tim's turn came, he could not resist this commanding position. He levelled an imaginary machine gun at them and swung it in a triumphant circle.

'*Pa-pa-pa-pa*! Gotcher! I'm the king of the castle! Everybody's got to do what I say.'

'Come off it, Tim,' called Zak. 'Columba's an abbot, not Osama bin Laden.'

'Maybe,' Margaret murmured to Brian, 'but I don't suppose that hut was built higher than the rest without a good reason. He was a bit of a control freak. He liked to get his own way.'

'Margaret, Margaret. You're a cynic. Let me keep some of my illusions.' His lips were wide with laughter, but his eyes seemed to beg something more from her.

She laughed and blushed. In front of everyone else, she did not know how to respond.

13

'If you're under eighteen, and you want to explore the island, there's a strict rule. You never go out in a group of less than three.' Don, more practical than Brian, was laying down the law at the start of their first free afternoon. 'I know it's not a big island. But there are plenty of places where you could fall and hurt yourself. So you need one to stay with you and one to go for help. Got it?'

There was a somewhat grudging assent. Margaret was acutely conscious of their delicate position. This was not a school trip, with a well-established code of rules and discipline. No one said 'Yes, sir,' to Don. A youth club was supposed to be more informal, to establish a relationship with a greater emphasis on friendship. But away in an alien environment for a week, *in loco parentis*, the sense of responsibility was more acute.

'So what if you're over eighteen and you break a leg?' Sean, who was fourteen, piped up.

'I'd strongly advise the older ones to do the same. Set a good example. If they don't, they may just have to lie there on their own, while their buddy goes for a stretcher party. And in any case, always tell one of us where you're going. Better still, I'll leave a book in the porch and you can sign out, giving us details. And woe betide anyone who forgets. We don't want to cramp your style, but we'd like to know where you are. And there'll always be one of us here, in case of trouble.'

It's not just broken limbs, Margaret thought. There's something else we're really worried about. Teenage boys and girls, let loose on an island that's sparsely inhabited. We need a third to play goose-berry, as well as run for help.

It was a calm and sunny afternoon. The wind had died, leaving trails of high cloud stretched along the sky, but barely moving now. The waves still danced. The sea would take hours to settle yet.

'I'll mind the shop today,' Margaret volunteered.

It was a sacrificial offer. The peace outside summoned her. She felt that all her life she had been waiting to be here. She sensed now what Brian meant. This was an island on the edge of space and time. The barriers were fragile. She did not know what she expected to happen here, but she knew that a life-shaking experi-ence was possible.

Besides, there was fifteen hundred years of history to explore, tall crosses carved with Celtic symbolism, the burial ground of Irish and Viking kings, the graves of Macbeth and John Smith. The little museum alone would hold enough to keep her happy for an afternoon.

She watched the other adults leave, dressed sturdily for walking. At first she thought they were taking Don's advice, setting a good example to the youngsters by staying in a threesome. But where the ways parted, Don went on towards the harbour, while Brian and Ruth followed the lane away from the sea.

There was no need for her to stay indoors. The sun was warm. She took out *The Early Poetry of Hy*, the purchase of which she had justified as research, but which was really self-indulgent holiday reading. She placed a chair on the porch, facing the abbey, and settled the book on her knee.

But self-indulgence that Sunday afternoon was, she found, to do nothing. It was not an occupation she normally found easy. She had no taste for holidays spent sunbathing on a beach. Yet there was so much to see, even from here, so much more to imagine. Her eye traced the range of stone buildings, placing each in its correct century. In front of the monastery, the slender cross of St John stood proudly high. Freestanding, it lifted a circle of stone too small to contain the arms of the cross. Christ breaking through the created world into the beyond. Unlike a Roman crucifix, the Celtic cross was not a symbol of suffering, but of resurrection glory.

Would it be deserting her post to cross the road and examine the carving on its shaft more closely? She decided it would.

'Shall we bring you back an ice-cream?' called Lucy, as a gaggle of girls came out of the hostel and headed for the village.

'It's a nice idea, but I don't think it would last till you got back here, at the rate you walk. And I don't know if the shops here are open on Sunday.'

'You what?'

The girls stared at her aghast, and then at each other.

'Go on. I'm only teasing. There are tourists coming across on the ferry all day. Even on Hy, I'm sure there are people who can see the commercial potential. Besides, it's a Christian duty of hospitality to feed travellers.'

She knew that they did not understand all that she meant. They were only half reassured. Well, good. Part of the value of coming away from home was culture shock, the realization that the world you knew was not the only possibility. Like finding yourself a character in a fantasy novel. No, more accurately, science fiction. An alternative future that could actually happen.

She watched them go along the road that Don and Ruth and Brian had taken. At the fork, they followed Don's path, down to the village. How many others had gone, like Ruth and Brian, to explore the interior?

She got up and went back into the hostel to consult the map hung on the wall. There were few roads, and few houses to connect them to. Even footpaths seemed sparse away from the coast. An island three miles long and a mile or so wide offered a surprising amount of empty space.

She pictured Brian and Ruth walking together. Did they chat as they went? Keep companionable silence? They probably had favourite places discovered on previous visits. Breathtaking views they anticipated before they reached them. With astonishment, she realized she was beginning to feel like a petulant, jealous child, left out of a game by the others.

She was grown-up. She had volunteered. Somebody had to stay at the hostel in case something went wrong. Tomorrow it would be her turn to explore.

But she might have to do it alone. She could not wish her company on somebody else, just because she had come without Maurice. Who else would want to linger, as she would, over the abstruse details of antiquities? But how far should she walk alone? Was Don right to warn even the older ones of dangers? Was this island strange, in ways that paths at home were not? Hy was a holy island. It should feel safe. Why did the thought force itself in on her that it was not?

As if in confirmation of her doubt, there were running footsteps on the path outside. Ceri burst in.

'Miss! Miss! Come quick! It's Tim.'

'What's he done?' Margaret's instinct was to cast that boy as culprit, not victim. But her heart was racing. She was keenly aware that she was totally unsuited to dealing with emergencies.

'We were playing on the beach. And he was jumping across from one big rock to another and he missed. He's cut his leg and it's bleeding horribly.'

Ruth was in charge of first aid. She was out of reach. Was it right for Margaret to leave the hostel?

'Which beach?'

Ceri pointed. 'There. Just the other side of the monastery.'

She must have run past dozens of people more competent to help than Margaret felt herself to be. She realized she had not even asked where the first aid kit was kept.

With relief she saw one of the Fellowship staff crossing the common room towards the kitchen. Ian, the chaplain, short, dark, slightly bow-legged, but with a sturdy look about him that matched his blue fisherman's guernsey.

'Ian!' she called. 'Is there a first aid kit? One of our more idiotic boys has fallen off a rock and damaged himself.'

'Where?'

'On the beach near the monastery.'

'It's his knee.'

Margaret and Ceri competed with each other.

'Let's have a look.' With reassuring efficiency, he fetched a scarlet box from the kitchen, put his head round the office door to

69

report the situation, and looked at Ceri. 'Right, lassie. Lead on.'

They found Tim huddled at the foot of a tall damp rock, hung with dark swathes of slippery bladder-wrack. There was bright blood coating the paper tissues he was clutching to his knee. A group of friends was kneeling round him, awed and frightened. They were, Margaret noted, the youngest of the party. They had left a space of sand around Tim, as though his wound might be dangerous to them, too.

'You need longer legs for that game.' Ian strode into the ring and knelt beside him. 'Leave flying to the gulls.'

'Don't touch it! Don't touch it!' screamed Tim. 'It's broke.'

'I'll need to see it before I give a considered opinion on that. Let me have a look.'

'I want a doctor.'

'You want to get a grip on yourself. I'm trying to help.' He looked up to Margaret for assistance. It came to her that she represented for Tim the nearest thing on the island to his mother.

'It's OK, Tim. We'll be very careful. But we need to see. And we can find you something more hygienic to stop the blood.'

Her voice sounded unbelievably calm and matter-of-fact. Tim looked up at her doubtfully under his sandy lashes. She smiled back. Slowly he took his dirty, protecting hands away. The blood was darkening on the saturated tissues. Aware that Ian was leaving it to her, she reached forward and gently peeled them away. Tim gave a gasp that was almost a scream.

Blood oozed down his sandy leg, where he had pulled up his jeans. The cut was deep, but the bleeding was slowing.

'Try straightening your leg,' Ian suggested.

Cautiously, and with dramatic yells at each pang, Tim extended the damaged leg in front of him.

'Dip that in clean salt water.' Sean ran to obey. Ian was preparing a dressing. He swabbed the blood from around the wound, then cleaned the gash with antiseptic and strapped the knee. 'It feels to me as if it's still in one piece. Bashed, but not "broke".'

'You don't know how it bloody feels,' shouted Tim.

'Bloody painful, I expect. But not life-threatening.'

Tim stared back at him. Margaret wondered if it was the chap-

lain's responsive adjective which silenced him, or his lack of sentimentality.

Ignoring his wails, Ian and Margaret hoisted him upright, one
supporting each armpit. His friends fell back, impressed at his
martyred cries.

'Don't I even get a stretcher? I can't walk, can I?'

'Try hopping, then.'

They got him, under protest, up the beach, ploughing a furrow
of wet sand behind them, and lifted him on to the grass above.

'Right,' said Ian, pointing to Ceri. 'You seem a sensible wee lass.
Run up to the office by the front door to the abbey and ask if you
can borrow the wheelchair.' He singled out a pair of younger boys.
'You go and help her with it.'

Margaret felt a wash of gratitude. This was an emergency, even
if it had proved a minor one, but it had been taken out of her hands.
She had not needed to do anything at all. Except that smile. And at
once she was aware that Tim was still gripping her hand while they
waited. He had been badly frightened. He still was. Never mind that
he had behaved like a baby, playing overdramatically for sympathy.
It needed Ian's tough common sense. But Tim had also needed
Margaret's . . . love? She tested the word. He needed her physical
reassurance, her smile, her hand. She shifted her grip tentatively,
put her arm round him and gave him a little hug. He grinned up at
her. She saw that the pale blue eyes were wet.

'Is it going to need stitches?'

'Oh, I think you deserve a wooden leg, at least.'

By the time the other leaders returned it had all been dealt with.
Ian had found a nurse. The wound was expertly cleaned, closed and
re-dressed. Tim was proudly seated in the common room, with his
bandaged leg stretched out on a table and an impressive bruise
purpling the exposed skin below. Margaret had made them all tea.

Ruth swooped to examine Tim and interrogate Margaret. It seemed
to her that Ruth's face had immediately been arranged in condemna-
tion. She felt almost pleased at her own apparent competence.

Brian was busy joking with Tim. He did not look at her.

14

After the first rehearsal on Monday morning, she felt exhausted. She had done her stint of holding the fort during their free time. This afternoon it was Don's turn to stay in charge, keeping company with Tim, who was making great play of the impossibility of walking on his damaged leg. Only once more, she thought, fetching her jacket from the shared dormitory. There can only be one more day when I might have to go through that again. A voice inside her protested that she should not be required to do even that much. Six free afternoons, four leaders. Surely the others would agree she had already done her share?

She looked into the common room. Don had got out a pack of playing cards and was teaching Tim conjuring tricks.

Margaret hesitated at the roadside. She had no clear plan. A walk around the coast tempted her. The hills of the interior looked more forbidding, alone. It would be prudent to buy a map in the monastery shop.

There was rain in the wind. As she neared the monastery, a softer part of herself reminded her that she had not yet explored what was here in front of her.

She was beguiled for a while by the tall cross in front of the little cathedral, every panel of its carving rich with meaning.

She wandered round the empty church, glad to let her intellectual curiosity go free. The intensity she felt in the liturgical morning and evening prayers here was beginning to alarm her. She distrusted emotion in religion. She felt herself dangerously moved, like a boat dragging its anchor on the sandy bed as the wind rose. Might she yet, before the end of the week, make some rash commitment?

She sat for a while in the carved choir stalls, steadying herself, and found she was praying again. When she stood up and resumed her tour, it was almost as if running away, like crossing the street to avoid talking to someone. She must justify the retreat to this more impersonal stance by finding something worth her attention.

Two stone carvings, high in the chancel wall, eroded enough to be ancient. A cat and a monkey. The unexpected iconography delighted her. And yet she was puzzled. What could they mean, here in the sanctuary of a Christian church? Every instinct told her they were imbued with significance. They had been carved by people to whom no image was inconsequential or frivolous. Was the cat wisdom, waiting to pounce on the mouse of truth? And the monkey mischief, the devil in disguise?

Would they carve a devil, looking down on the altar of Christ?

Be wise as serpents and innocent as doves. Perhaps the monkey was worldly wisdom, Christ's practicality.

She gave it up and went in search of other images in the monastery museum. Visitors moved softly across the shaft of sunlight which had broken through the cloud and was shining through the window. It was an unexpected pleasure to find the chaplain, Ian, there. The tall cross he was gazing at looked oddly familiar.

'But I've just been looking at that standing outside,' she protested as she joined him.

'No, you haven't. There's only one St John's cross. This is the real thing. We brought it in here out of the acid rain. The one in front of the monastery is only a copy.'

Her eyes traced the wheel of glory, the grapes of the true Vine, the arms of love. Eighth century. For thirteen hundred years it had been telling the story of salvation without need of words. She studied the original with a historian's respect.

'Of course,' said Ian, smiling sideways at her, 'I could be wrong. Maybe the replacement is the truth now, standing where St John's cross always *has* stood. It's proclaiming the same gospel to everyone who approaches the monastery. So maybe this one isn't the reality any more, put aside in a museum. A bit like an ex-wife. How's Tim?'

She was startled back to the present day. 'Complaining. And loving every minute of the attention.'

'He looks like a lad that hasn't been given enough attention.'

'No. I don't suppose he has.'

'But you seem to have got through to him. He trusts you.'

'Me? I'm not really part of this group. I feel like a fraud. I'm only here because I helped Brian write his musical.'

'But Tim will remember you. And you'll remember Hy.'

He stared at her for a while, smiling, but his dark eyes intent. She felt he saw more in her than she did herself. It was oddly strengthening. His eyes did not have the power to disturb her, as Brian's did when they stared too deep. For a rash moment, she even wondered whether she could confess that to him, and ask for help.

'Enjoy your afternoon.' His gaze released her and he was gone.

She felt a moment's disappointment.

She amused herself among the collection of retrieved gravestones, fragments of carved masonry, excavated pottery. One motif carved on old tombstones intrigued her. A mirror and a comb. The label informed her that this identified the body in the grave as that of a woman.

Margaret eyed it with a stirring of frivolous doubt. Something tugged at the corner of her memory. The mirror and the comb. Where had she heard that combination before?

It sprang into her mind with all the pastel colours of a children's picture-book. A mermaid with an iridescent tail, sitting on the rocks. Butter yellow hair streamed over her naked shoulders, and through it she pulled her ivory comb, while she gazed at the beautiful face in her hand-mirror.

Not ordinary women, then? Or was the prosaic archaeologist saying that every woman was a siren? We all have rainbow-hued tails and perch on rocks to flaunt our beauty and sing the songs that will lure men to their deaths.

But it was these women who were dead. Their families had

carved the mirror and comb above their names. By this, the future would know and remember them. Was it like a grave-cross, which told everyone who passed that here lay a Christian? If a woman bore instead the mermaid's mirror and comb as her symbol, what did that tell you about her?

The nights were the worst. For eight girls and two women there were two rooms, each holding six beds. This arithmetic had dictated that Ruth and Margaret could not sleep separately from the girls. Margaret would have found it difficult to share a room even with adult strangers. To be thrown into such intimacy with adolescent girls, and ones she must go on meeting afterwards, was a low-grade torture. Hers was a shy privacy, not an aggressive assertion of personal space. It was a sense of inadequacy, that Dr Margaret Jenkins, the respected academic, would prove at close quarters a sham and the reality be revealed as soiled pants, sagging breasts, and a nightdress nearly twenty years old.

The girls, in T-shirts that barely covered their buttocks, were friendly, but their sidelong smiles did not escape her. Nor the pregnant silences when the lights were out and the air hung heavy with the indiscreet gossip they were bursting to tell each other.

At home, she would have read a novel until she grew drowsy. Maurice usually came late to bed. Here, she wanted to vanish into the darkness. But she could not sleep yet. She heard Lucy's tentative whisper.

'What about Pete, then? Isn't he drop-dead gorgeous? I'll kill myself if I don't have it off with him before we go home.'

'You'd better watch it,' Emma murmured from the top bunk. 'I think Annie's beaten you to it.'

'Me? No way. I can't stand the way he ponces around with that blond quiff. Thinks he's God's gift to women.'

'So what were you doing behind that wall this afternoon? I saw you. It wasn't exactly a threesome, was it? Don said we shouldn't go off in twos.'

'Ssh!'

She felt all their eyes turn towards her bunk. The room was a ghostly grey from the half moon beyond the curtains. Should she speak? Let them know she was awake? Stop this now? But she could not think what to say, or what tone to say it in. She took the coward's way and tried to make her breathing slow and even. Perhaps, she told herself, it's my duty to be aware of what they're up to.

Annie lowered her voice to a virtuous hiss. 'I told him he wasn't taking any liberties with me. I wouldn't soil myself.'

'More fool you,' Lucy said. 'I would, tomorrow. And I bet I could show him a thing or two.'

'Go on,' said Emma. 'You're just talking big. I bet you've never done it.'

'Course I have. Do I look like a virgin?'

'Who with, then?'

'None of your business, is it?'

'Shut up talking dirty, both of you,' Annie cut in. 'Ceri might be awake.'

'You think she doesn't know the facts of life yet? This is the twenty-first century. Get real. Even kids of eight know all about it. Isn't that right, Ceri?'

There was a strangled snort from above Lucy's head, then a gentle snoring.

'Knowing's one thing. Doing's another. She's just a kid. Lay off her.'

I should have been the one intervening to protect her, thought Margaret. Not Annie.

'Oh, high and mighty, are we? Don't tell me you've never had it off with a boy.'

'As a matter of fact, no, I haven't. And I'm not intending to until I'm married.'

'*What?*' Emma and Lucy chorused.

'Come off it. You don't expect us to believe that! With that skirt?'

'I can wear what I like. But it's my body, like my mama said. I'm my own woman.'

'Blimey!' said Lucy. 'I always wondered what you were doing in a church youth club. I never thought you took what they tell you for

76

real. You don't go for that line, do you, Emma?'

'Yeah, well, you've got to live while you can, haven't you? I might be dead before I'm twenty.'

'Once you get to twenty, you might as well be dead.'

They lay still, silenced by the prospect of the years ahead of them. Margaret's mind adjusted her images of them. Emma's sweet, plump face, the long fair hair falling round it in soft waves, the purity of an English rose. Lucy, smaller, sharper-faced, aggressively battling for parity with the older ones. And Annie. Vibrant, gorgeous, sexual Annie, who must surely make any man in the room with her pulse with desire.

Biology made no such obvious laws for reproduction. It was not the most beautiful, the most talented, the healthiest girls, who got pregnant too soon. *Blessed are the meek, for they shall inherit the earth.* No! She pulled herself up, shocked. Yet, in a way, these were the madonnas of the estates, acquiring for the first time in their lives significance through an unintended but cherished baby.

What about the young fathers? Were bragging claims even now being whispered in the boys' rooms, under the nose of Don or Brian?

She began to imagine Brian, lying as she was in the darkness. He had probably not been embarrassed as she was, undressing in public. What did he wear in bed? Sensible pyjamas? A pair of shorts? Or did he sleep naked? She smiled, and then gasped in surprise at the response of her body.

Could biology betray even me? I must stop this, now.

The older girls were breathing more sleepily. Ceri snored. Could Annie protect her from her cynical sister? Would Ceri need to be as beautiful and glamorous as Annie to have the confidence to wait? Was Lucy boasting of what had never happened, ashamed of her innocence?

Sex had played little part in Margaret's life for several years. Why now? Was it just the hormones warning her it was nearly too late for more children?

Her mind went back, with a shiver of delight, to that morning in the garden. Brian kissing her on the lips. It had meant only friendship on his side, hadn't it?

15

It was the urge for privacy, as much as spirituality, which drew her out to pray in the early morning now. Sometimes she saw Brian in the distance, a lean dark brushstroke on the beach or the road. She fled from him. She was as much afraid, though in a different way, of meeting him alone as of meeting God under this vast Hebridean sky, with the ocean dancing dangerously all around them. Too much light, too much silence, too much depth, too much beauty. She would not know how to withstand the impact.

The cast threw themselves into rehearsals with abandon. They had cast off their last inhibitions and teenage lethargy with the ship's hawsers at Oban. The band played their hearts out, visibly revelling in the music, the freedom to pound it out, the admiration of the other young people in the hostel. Yet it lacked the punch of Laurie's drums. Margaret thought wistfully how much he would have enjoyed this week, if only she had been able to persuade him. She had lost her unsuspecting chaperon. She must keep her inhibitions in place herself.

Michelle, the Fellowship's director of music, heard them rehearsing. She scheduled them to perform for the whole island on Friday night. She had other plans for the band, too. Soon the guitars and saxophones and keyboard were skirling with the unaccustomed lilt of Scottish folk tunes. The toes of the dancers tapped to a different rhythm.

After the Tuesday rehearsal, cast and musicians slumped, sweaty and exhausted, on the floor around Brian.

'Tell them a story,' he smiled innocently at Margaret. 'Tell them how Columba stole the book.'

She was startled out of near-anonymity. By this third day she had found a routine for herself that enabled her to feel useful, but was not too threatening. There were gaps in the cast list, as well as the band. She read whatever part was required: the chief Druid, a woman weeping over the battlefield, she had even mimed the monastery's old white horse. She took turns with Ruth and Don at keeping busy anyone who was not immediately needed on stage. They were creating a frieze of the sea: found objects from the beach, paintings psychedelically marbled in swirls of blue and green, indigo and purple, gold and scarlet. They added collages of Celtic coracles, mermaids, dolphins.

Brian was gazing at her expectantly.

'But they know it already,' she protested. 'It's in the script.'

'Tell us,' he compelled her. 'Tell it here. Show us what it meant.'

It was unfair. He should have warned her. She hated to perform extempore. She needed to consult her sources, make notes, arrange her points. He was the bard, not she.

She did not know how to resist the smile in his eyes.

'Columba was born a prince of the O'Neill, the ruling clan in Ulster,' she began, and heard her voice strengthen as she warmed to her theme. 'There was a High King in Tara over all the kings of Ireland, but the North always thought itself different from the rest.'

So it went on. The high-blooded prince who could have been King of Ulster one day, but chose instead to become a monk.

'But that didn't stop him being as proud and hot-tempered as he was before. When his cousins were out raiding the borders for cattle, he'd be raiding the monastery library to see what treasures he could find in the books. And what do you think the most important book in a monastery would be?'

'The ferry timetable to get out of there,' Pete murmured.

Margaret ignored him. She painted for them the picture of a scriptorium in the days before printing, when every book had to be copied out by hand. It could take weeks to write a single book of the Bible, years for a splendid Gospel to display on the altar. There would be whole pages of intricate pattern, or a single capital letter coming to life as an animal.

'For these really splendid copies, it took the skin of one calf to make each double page.'

'Ugh! That's gross!'

She had them leaning forward now, both fascinated and repelled. She told how, when Columba was already famous, his old teacher Finnian came back from his travels with a new version of the Psalms. This was the most precious book to the Celts, next to the Gospel. They sang through the whole of it every week.

'So Columba set his heart on having his own copy of Finnian's new book, but he was either told or he feared that the abbot wouldn't agree. Columba was a proud prince, and he wasn't a man who liked to be said "no" to. He copied it in secret, probably at night by the light of a single candle. All one hundred and fifty psalms. It was a tremendous work.

'But once it was done, a treasure like that couldn't be kept secret. Finnian said Columba had stolen that copy. Since Finnian owned the original, then the copy belonged to him, too. He demanded that Columba hand it over.'

'The old meanie!'

Margaret laughed. 'We have laws today about pirating other people's work, words or music. Anyway, Columba wasn't going to give in without a fight, any more than his warrior cousins would have given back the cattle they stole from their neighbours. He refused.

'Finnian took him to the court of the High King at Tara. And the High King ruled against Columba. He said, "To every cow belongs her calf." He ordered Columba to give back the book he'd worked so hard to copy.

'And that was a red rag to a prince of Ulster. There was bad blood already between the North and the High King. Columba went rampaging home in a furious temper, taking the stolen book with him. And all his family rallied round him. The honour of Ulster had been insulted. They'd rather go to war than give in. So, for Columba and his holy book, they fought a great battle at Culdrevny, in the west. Thousands were killed.'

'Just for a book?' said Ceri.

'For pride. Because Columba wouldn't be told he had to give up what he'd stolen.

'The Church was appalled at the bloodshed. Columba was a priest, an abbot. They called him before their council, and that was much worse than the High King's court. They voted to excommunicate him, throw him out of the Christian Church. Just two men pleaded for mercy for him. One was Finnian, the very man Columba had stolen his book from.

'And because of Finnian's pleading, the council didn't throw him out of the Church. Instead, they threw him out of his country. Columba had to turn his back on his abbeys in Ireland and set out in a boat. And when he reached a land from which he could no longer see Ireland, he must work at saving life. He was to rescue as many souls from darkness as the thousands who'd been killed at the battle of Culdrevny.

'And the land where he chose to begin a new life was Hy.'

Her heart was beating hard as she watched their faces gaze beyond the windows at the sea-bright sky, the little cathedral church, the monastery risen again from its ruins. Ruth, she noticed, was staring down at her lap, plucking at the crease in her trousers. She put up her hand to brush her eyes, as though the story of that long-ago theft had moved or upset her.

Margaret caught Brian's eyes. They smiled for her, brighter than the dancing sea.

'Should have posted that book on the internet,' said Sean. 'That'd have sorted it.'

That afternoon, it was Ruth's turn to stay behind. Margaret was tempted by the offer of a boat trip to see puffins on the island of Staffa.

Ian warned, 'The wind's fresh. It's unlikely that wee boat will be able to get in to the landing stage. But he'll cruise round the island and you'll see plenty birds.'

Margaret imagined the small open boat on the heaving swell,

under the glistening basalt cliffs, gliding among the rocks with its engine cut. She thought better of it. Don went, with a couple of the boys.

Two hours of leisure stretched in front of her. This was her opportunity to venture further than the early morning search for solitude. It felt strange, setting out alone. She felt herself unexpect-edly missing Maurice, striding out beside her, confidently taking over the map, telling her where he thought they should go. It was not the loneliness that disturbed her, but the knowledge that, here, all such decisions were hers. Marriage, with its commitment to consider someone else's wishes before her own, was temporarily laid aside. And, of course, it was only temporary. Now that she thought about it, the independence tasted sweeter, perhaps not threatening at all. She smiled, a sense of responsibility lifting from her. She really was free. She could do what she liked.

But what? She had made no plans. There was nothing outside the monastery she specifically wanted to go and see by herself. Tomorrow, members of the Fellowship would lead them on the weekly pilgrimage around the island. They would guide her to remote places, like the bay where Columba landed. Perhaps this afternoon she should forget history, revel instead in the present of pale beaches and turquoise sea. She would just walk where the fancy took her.

Prudently, she put the map in her pocket. Wherever she went, she would need to find the way back.

She stepped out on to the path, and was greeted by half a dozen of her party, sprawled in a patch of sunshine.

'You're not going to sit there all afternoon, are you?' she chided them, smilingly. 'You may never come back here again, you know.'

'Did you remember to sign out, miss?' Lucy raised her crafty, challenging eyes.

'You're right. I'm setting you a bad example, aren't I?' Conscientiously, Margaret turned back to the porch.

She signed her name in Don's book. Her hand paused over the space beside it. She had no idea where she was going. After a moment's thought, she wrote: 'Walk round north end of island.'

She went through the gate and almost immediately regretted her decision. North was the direction she took every morning, away from the village. True, she had never gone on beyond the headland, round to the western shore, but the south and the interior were all unexplored, too.

Still, she had committed herself to the north. Where everything was unknown, any direction promised the discovery of a small miracle. She would trust herself, like a Celtic pilgrim, to the wind of the Spirit.

Freed from the purposefulness of prayer, she could look about her more eagerly and find nuances in the beauty that might themselves become occasions of prayer. The sand was not, after all, silver, but washed with the palest warm gleam, like semi-skimmed milk. Rocks were not only black and grey, but also a startling pink, sparkling with crystals. When the breeze brushed over the gorse bushes, it released the fragrance of coconut.

She let down the barriers of her mind to allow all these physical impressions in. But at the same time she was raising a hedge of protection. She would not let her thoughts turn inward. She would simply be where she was. It was dangerous to daydream here.

She rounded the northern headland, where the road ran out. Now, for the first time, she took the path that bent south, along the western shore. As she turned to face a different sea, the wind caught her with its full force. Her mind flew to Don and the boys in their little boat. She would not have enjoyed its pitching. She had been right to change her mind.

It was almost hard to breathe. She thrust her hands into the pockets of her jacket, hunched her shoulders and felt the wind tearing at handfuls of her hair. It was not Ireland she was facing towards, over the horizon, but a vaster ocean. Nothing between her and Canada.

She left the path and trudged along the beach. There were a few people scattered across its shimmering expanse. Walkers like her, others more slowly beachcombing for curious stones and shells. She preserved a distance. This brief independence, which had struck her as unfamiliar, was now precious.

Rocks barred her way. She glanced at her watch. Not half an

hour had gone. She could go much further yet.

Retreating to the grassy path, she made her way above sea-washed slabs, past pinnacles where lichen blazed yellow as gorse, until the path skirted a knoll and the path dipped down into a sandy cove. Her legs were weary now, the afternoon half gone. There was no one else in view.

She opened the map. It was not easy to be sure where she was, even so. There had been so many indentations in the coast, so many sea-girt rocks. She had no compass. But since this beach was sandy, it might be Port Ban, the White Bay, sheltered by the Island of Protection.

She retraced her steps and climbed the knoll. She was facing south, to where the coast swung round into a wider bay. Vivid against its pale sand waved a vast green meadow. It was unlike anything she had seen on the east of the island, where there were only a few small rough fields, with sentinel bulrushes. She did not need to check her map. Her mind instantly supplied the historic name for it: the Machair, the monastery pasture. It was not difficult to people that sweet, succulent turf with contented cattle. Here was the source of the monks' milk and butter and cheese. Here would have staggered slender-legged calves, their delicate hides destined to become pages inscribed and illuminated for such treasures as the Book of Kells. Here, the milk churns were loaded on the old white horse, Columba's friend, who had nuzzled the old abbot on his last walk round Hy.

Enough. No more history. She was going to be resolutely physical this afternoon. Time was passing. She needed to decide her way back. She sat down, crouched over to shelter the map from the wind as she unfolded it again. She could, of course, go back the way she had come. Every walk looks different when traversed in the opposite direction. She might catch a sight of the boat coming back from Staffa. But retracing her steps seemed like a defeat of her new-found adventurousness. She studied the map for some other way back. There was a road across the middle of the island, from the Machair to the other coast, well south of the village. But it was too late to attempt so large a circuit. A tangle of footpaths ran more directly back, threading through the northern group of the island's small hills.

It was a risk. The path she chose might prove a clear track, with no possibility of mistaking it, or it might lose itself amongst grass and heather, indistinguishable from a thousand rabbit runs. Habitual prudence counselled her to stay on a known, frequented route. She was alone. If she got into trouble, there would be no one to go for help. She had written nothing in the book to suggest a journey into the interior. But the challenge was there. Surely, with a map and common sense, on an island only a mile wide, it should not be beyond her intelligence to get herself back safely.

16

As she turned her back to the sea the sense struck her, like the wind between her shoulder blades, that this might be foolish, that she was leaving behind the path she knew, which would bring her surely home. Here, in the Dark Ages, the sea was the familiar highway that linked people together. Inland was the dangerous unknown.

You're exaggerating, she told herself. It's only a mile or so. You can't get lost.

The path forked disconcertingly often. Her map, she found, was a bold sketch, rather than a detailed survey. It was hard to know whether every trail across the hillside was shown. She looked behind her, to where the sun was slanting down towards the western sea. Without a compass, she tried to gauge her direction from it. But she did not know its trajectory at this time of year, this far north. It must, she thought, be near the spring equinox, when days and nights are equal, but she was uncertain how to interpret that knowledge.

She must rely on instinct. Somewhere, over these small, rough hills, lay the hostel. If she walked away from one coast, she would reach the other.

As she climbed, Margaret began to feel more positively adventurous. With each decision made, she was penetrating deeper into this wilderness of boggy grass, boulders, the wiry stems of last year's heather. If she persisted, the time must come when she passed the middle of the island and glimpsed the Channel of Hy again.

The path she had chosen was rising, taking her up perhaps higher than she had intended. She paused at a stile in a fence. Now one track rose sharply away up a considerable hill. Another wound on, through the softer, wetter ground around the contour. Common sense dictated that the path through that gap would be muddier but shorter than the hill route, and that the latter would only add height she must lose later. She spread out the map on the bar of the stile, trying to disguise from herself the panicking realization that she no longer knew where she was. If she climbed the hill, would she see the hostel and get her bearings?

'I should have known you'd find it out for yourself.'

His voice hailed her from a distance, the teasing warmth of his laughter instantly recognizable.

Pure delight washed through her. Magical, as always, Brian had appeared like the wizard of fairy tales, when the protagonist most needs direction. In place of a pointed hat, he was wearing that ridiculous blue bobble cap, which made him look like a long-legged gnome. She watched him come. Already she was folding up the map she no longer needed. Brian surely would know the way back.

She was laughing too before he reached her, her anxiety dissolved.

'I haven't found anything! But I've lost my bearings. I was rather rashly trying to take a short cut back to the hostel.'

'Not found anything? Margaret, you should give your instincts more credit. They've been leading you to holy ground, one of my favourite places. After you.'

He was indicating that she should cross the stile.

'Is this a good idea? Wouldn't it be quicker if we stayed on the low path?'

'Trust me. It's only a little climb, but it'll lead you to great heights.' His eyes were close to hers now. They were dancing with laughter, like the blue-grey waves, willing her to do what he wanted. As always, she let him have his way.

He steadied her as she mounted the stile, though she did not need his help. Yet he left a distance between them as he strode forward. She felt his attention had turned away from her, towards their goal. She studied the hillside above. A narrow gap between the pink-washed boulders. Yellow flames of gorse. Brian turned to watch her follow him through the gap in the rocks. Then he went bounding ahead up a steeper scramble.

They were in a small meadow on a natural shelf facing back to the western sea she had left. Margaret realized with a lurch of anxiety that they must still be further from home than she had calculated.

But Brian's attention was absorbed by this place. He was standing now by a ring of built stones, lost to the lateness of the time, the waiting teenagers, to Ruth, and even, she realized, to her. Margaret's practical worries were beguiled by the magic emanating from him.

As she came up to him, he turned. And now there was delicious laughter again as he anticipated the discovery she was about to make. He was like a small boy waiting for his mother to unwrap her birthday present. Yet there was something else deeper under the surface. He had been coming here anyway. This place mattered to him.

It became important to her that it should matter to her, too.

He stepped away to allow her to see better. Leaving her with a confident grin, he sat down with his back towards the stones, careless of the damp turf. He linked his hands round his bony knees and stared out at the bright line of surf rippling away from the outlying rocks. He had gone beyond her.

She could not turn her back on this circle of stones as readily as he did. It was the remnant of a small building, obviously. But what? A recent shepherd's bothy? Something much older?

After a while, he tilted his head back up to her. 'Well?'

'It could be any age. The building techniques haven't changed much, although we're fonder of right angles nowadays.' But the smile could not help breaking through. 'Still, since you've dragged me up here to see it, it's a safe bet that it's more than a nineteenth-century shieling. Has it got something to do with Columba?'

His smile sparked out to meet hers, approving.

'His hermitage.'

'The *dysart*? His "dear desert", where he would come to meditate alone.'

'You knew that?' He sounded a little disappointed.

'I didn't know where it was. But I knew he'd have one. They all
did. Aidan on a rock off Lindisfarne. Columbanus in Burgundy,
turning the bear out of her cave. Kevin at a Bronze Age barrow
above the lakes of Glendalough. Every abbot needs a place to be
alone with God, like Jesus in the wilderness. That's why their desert
was dear.'

'Aye. We need solitude.'

She looked down at him tenderly. His eyes had gone back to the
horizon. Below the knitted cap, his face looked taut and lined. The
smile had withdrawn.

'I'm sorry. I'm in the way. You were going to come here alone.'

'No. I wanted you to be here.'

Professional courtesy? The minister conscientiously setting aside
his own needs for one of his congregation?

'Sit down,' he commanded.

After a moment's hesitation, she obeyed. It seemed too calculat-
ingly careful to take off her jacket and spread it out first. She knew
he meant her to give herself to this experience without reserve. She
settled a little distance away, unsure how much space he needed.
He turned his face to the sea again. He was expecting her to do the
same.

She was aware of what he was inviting her to do. To go beyond
facts. To abandon all academic scepticism about whether the turbu-
lent fortunes of Hy could have preserved a memory of the exact
location of Columba's hermitage. If not here, then it must have
been somewhere like this. This was reality. He was willing her to be
where she was, to suspend disbelief, to imagine truth.

The sun was shining directly in her eyes. It laid a bright barred
sea-road towards Ireland. To the Blessed Isles of Paradise. To the
fairyland of the Ever-Young.

But soon they would have to turn and face the east. Return to the
monastery, and all the responsibilities that waited there.

Columba had sat here, far more grievously burdened. The care of his monks, body and soul. The call from the Scottish court, to be their kingmaker. The forbidding mountains beyond that must be penetrated through the deep Great Glen, to challenge the Picts and their Druids and win them for Christ.

What were the cares that Brian brought here? She stole a glance sideways. The sun picked out the little tufts of hair at the side of his jaw, which made her think he secretly would like to grow a beard. She noticed with a start that they were not fair, as she had supposed, but white. For all his youthful zest and laughter, time had not stood still. How much of an effort was it for him to attract and jolly the youngsters into doing what he wanted, making it seem so spontaneous, like a rock Peter Pan? She felt a rush of protectiveness, so that she had to will her hand to stay still and not reach out across the daisy-starred turf to cover his.

'I love you,' he said, still gazing before him out to sea.

The wind seemed to halt. The words hung in mid-air, too dangerous, too dear, for her to accept.

After a long silence, he turned his face slowly towards her. She dared not look directly at him. He looked so sad. She was aware of the nakedness of need and the restraint that was forbidding him to ask her what he wanted. It seemed so different from purely physical lust. She sensed an ache that made her yearn to get up and throw her arms around him. She willed herself to sit still.

'I know. It's a very precious friendship,' she said carefully. She was pleading with him. A word more, one movement, could wreck it.

And yet she wanted him to move. His eyes held hers.

'Did you think it was no more than that?'

'I thought I could help you.'

'You do. Are you afraid because I give myself back to you?'

'Ssh. Don't say anything else.'

'The truth shall set you free.' He was still not smiling.

'But we're not free. There's Ruth.'

'Not Maurice?'

She blushed at her own omission. 'And Maurice.'

The silence lengthened. She dragged her eyes away. The wind

was streaking long banners of clouds above the horizon. Their parallel gazes avoided the knowledge in each other's faces.

Then he spoke again, 'I wasn't going to ask if you loved me. It seemed unfair. But I think you've answered.'

'There's no point in discussing it. Neither of us can do anything about it. It's only going to spoil what we have already.' Her voice was rising in desperation.

'Margaret. Don't be afraid. *I love you.*' He said the words over again, joyfully now, as though he was tasting a new line of poetry.

'Don't say it.'

'I should like to hear you say it. Just once.'

'We can't.'

'Just say it.'

'I love you.' Like a little girl repeating a lesson. Tears were running down her cheeks.

'It's all right. That's all I'll ever ask. Though you're making it very difficult for me not to put my arms round you. I wasn't going to.'

It was she who turned, shuffling close to him, till he could pull her weeping face down on to his shoulder. He held her with studied lightness. His hand played in her hair.

'The wind's tangled it.'

'We've got to get back. I'll look a mess. Red eyes and covered in grass stains.'

'A fallen woman. Don't worry. I promise I won't hurt you.'

She felt herself tremble in the comfort of his arms, unsure what that meant. She was longing for him, as her body had not longed for a man since she was a student. Had she really loved Maurice with a passion like this? Held close, she could feel the tenseness of Brian's own body, too.

'Margaret, be still. It's all right. Or all wrong,' he whispered. 'We've both made promises to other people. We're neither of us about to break them.' He put her away from him. She wanted to protest at the cruelty of separation, but she must not.

'Then we shouldn't be here, saying what we have said.'

'You can't tell me I shouldn't love you. It's impossible not to.'

'But we can't do anything about it.'

91

'You've done what I never believed would be possible. You've said "I love you".'

'I shouldn't have. *You* shouldn't have.'

'I didn't plan this. To find you here. To tell you I love you. But when I did it, it seemed so good, so natural. You felt that, didn't you?'

'What if Ruth had come round those rocks and found you holding me?'

'Ruth's looking after the hostel. I promise you, we won't either of us do anything to hurt her. You know we can't.'

'Or deceive her?'

He turned to look at her, his blue eyes steadily burning. 'Nothing physical will happen, Margaret, I promise you. I'm flesh and blood. I wish that it could, but that's not possible. And you don't have to tell me I shouldn't even think that. *He who looks at a woman to lust after her has committed adultery already in his heart.* Only today, just for once, I'm being wonderfully honest. I can't tell you how that feels, to know I can trust you. A minister spends most of his life acting the part. Sometimes I think I can't go on. I need you, Margaret. I still love Ruth, but just now it's you I need.'

'That's what I thought I was doing before. Being the person you needed. But it can't be like that ever again.'

'Don't leave me!' She saw the panic in his face, like a small boy, the startled move towards her.

'How can I leave? I wish you hadn't said anything! The sort of friendship we had together was something I've never known before. It was the best thing that ever happened to me. But we can't pretend it can go on now.'

'Can't we? If I can act a life because that's what people need from me, can't you?'

'Oh, don't be ridiculous! Do you think I can go on meeting you? Giving you tea? Trying to chat about poetry as if nothing had happened and wondering . . .'

'If I'm ever going to kiss you?' His eyes began to dance again.

'Don't! You mustn't.'

He put his hand over hers to still them. They were still apart, but she could feel the unbearable warmth of his nearness.

'Margaret, Margaret. We have to find some way to live with the truth. It's got to be an honourable way. I'm not going to believe the gift of your love is something dirty, something shameful. You're too fine a person. And yet you love me.' His voice curled upwards in wonder.

'I can't see you alone again. I can't bear to. Why did you have to tell me?'

'We've both said what we needed to say. The plain truth. I warned you Hy was dangerous. A thin place, where the skin between the physical and the spiritual can easily be stepped through.'

'And that's what's wrong. That you and I can't separate the physical from the spiritual any longer. That's what I mean. It *isn't* holy.'

'In an incarnational religion the physical should be sacred . . . You're right. We have to go home.' He stood up, so that his words had a doubled meaning. 'Put our lives back into the old tidy compartments.'

'You told me Hy would change me.' She stood facing him. 'Is this what you meant?'

'Are you angry with me? Do you want me to leave Boulton? Find another church?'

'No. . . ! It's not just for me,' she added, but the cry had come too quickly.

'Then help me serve this one.'

'I was doing that. Why did you have to say it?'

'You said it too. You didn't deny it. You couldn't.'

Even now, they were half-laughing as they argued helplessly. Brian was still holding her hand. He drew her towards him swiftly, so that she thought he was going to kiss her, then released her, leaving her desolate. He lifted a rebellious strand of hair from her face. 'The wind makes my eyes water, too.'

There was a long walk ahead of them. In the distance she glimpsed the hostel as they rounded the hill. She longed to be back there now, protected by the crowd, by the necessity of duty to lay tables, supervise painting, help Tim telephone his mother.

93

'We're going to be late back.'

'I'll tell them the truth. You were lost and I found you.'

The hostel had been in view for nearly half an hour, as they picked their way down off the hills, over saturated fields, across stiles. Margaret wanted to separate as they drew near it, but Brian would not let her.

'I met you by accident. That's the truth, isn't it? In all innocence, I'd have walked you home.'

'You're going to pretend things are the same as before?'

'Nothing else will happen. We love each other. That's all.'

She shook her head, incredulous.

The big common room they used for rehearsals was full. Tea was over. They were late. Margaret fled to her room to shed her jacket and change her boots. She felt like an embarrassed teenager, sidling into the common room, knowing that everyone would have seen her arriving back late with Brian.

He was ahead of her, forging a path through the crowd, waving to Don.

'You didn't get shipwrecked on Staffa, then? Did you see the puffins? They never come out on film the way you hope, do they? I'm always pointing to these little specks on the crest of a wave and telling people, "That's a puffin. Honest. Trust me." '

Margaret wanted to avoid Ruth. She crept round the side of the room towards the fireplace. But suddenly Ruth was there. Her shoulders, in the newly bought sweatshirt, were squared. Her face bore that habitual humourless, slightly accusing air.

'Did you have any more crises this afternoon?' Margaret got in first.

'No. I had a quiet shift. And a long one. Where were you?' It was, like most things about Ruth, direct.

'I went exploring round the north coast. Only then, I rather rashly decided to cut back across country. The map I've got leaves a lot to be desired when it comes to marking footpaths. Or else I'm a rotten navigator. Fortunately, your husband caught up with me and showed me the way back, or I'd probably still be paddling around in a bog.'

94

The flow of words came out so easily. All of them true. Ruth stared at her in silence.

'I suppose Brian would have got back faster if he'd been on his own.'

'Yes. I'm sure he would. I did tell him to go on ahead.'

It was all so plausible. They both knew it was exactly what Brian would have done, overtaking one of his party who was lost. He would not have left a lost sheep to struggle back alone.

Ruth turned away. 'It's Columba's death scene. We're short of someone to play his servant, Diarmit. Could you read it?'

It was a major part. The devoted monk who wakes to the midnight bell and finds that the dying Columba has run from his bed and light is blazing from the abbey church. He rushes in to find his master prostrate on the altar steps. As the monks pour in behind him with torches, he cradles Columba in his arms and raises his hand to make the final blessing.

It was both a relief and an ordeal to be centre stage. There was so much for her to do, a part laid down for her, so that she could cease to be Margaret Jenkins. While she was absorbed in the part, it was impossible to think about what had happened.

But she felt their eyes on her. Annie, waiting between the cascades of song which were the linking narration. Dark, thoughtful eyes fixed on Margaret. Emma, watching her over the rim of her saxophone. Lucy and Ceri, whose faces in performance would be shaded by monks' cowls, now openly curious. Margaret knew enough about the ways of teenage girls to guess the gossip that would be going on just out of earshot. So her schoolfriends had discussed their teachers with casual speculation or slanderous innuendo.

She concentrated on the script, line by line.

There was a giggling in the darkness.

'Miss,' came Lucy's whisper, 'do you fancy Brian?'

Margaret was startled out of the silence of sleepiness into a different silence. She was alert, terrified.

Annie's voice cut across the room. 'Lucy! That's rude.'

'Oh, hoity-toity! I only asked, didn't I? What with her coming in late with him like that. Did you see Mrs Hargreaves' face?'

It took a second for Margaret to connect the rarely used surname with Ruth's direct, unsmiling stare.

'I got lost,' she said. 'Brian overtook me and showed me the way back. I don't suppose I walked as fast as he would have done on his own. It just shows it's really not a good idea to go off on your own, even at my age.'

'Is that how you both got grass stains all over your trousers?'

Annie sat up. 'You've got a dirty mind, Lucy Pargeter. You just apologize to Margaret this instant. Do you think a person can't be friends with a man without it having to be sex? We're not all like you.'

'Oh, pardon me, Miss Chastity! If your nose turns up much higher, it'll scratch your eyebrows.'

'Shut up, you two. Some of us are trying to get some sleep,' moaned Emma. 'What's the big deal, anyway? People are having it off all the time.'

'Not *them*. He's a Methodist minister, isn't he?'

'Of course he is. That's why you're talking nonsense.' Margaret felt authority slipping away from her. At the university, her students respected her. They wanted what she could give them – knowledge, success. These girls barely understood why she was here. An extra body, to improve the ratio of adults to teenagers. It was Annie who had authority, because the younger ones wanted what she had – beauty, glamour, a heart-stopping singing voice. But Annie's morality was uncomfortably further away from the truth than Lucy's snide questioning.

She felt soiled. Why was she here? Because Brian had wanted her company? He had needed to share the island he loved so much with her this time, not just with Ruth. She tried to cradle that first moment, like a jewelled bubble she was terrified would burst. Sitting near her, yet not touching, gazing out to a limitless sea with that naked honesty in his face. *Margaret, be still . . . I love you.*

There must be no before and after. Only that moment was permissible. She could not bear to cancel it and wish it had never been. But it must never happen again.

17

Wednesday was the pivot of the week. There would be no rehearsal today. All twenty of their party were gathered by St John's Cross outside the monastery for the pilgrimage around Columba's island. Even Tim, still manfully limping, refused to be left behind. The crowd was spread wide in the whipping wind, others from the hostel and the monastery, a few from hotels and guesthouses. They were colourful in their anoraks, picnics stowed in knapsacks, faces turned expectantly to the leaders.

Michelle, the Fellowship's musical director, was in charge today. She stood tall, the wind tangling her long brown hair, surveying them all with a shepherd's smile.

Is this a chore for them? Margaret wondered, assessing other young staff beside Michelle. Do some of them get detailed for this every week, while the others get a day off? 'Oh, bother, I'm on pilgrimage tomorrow.' Or is this always as special for them as it is for us?

She remembered how easy it had been to get lost, just crossing from one coast to another. Today they would be venturing much further, into the wilder south of the island, to its very extremity. She must not let herself imagine making that journey alone, nor what had happened on her far shorter exploration. She could not deny it had occurred, but she must put it behind her. Nothing must come of it, and nothing would.

Yet however hard she tried, it was impossible not to remember. Brian's arm around her as she wept into the hollow of his shoulder.

The effort it cost him to hold her gently. The rebellious longing of their bodies to meet, whatever their consciences protested.

She must not think about it, but it was difficult to think of anything else. Brian was standing close to Ruth this morning. For protection?

Michelle was speaking. The words floated past Margaret, uncomprehended. Even now, she found it hard to focus her attention. Michelle was telling them about the day ahead, leading them into the prayers of departure. No Celtic Christian would rise from bed, open the door, set out on a journey, without the appropriate three-fold blessing.

She tried to empty herself of historical knowledge. Live this day as it comes. Listen to the story as Michelle tells it. Hear it with the ears of Lucy and Annie and Tim. Let Hy speak to you as to a child.

If only.

The procession moved off. There were stops along the way. St Martin's Cross. The ruined nunnery, where Michelle's prayers made a spirited pitch for the femininity of God. She said nothing about the carving on the wall behind her, of the Sheela-na-gig with its blatant sexuality. She led them out beyond the village for the hills of the south.

They climbed into an increasingly beautiful day. Torn clouds were flying apart to reveal the duck-egg blue of the sky. Waves threw up ruffs of foam around the rocks. Skylarks ascended ahead of them out of cities of gorse to pour down a piercing clarity of song.

As they crossed the plateau and dropped down towards the southern sea, the way grew rockier and narrower. Brian stood long-legged over a rushing burn, steadying the less sure-footed across. Margaret cast wildly around for some other crossing place, even at the risk of wetting her socks. But Brian's hand was reaching out.

'Go on, Margaret. You can do it,' Annie urged.

She let him hold her. His smile almost undid her balance. Then he let her go and she was on the other side. Ruth, already across, had her camera trained on the scene as Annie followed.

Margaret paused. If Ruth had been anyone other than Brian's wife, she would have clutched at the security of another woman's company. She should, of course, be journeying alongside her teenage charges, using this opportunity to know them differently. But she was finding it hard to make sense of her thoughts this morning, let alone find conventional words.

She fled on ahead, before Brian could finish helping the others over. She found herself striding downhill beside an Irish nun, who talked non-stop about the thrill it was to her to be here on Columba's island, where the sainted man had walked himself.

'And him the Dove of the Church, the sweet man.'

Margaret bit back a crisp reply about Columba the wily fox and settled instead into grateful listening.

They came at last to the rocky shore. It took a while for the whole expedition to funnel out of the defile, spread across the grass and find the stony beach. They began to spread out, some beachcombing, others going down to the very edge of the waves to look out past the sentinel reefs, the way Columba had come sailing in. Some of the boys started to climb the rock stacks, golden with lichen, and Don went after them.

Margaret had lost her nun. She stood, feeling vulnerable in her solitude, but reluctant to make the effort to break out of it by approaching anyone else.

'Miss, miss. Look what I've found.' Tim was running to her, his bad knee forgotten, ploughing over the slithering shingle.

'What is it?' The smile she found for him was genuine.

'Look at that!' He was crowing with triumph. 'This is Columba's beach, innit? Where he landed? And look what I went and found.'

The stone had been scooped out by the sea, creamy-white on the ridges of its bone, yellow in the hollows. And marked across its concave face, as though by the ink of a scribe, was a black cross.

'That's magic, innit? It's got to be a holy stone, hasn't it?'

Geology was not among Margaret's accomplishments. She had no way of knowing how unusual this might be, what caused it. For once, she could not respond with information, only enthusiasm.

'It's lovely, Tim. Well done. I shouldn't think anyone else has found anything as special as this.'

He passed it to her. The stone had a smooth, warm feel, moulded by its history. It must have been ground out by its harder fellows, constantly dashing against it, wearing it away. But it had let itself be hollowed out by them, its own angularities giving way to accommodate them. Aeons of exposure to jolts and pressures had formed the beauty in her hand. But the cross had always been there, written into its structure long before it broke away to become an individual pebble. Her thumb caressed its contours. She was almost unwilling to hand it back. Slowly she held it out to Tim. He backed away.

'It's yours. I found it for you.'

'But it's so lovely, Tim. A stone with a cross, from Columba's beach. Don't you want to take it home for a souvenir?'

'You keep it, miss. Sort of like a present. Well, it's not much, is it? It's only a stone.'

'A very special stone. Thank you, Tim.'

She knew by the pride in his smile that she had done the right thing. Perhaps the chaplain Ian had been right. Perhaps she had touched Tim, somehow, for all her sense of inadequacy.

He dashed away, to throw wet seaweed over the girls. Soon there was a fight with sand, which she felt she perhaps should stop, but did not.

She still had the stone curled in the palm of her hand. It felt both solid and pliable. It fitted the curve of her fingers. It was oddly comforting.

'Penny for them?'

Brian was smiling, as always. She mastered her panic.

'I was thinking about my present.'

'Not about your future?'

'Not that sort of present. Tim gave me this.'

She opened her hand.

'Ah! I've sometimes gone looking for one of those, after other people found them. But I never have. Maybe it only comes as a gift, to people who aren't looking for treasure.'

She wanted him to go away. It was too difficult not to fall into that intimacy of talking with him, here on the open beach, surrounded by dozens of witnesses. Surely anyone looking at them must see how she felt. She did not dare to imagine what he was feeling.

A louder than usual yell from Ceri diverted their attention from each other.

'Heigh-ho. I think they've started the battle of Culdrevny all over again.'

He ran over the stones to haul Tim away. Margaret followed more slowly to comfort Ceri and wipe the grit from her eye.

She was alone again. Brian was surrounded by boys and girls. How could he be so light, so in charge of himself, so open to others, only a day later?

Does he really draw some of that strength from me? Am I necessary, to make it possible for him to do what he does? She was looking down at the stone, at the black cross embedded in the creamy pebble. He's a minister. I can't begin to understand the time he spends in prayer, studying the Bible, meditating with God. It's colossal pride to think I could have anything to do with the task he's given his life to. It's him. It's what he is. It's what he does. Him and God.

But the tufts of hair on the corner of his chin were turning white. The set of Ruth's jaw might mean she was cooling, hardening. And Brian was growing older, growing more tired. Each year it would be more of an effort to do what he had done before.

Did prayer cool and harden too, even for a minister of God? Did you wake sometimes with the icy fear that you had committed your life to the service of a God you were no longer sure you believed in? Even if the will approved, did the heart no longer feel the rush of love that had carried all before it?

The stone had grown warmer by her handling of it. It was an oddly precious gift. So unexpected. Both hand and stone were hidden in her pocket now, still twined together. She could not see the cross which marked it out from every other pebble. It was just a stone in her hand, but they felt good together.

The scattered pilgrimage was drawing together near the edge of the sea. Don had herded the boys down from the rocks. Belatedly, Margaret started to stumble down the shingle to join them.

'This is the Port of the Curragh,' Michelle was saying, her clear musical voice ringing across the wind. 'The southernmost point of

Hy. This is the beach where Columba landed, when he was driven out from Ireland. When his curragh grounded and he stepped ashore, he knew he had found the place of his exile, and the place of his resurrection. He was beginning a new life. He put the old painful things he had done behind him. From now on, he would throw his heart into doing good.

'We have a tradition on the pilgrimage at Columba's Landing. We invite you to pick up one of these stones. Hold it in your hand and think about it. That stone represents something in your life that is a burden on you. Something you did that was wrong, something that is stopping you doing what you feel you should, some thought that is spoiling your life. Put it into that stone. Think of the freedom that will be yours if only you could get rid of it.

'When you are ready, walk down to the water and cast it away from you into the ocean. Then turn your back on it and walk away, into God's freedom.'

For some it was part game, for others more serious, as everyone began to look for their particular stone.

Margaret stood rigid. She already had her stone, clutched in the secret of her pocket. She did not need to take it out to see its meaning.

But she could not throw this away. It was a present. Tim would be hurt if he saw her cast it into the sea.

It was not Tim she was thinking of.

There were thousands of other stones on the beach: grey, white, sparkling with quartz, marbled with green. Each one uniquely beautiful, tempting one to keep it. Any one of them would do. It did not have to be *this* one.

But she knew that it did.

Arms were swinging against the sunlit sky. Stones arced through the brightness to fall with the lightest of splashes into the running waves. It was so quick, for such a defining moment. Seen, then gone. Her breath stopped for a moment as she saw Brian hurl his in a spinning arc. What did he mean by it? What had he done? Zak, Emma, Ceri, even the young ones' faces had a solemnity printed upon them as they walked up from the tideline, not looking back.

Ruth approached her. 'Haven't you got rid of yours yet? Just pick a stone. Don't agonize over it.'

'You're right. I'm being too portentous.'

She found, at random, an egg-shaped pebble, half green, half reddish-yellow. Briefly she saw how the colours would intensify if she dipped it in water. She hurried down to where the ripples were pushing a wash of silver higher up the stones. She bent her elbow to throw, and only checked when at the last moment she realized her stone had no meaning. What else could she throw away? It was like scrabbling around for a New Year's resolution. She thought of the painstaking insistence with which she criticized every detail of her students' work. She must be warmer. She should praise more. Value the fiery red as well as the cool green. Allow them to see more of her genuine enthusiasm for their work. She hurled the hard, cold stone away. Her hands had not had time to warm it. It fell with a satisfying plunk. She turned, relieved. It had not cost her much.

The cross-marked stone hung in her pocket. She had needed to let go of it to throw the other. But she could still feel the weight of it dragging on her side, as she followed after the others.

They came down off the highest cliffs to a bay of opal brilliance, an impossibly turquoise sea, shot with purple, and laced with the pale fire of the sandy beach. The colours were so vivid that Margaret knew, even as she photographed it, no one would believe she had not used a filter. For a mile or more the rugged shore dropped into the flat calm of a vast bright green meadow, puckered only by sand dunes.

Now she had drawn the string of the island full circle. This was the plain she had seen from the northern rocks, the Machair, the monastery's pasture. A knot tightened in her stomach. Soon today would be meeting yesterday. She could not put it away from her. The stone still weighted her pocket.

Perhaps it was not too late. She could take it out now, drop it unnoticed on the downward path. She had it in her hand. She tried gently loosening her fingers. It almost slipped. She clutched it back in a panic.

What would it mean to let it go? Whatever she held was so newly discovered she hardly knew what it was, except that it was precious. Perhaps it was no more than the delight they had shared in each other's company for so many months, innocently. It had become explosive only because Brian had dared to name it.

The stone in her hand was both hard and warm. Physical. She could not deny the joy she had felt, shaken by tears, to be lying in his arms. It must not happen again. It would not. But she perhaps did not have to deny herself the childlike pleasure of those afternoons, sharing tea on the flowered cushions of the cane chairs, watching the koi leap in the sunlit pond and talking of poetry. Surely that could still go on? It must, for Brian's sake. He needed her.

The turf welcomed their tired feet. Some of the teenagers started to run towards the beach. Brian strode on, like a man who knew where he was going, to a stack of great boulders that formed the half-way mark.

Margaret had placed herself in the role of back marker, to encourage the stragglers. Lucy looked pale and was limping slightly.

'I don't expect you're used to a route march like this,' Margaret tried to sympathize. 'You're doing well.'

'S'nothing. I can keep dancing for six hours, Saturday nights. It's just there's nobody selling you E's here.'

She's hoping to shock me, Margaret realized. She thinks I'll hold up my hands in horror at the notion of drugs. If a church youth group isn't her scene, why does she keep on coming? She knew the answer, of course. It was the same with her own son, Laurie, who would have fled the church long since. They all loved Brian.

She saw that he had settled himself down with an air of justified bliss, his back to the great rock. He had taken out his picnic box and placed it on his upraised knees, but not opened it. He was visibly enjoying the sun on his face, the cries of the youngsters charging over the grass, the sense of centuries of sanctity permeating this landscape, devotion physically expressed in the mooing of the vanished herd, the warm udders spurting milk, the staggering calves, the sheep cropping this jewel-bright turf.

Ruth had seated herself a little way away, and Don joined her. For all his professional gregariousness, Brian managed to create a space around him, an invisible halo of joy, that asked to be respected. Margaret felt the tug. If it had not been for the others, she felt she could have sat on the edge of that shimmering circle, silently sharing his joy, creating her own halo. He would not have turned his head or spoken. He would have known she was there and welcomed her. When she was with him, it was for him not an intrusion but a completion of himself.

That is what love is, more than a physical joining. Brian would simply be less than he was, without her. Her thumb stroked the hollow of the stone she could not let go.

The afternoon was the hardest, for both of them. Margaret almost recoiled when she saw where Michelle was leading them, over the stile, up the hill to Columba's hermitage. Brian had known. He had been on this pilgrimage before. He had not warned her. She should have seen the inevitability for herself.

She was still the back marker. There was safety in letting the others stream up through the defile and find the grassy plateau ahead. By the time she reached it, the space was bright with anoraks and backpacks, bodies slumped down around the stone walls, or exploring the cliffs behind, or gazing for the last time on the western waves. Brian, she noticed, had taken himself off some distance from the hut.

She made herself concentrate, as though she had never heard it before, on Michelle's explanation of what a Celtic hermitage was for. The extravagance of prayer and fasting. The love of wild animals, who so often crept or flew to a hermit's hands. The simple food that the earth provided.

'But the sea had become a dangerous road. After Columba's time, the Vikings began to arrive. Now it wasn't the Spirit flying down the path of the sun, but the square striped sails of the longships. The monks of Hy were tortured and killed, to make them tell where they'd hidden the monastery's treasures. But the survivors took the most precious bones and books with them, fleeing back to Ireland. Hy was left desolate.'

It moved Margaret almost to tears, though she knew *every* word of it. So dear had been this island. So deep the loss.

She stood, gazing at the grass, flattened by so many tramping feet. The air was loud with the singing of a hymn, with excited chatter. She heard none of it. The wind sang in her ears.

I love you.

The pilgrimage ended fittingly in the little graveyard, the ancient burial place of kings. In death, Macbeth was startlingly revealed as a real human, not just a character on the stage; a revered king, not a reviled murderer. Margaret fingered the physicality of his tombstone almost with awe.

It was over. The pilgrims were separating. Margaret could walk away, alone at last.

She had one last visit to make, privately. Tucked in an angle of the cathedral wall was a chapel so tiny she had walked past it on the first day without even noticing it. But she knew now what it was. The site of Columba's oratory, the monastery's first church, the place where the saint had died.

She went in, down the stone steps. It was so small it made her think forcibly of the fragility of that early community. So few of them, so many dangers.

She wanted to pray alone, but there was someone already there, kneeling.

Brian turned his head. His smile, when he saw her, was slow and sad. For once, the blue eyes did not dance. He nodded his head, gesturing her to the few seats on the other side of the aisle. It was at once a welcome and a separation.

They prayed in silence, probably the same prayer.

18

The liturgy of Hy delighted Margaret, with its blend of Celtic cadences and the needs of the contemporary world. But on Wednesday there was a break in the pattern of the evening service in the monastery church. For this one night, after the pilgrimage, the young staff of the Fellowship did not lead the worship. They made a gift of this sacred space to their guests.

Brian had waved away the possibility of being involved. 'I'm on holiday!' So another group of guests had taken charge. Don had volunteered to represent the Boulton party and persuaded a few of the teenagers to join in.

As the service began in the candlelit cathedral, Margaret felt a pang of regret. She had stood back modestly, making way for others, but she realized now how dearly she would have loved to be up there in the choir stalls, reading a lesson in the shadows of an April evening starred by candle flames. Listening, she heard the resonance of centuries of other voices, reading this same Gospel, in this same place, back to Columba himself.

Annie sang, and Margaret sensed the thrill that ran through the congregation as this tall black girl opened her lips and sent the deep power of her voice rolling around the rafters, a sound as dark brown as their shadows.

Zak read a prayer, a little awkwardly, as though he was both proud and embarrassed to be standing at the lectern, in front of all his mates. Margaret listened amazed, half giving herself to his words of thankfulness for this day outdoors, half imagining the effect on her son Laurie, if he had been here to see his friend pray in public.

Then a woman Margaret knew only by sight made her difficult way up the chancel steps. She was elderly, but the upright carriage of her grey head said she would stand no nonsense from her infirmity. And infirm she was. She walked with a stick which was also a crutch, supporting her weight under the elbow. It was clearly an effort to hoist one side of her body up the shallow steps. But she willed herself on, until she stood before the high table. There she turned.

Don moved to the lowest step. A pile of stones rattled in the silence as he spilled them out from a basket. A hard sound.

The woman spoke, in a crisp voice with an Edinburgh accent.

'You'll have guessed I wasn't on the pilgrimage, though I would dearly have loved to walk this island with those of you who did. There are others here tonight who couldn't make it, either. But we can all make a pilgrimage of the heart. You've heard the lesson from the Gospel. A rich young man comes up to Jesus, wanting to know what he shall do to inherit eternal life. Jesus reminds him of the Ten Commandments. And the young man protests, "I've been doing all that since I was a bairn." But those old commandments were mostly about things you shouldn't do. Jesus's commandments are positive. Love God and love other people. He set the young man a challenge. There was something positive still waiting to be done. "Sell everything you have and give it to the poor. And then, follow me." And the young man went away with a long face, because he was very rich.

'If you went on the pilgrimage today, you'll have stood on Columba's landing-place and chosen your stone. You were challenged to cast it into the sea and free yourself. But for those who weren't on that beach, and maybe for some who were, I've got a different challenge. There's a pile of stones in front of you here. This may be the night to choose one. I'm not asking you to throw this one away. It's not a sin. It may be something you have and treasure, which is good and precious. I'm inviting you to pick it up from the pile and bring it to the cross. I have another basket here. Take the stone of your riches, whatever form it takes, and give it away to

God and other people. Drop it, not because it is wrong in itself, but because only by giving it up can you show your love to somebody else. It may leave an awful empty hole, but it's then that Christ can fill you with life.'

She staggered slightly, and the stick clattered on the old flag-stones. There was a sigh as she steadied her balance. Then the church was filled with a deep hush. Margaret had a sudden fear that the organist would feel it necessary to fill this silence, but he let it deepen.

Slowly, there was a stirring in the dim pews. Feet shuffled in the aisle. Shadowy bodies began to move towards the chancel. There was a clink of a stone being lifted from the pile, disturbing others. Then another. One by one, people were moving on up the candlelit sanctuary, stooping to drop a stone into the waiting basket. They came away with an intense look on their faces, as if they were still contemplating what they had done, or with a relieved smile and a lighter step.

Margaret sat, growing tenser with the knowledge that this challenge was meant for her. She could not be just a spectator of other people's spiritual journeys. Her hand was clenched on the stone in her pocket, which she had not been able to throw away. It was definitely not a sin, her love for Brian. It was not a sin.

But it could be a gift, a richness she did not deserve and had not thought possible. Brian's love for her. She was being asked to give it away. This was not a burden of guilt to be tossed from her, like those arching pebbles buried under the waves. This was a jewel, the most precious thing she had to give. To ensure the happiness of Ruth and Maurice she must make this sacrifice of love.

And what would this mean for Brian? She must not think of that. He was sitting here, three rows away from her. He must be subject to the same challenge.

She moved. Lucy looked round in astonishment, as if she could not believe real people she knew would do this. Someone else was moving, too. Emma had risen and was working her way past the knees of her friends, towards the aisle. Her fair baby face was solemn, a little flushed with resolve.

For a moment, Margaret forgot her own impending sacrifice. She could not guess what was going through Emma's heart. Whatever decision the stone she would give represented, this was something the girl would always remember, this night in a shadowed church on Hy, at the close of a day of pilgrimage.

Margaret stood waiting for Emma to reach her and gave her a brief supportive smile. Then she led the way.

The line was thinning. She had almost left it too late. Before she bent over the pile, Tim's stone with the cross was already in her hand. She let the heap of remaining pebbles clatter under her knuckles, as though she had lifted one of them, then she straightened up and mounted the chancel steps.

It was over so quickly she did not have time to experience the meaning of what she was enacting, no chance to ponder the extent of her loss, the fact that neither Ruth nor Maurice would ever know how great was the gift she was making them. She turned away, and Emma took her place. Her step really did feel lighter as she returned to her seat, even though she did not yet understand what she had done.

She trudged up the now-familiar road in the early morning, putting distance between herself and the hostel. There was nothing in the surroundings to lift her spirit and give her hope. A mist hung sullen over the Channel. The hills of Mull loomed darkly through it.

Yet as the little fields petered out towards the wilder north, she lifted her head to the first light breeze and found a temporary peace. She still did not see how it was to be achieved, this giving up of Brian's love. But there were small, practical things she could do.

He must not come to the house. No, she was deceiving herself! This would be a huge sacrifice, to lose those brief, sweet, innocent meetings. Never to hear him bare his heart to her in poetry, to meet his look, half-fearful, half-longing, the flash of delight at her approval. But they would have to stop. She could no longer trust herself, or him.

She must not send Brian away from Boulton. Others needed him too much. It would be a daily grief to cut herself off from that intimate, delicate friendship with him and yet remain so close. Still, it must be done.

She need not work with him again once this musical was over. Or if she did, there must always be the safety of other people around them.

He must not touch her. Not even the pastoral kiss he shared with so many of the women in the congregation. Even a conventional hug would betray her. She was quivering already at the thought of his arms around her, hot with the longing it aroused.

She had put all that behind her.

All this she thought, sensibly and determinedly, striding faster now towards the dunes. This morning, as never before, she felt driven by the need to pray alone. It was no longer just being on Hy, a spiritual tourism. Now she was asking something of herself she knew she was too weak to sustain without help. Only God could give her the comfort she needed, sustain the hard, pure resolve.

Her feet left the metalled surface and she felt them sink in the softer sand of the track to the beach. As she came face to face with the sea, her lips curled in a wry smile. If her university colleagues knew the scruples she was struggling with, they would shake their heads in incomprehension. Affairs were commonplace. Few of her department were still with their first partner. Surely, they would say, if Brian attracted her, why not go with it? The last of her children was almost grown-up. What quaint, prudish hang-ups these church people had. Unhealthily repressed.

She paused, picking at the bladder-wrack that clung to a rock. Of course, they would allow, we do see your problem. The tabloids love a sexual scandal involving the clergy. But a Methodist minister? Really, so unglamorous, my dear. It's hardly the same circulation-booster as a Catholic bishop or an Anglican vicar caught with his trousers down. Who's interested in Brian?

Not only sordid, but dull. That was the level to which the world would reduce the magic between them. She would not give them that satisfaction.

A gull flew in front of her, laughing raucously.

Of course, the colleague's eyebrows would lift, 'I don't know what

111

you're worrying about. Maurice and Ruth need never know; my partner didn't.'

She was ploughing deep now, through the dry pale sand above the tideline. It did not matter this morning where she stopped to pray. There was no ideal spot. It was not the beauty of sea and sky she was seeking. It was a child's need for her Father.

She sat down on a flat rock almost buried in the sand, with her head bowed over her knees, telling her troubles to someone who must already know truths she had not yet admitted to herself. She thought, fleetingly, that there was a chuckle on the wind, as though he knew of larger griefs than this. But then the breeze stroked her hair, caressingly.

Margaret ran out of words. She was left with a dull, empty ache, which yet seemed like a massive obstruction she could not swallow. But she must. She had come out here to find the nerve to do what she had promised last night, not once, but over and over again, every week, every month, for the five years Brian could remain with them.

What about Brian? She had almost forgotten the reality of him. She should be praying for him, too. She gasped at the thought of her own selfishness. What kind of love was that? But the rush of her heart quieted. It was because Brian was so close to her that he hardly seemed like a separate person. When she prayed for herself, she was inevitably praying for him.

She shook herself, opening her eyes wide to the waves, where the grey horizon was coming into view.

She was cheating herself. Brian's life was nothing like hers. The loss would, though it was hard for her to accept this, be harder for him. She needed to stifle a rise of pride at the thought. When he said 'I love you', it had spilled out from a deep need that could not be kept down any longer. A smile was beginning to warm her face . . . No!

She grabbed a handful of sand and sifted it rapidly through her fingers. That's all over. It shouldn't have happened. You let go of it last night. It has to stop.

She had lost the calm assurance that had comforted her for just a few minutes. She was not really praying now, only arguing with herself. She turned her head along the line of coast. The sea was grey, whipped by the breeze into cold white caps. The sand was damp.

She rose, disconsolate. There could be nothing glamorous in this renunciation. The idea of making it her gift to Ruth or Maurice was unrealistic. She had expected to feel heroic, even martyred, after sacrificing her precious stone before the cross. Instead, she was only rather tired and cold. The seat of her jeans was wet from sitting on the stone.

She glanced at her watch. Twenty minutes yet to breakfast. She trudged back along the shore, following the tideline of seaweed.

She skirted the last rock. Brian rose from its shadow.

The shock ran through her, convulsive as electricity. His smile of greeting showed no such surprise. He must have seen her long since. Had he watched her while she prayed to be separated from him?

She exonerated him at once, with a swift reproof to herself. Brian, of all men, would respect her privacy. It was probably because he had seen her that he had settled on the far side of this rock, like a drawn sword between the chaste lovers of romance.

'When you went up and dropped a stone in the basket last night, what were you giving away?' She saw the bright pain of struggle in his eyes. Then, 'I'm sorry. I didn't have the right to ask you that. I was just afraid it might be me.'

'It was.' Defiant as a rebellious child. Lucy might have sounded like this.

He watched her through a long silence. He did not move towards her. The mask of his face, for once bereft of laughter, did not stir.

At last he said sadly, 'You're stronger than I am. And I *have* been trying. I know it has to stop here, but I don't know how I can bear it. I can't imagine how I can lose you and still stay on in the same church. Or how I can move away and never see you again.'

'Don't. It's quite simple. You stop coming to the house, unless Maurice is there. We don't meet alone anywhere. You don't touch me.'

113

'Margaret! For pity's sake. . . !'

'No. Not even in public. I couldn't bear it.'

They were still standing apart. One more step would have taken them into each other's arms. The force of her need was hard to resist. She could not even trust herself to meet his eyes, though she felt him gazing at her intently. She kept her head resolutely lowered, staring at the crook of the sleeve of his navy blue anorak. Past him she could glimpse the restless waters of the bay.

'That is the last straw!' Ruth's voice cut between them, sharper than the wind.

They instinctively leaped apart, turning to see her standing on the lowest step of rock. Her jaw was set in accusation.

'It's one thing when you take yourselves off for a walk together, knowing I'm tied to the hostel for the afternoon, but to tell me you're going out to pray and use *that* for some mucky assignation . . .'

'Ruth! Stop it there, love.'

'Don't you "love" me ! Even the girls can see what you two are up to. Can you imagine how that humiliates me?'

'Ruth, you've got it wrong.' Margaret tried to hold her voice steady. 'I've never once arranged to meet Brian anywhere. Not the day I got lost. Not this morning.'

'He always knows where to find you.'

Margaret turned her head to Brian involuntarily. Could it be true? Were the encounters less accidental than she had supposed?

'Ruth.' Brian moved towards his wife. 'Don't blame Margaret. We need to talk.'

He reached out to take her arm, but she shook him off.

'Do you have any idea what it's like, being a minister's wife?' she said, speaking directly to Margaret, ignoring Brian. 'Having to share him with the whole world, seven days a week? He's supposed to have a day off, but how many of you bother to check which day it is? Even if we leave the answerphone on, Brian twitches every time it rings, in case it's something really serious. We have to go out of the house to get any peace by ourselves. And whenever that phone rings, it's someone wanting to suck blood from him. It's never ring-

114

ing for me. I've sacrificed my whole life for people like you. And you come along and think you can take what little I have away from me, when you've already got so much.'

She turned, slipping on the seaweed, and began to stumble away.

Brian and Margaret stood looking at each other helplessly. She was so wrong, and yet so justified.

Brian started after her. Ruth tried to throw off his hand. Margaret could not hear the argument between them. She could only guess at the hurt of Ruth's accusations, the reassurance Brian would try to give her. How much of the truth was he going to tell her?

Margaret stood in the rising wind. She felt a colossal weariness of failure. She had raised herself to such a pitch of idealism last night, to drop her treasured stone in the basket on the chancel steps, with all that gift meant, and walk away from it. She had strengthened her resolve this morning, shoring it up like a sea defence. The folly was over, before it had even begun. She had convinced herself of that. She had told Brian.

The cackling gulls were the screams of laughter of her university friends. Such guilt, such angst, such self-inflicted torment, for *that*? Nothing, in their terms, had happened at all. How ridiculous could these Christians get about sex?

Duty. Commitment. Words that were dropping out of the language.

But it had happened, in spite of both of them. A sweet and lovely passion, which had burst out like a flame for everyone to see. It would not be smothered from Ruth under heaping turfs. She would only burn herself trying to beat it out.

Margaret felt sick with helpless dismay.

19

The island where Margaret had so longed to be had suddenly become too small. She stared out of the window at the gorse-starred hillocks crowding them in. The room was too full of people. This has all the murderous tension of an Agatha Christie house party, she thought wryly. A small community, thrown together in isolation. We cannot escape from each other until the end of the week.

She was aware of herself going through her duties with a numb efficiency. She had never been one to display emotion. No one would know how she longed to run, tears streaming, to the jetty, jump on the next boat and flee. Never meet Ruth again.

It was not possible. They were both too responsible. Orderly Methodists, doing what had to be done. Labouring on. Ruth had even spoken to her – curtly, it is true – as they set out the makeshift props for the next rehearsal.

It was Brian who made her ache. He looked stunned. Colour seemed to have bleached from his wind-tanned face, leaving it yellowish. The blaze of enthusiasm and the laughter had left him. Although Margaret, astonished, even caught herself joking with Annie, Brian moved like a sleep-walker. He spoke to the cast, still directing them, but as though the words came from a great remove. It was as though Brian himself was not *there*, but passed his messages through some intermediary. He did not look at Ruth, except just once, with the pleading eyes of a scolded dog. Ruth watched him. Brian never turned his face to Margaret.

Have I done this? she thought, appalled. Wrecked what I meant to support? I thought I couldn't leave him; he needed me too much. And I've destroyed him.

Don't be so melodramatic, her sensible university staff-room self mocked. Couples who love each other dearly often row. Afterwards, they come together passionately, making up. Brian and Ruth still love each other. That's why Ruth cared.

And *my* marriage? She tried to imagine the conventional courtesies into which she and Maurice had subsided breaking apart in sparks and fury. Her lips curled into a small smile. She could not think what might provoke that. What would she feel if she found out that Maurice was having an affair? The idea amused her with its improbability.

Am I being complacent? Do I know Maurice as thoroughly as I think I do? I'd feel humiliated. It would make me feel older, more unattractive, than I already do. Is this just the flattery Brian was offering, making me feel seventeen again?

Exploratively, she began to imagine her anger against Maurice, or the other woman, fury at losing him. Did she still care enough? Was it only her pride which would be hurt?

Before she could come to a conclusion, she was startled into the reality of the present. Ruth was thrusting a script into her hands. She spoke impatiently, as though Margaret were an inattentive and deliberately obtuse child. Probably she had already said this once.

'Diarmit. Columba's servant.'

Margaret had been the stand-in for this part before, in earlier scenes. It was a major role, Columba's faithful attendant in his declining years. Now the saint's death approached. He made the round of Hy's farms, assuring himself that the monastery's barns were stocked with corn, the future golden. Some of Brian's most lyrical music conveyed Columba's blessing on Hy and all it would mean for the conversion of Britain.

And now his last meeting with the old white horse who pulled the milk-cart from the dairy. This was to be a pantomime creature, a girl and boy dancing skittishly under a painted skin. It was a scene of both tenderness and laughter. Diarmit wanted to send the horse packing for troubling the weary saint at the end of his last journey.

Instead, Columba went to meet her, open-armed. On the night, Lucy, as the front half of the horse, would make it weep real tears down its papier mâché nose, as the two joined in a last embrace.

Margaret, as Diarmit, stood to one side, rejected. She felt the reality of that this morning.

Brian was not Columba. He was not a . . .

What *was* a saint? She listened to the serio-comic duet between Zak, as Columba, and Lucy, the horse. Columba, that passionate Irish prince, had provoked a war that left thousands dead. He had had to be packed off across the water to begin again. And Hy had been gain, not loss.

If Brian had to leave Boulton, he would touch other lives, permanently, other people's children.

There was no horse's mask in rehearsal, no tears on the papier mâché cheeks. Lucy brought an earthy humour to the role. It needed the painted horse's eyes to express the sorrow. The tears were on Margaret's cheeks.

She went through the motions. Diarmit supporting the abbot in his cell as he wrote his last words. Waking in the night to find Columba gone and light blazing from the church. Rousing the monks and running to find Columba slumped on the altar steps. Lifting the saint's hand to make the blessing he could no longer speak. Grief and loss, swelling into the triumph of angels.

Heart-stirring. Brian knew how to play on emotions.

Margaret took a mug of coffee, to sit around the stove in the common room, at once deeply moved and detached. She should, she knew, be helping Ruth supervise the tidying of the rehearsal room, the safe and orderly stowing away of props. Don was organizing a football game for the afternoon. Brian was . . . just being Brian. He had recovered something of his colour and warmth, though he was more subdued than usual. Music and poetry were healing him, even though they were his own, as they had allowed her something of release.

Older poetry chanted in her head.

Isn't it delightful to rest on the breast of an island, on

a peak of rock? To gaze out on the calm sea?
To watch the waves roll in over the glittering ocean,
chanting music to their Father on the eternal round?
To know the ebb-tide and the flood-tide in their turn?
This is my name, this is the secret I tell you , 'I am he
who turned his back on Ireland.'
It is good to feel repentance break over me as I gaze on
God's creation, to give voice to my grief for many sins,
so hard to speak.

Columba's words. And now Brian's.

Margaret went and stood by the window. There was no sun today. The grey Channel of Hy drove its white lines of breakers hard at the rocks. The mountains across the water rose into the cloud. The unknown land, Scotland. The challenge. Out there the monks must go, without Columba now. On into the south to found Lindisfarne.

No, she thought. I can't do it. Not without him.

'Don't you wish you were twenty years younger?' Ian the chaplain was standing beside her, short but burly in rugged layers of sweaters, nursing a steaming mug with chapped hands. His head nodded at the chattering teenagers. 'I was reciting Bible verses and singing "I'm H. A. P. P. Y." when I was their age, the younger ones at least.'

'I'd need to lose thirty years, not twenty,' she said self-deprecatingly.

'Whatever. Funny how age doesn't seem to matter with guys like Brian, isn't it? He's still a kid at heart. You have to be like a child to get into the Kingdom of Heaven.'

She could not answer. She had loved the child in Brian, had wanted to protect its sacred space. But now he had moved her as a man, held her as a man. She ached for him to kiss her like that.

'You don't look happy. I doubt if your Lucy's a good enough actress to bring those tears to your eyes.' Ian glanced sideways. She sensed he was assessing whether she was affronted that he was invading her personal grief. But he was like a determined sheepdog

119

going after a ewe in danger, wary of startling her into running, but intent on fetching her back.

She felt the release of trusting someone else. The week was nearly over. She need never see Ian again. It offered the anonymity of a confessional in a foreign church. No, it was more immediate than that. Ian was a very real person. A strong physical presence standing beside her at the window. A distinct, rather disturbing personality, who might challenge her. She was not attracted to him, but her acute awareness of his closeness suggested she could be.

Confused, she said, as much because he seemed to expect it of her as because she wanted to, 'Could I talk to you?'

'Of course. It's what I'm for. Are you needed for this football match? No? Come across to the monastery. There's a wee room round to the left, just inside the side door nearest the sea. We'll be quiet there.'

His eyes looked over her face. She wondered how plainly he could read what was written there.

'I thought I was coming to Hy for a holy week. I seem to have made a bit of a mess of it,' she laughed, nervously.

'Hy's a thin place. The barriers are easily crossed.'

'That's what Brian said. I thought he was talking about the spiritual and the physical.'

'Aren't we?'

She felt the blush mounting. He studied her a moment longer without smiling, then turned away.

'Two-thirty.'

A moment later he was teasing Tim about the bandage still swelling the knee of his tight jeans.

The shouts of boys and girls flew through the air like darting gulls. Margaret stopped, hands in pockets, wind whipping the hair back from her face. A clean feel. Might it not be better to be out of doors, letting the naked elements wash that soiled, grubby feeling from her? She felt sick at the way Ruth had twisted so delicate, so barely expressed a relationship, and made something dirty of it.

Don was racing up and down the field, whistle ready. Brian was somewhat ineffectually wielding a flag as linesman. Ruth stood, dutiful among a knot of the less athletic girls watching. Nothing deflected her from her purpose, her duty.

I should be there, Margaret thought. I'm weaker than she is, more concerned with myself.

The prospect of that 'wee room' in the monastery was more threatening now. It had sounded as if it might be a place to take her troubles, and Ian a shoulder to lean on. It would not be like that, she knew it now. He would be too strong, too honest, to let her get away with self-pity. She had been responsible. She must have been, mustn't she, for this to happen?

For what to happen? So little. So quickly over. Three words of confession. A chaste embrace. A stone dropped in a basket. A book closed.

Columba's bloody battle had happened because he wouldn't let go. He had held on to his copy of another man's book. It didn't matter that the copy was a work of beauty, precious Psalms written to the glory of God, fit to be shouted aloud to the whole world. It was their physical embodiment in a book that was one person's property, the tooled leather of the cover, which fingers might stroke, the carefully penned pages, the flashes of illuminated letters, making the heart leap like a sudden smile. The original had been a private possession, not to be duplicated by anyone else. Columba had taken his copy by subterfuge.

It was hard to sustain the metaphor, she thought as she walked on, tearing her eyes away from Brian's skin, the flash of light on his face as the team raced towards the goal. The words are for sharing. They need that physical binding many times over. One is not enough.

The monastery loomed over her. From the ferry, it had seemed a low building, crouched against the wind. It was taller and more forbidding now she stood in its shadow. She had no memory of the side door Ian had designated. She walked along the walls of the cathedral to the seaward side and felt the breeze lift her hair more strongly. There were benches here, but nobody was sitting in the keen air. More nervously now, she rounded the far corner. There was the small dark door. She stepped inside, and the room waited for her, the inner door open.

Ian sat at a desk, but he lifted his head as she entered with a tentative knock, and swivelled his chair. He motioned her to a more comfortable one, battered mock-leather, but deeply cushioned. She sank into it, and at once felt herself lower than the chaplain. Not quite on her knees, but more nearly the penitent than she had been, standing with him at the hostel window. Physical symbols are important, she thought. It's not just the words.

'Tea?' He handed her a mug. The kettle had already been on the boil. There were sweet biscuits with jammy centres, which for once she accepted gratefully. Comfort food.

He sat leaning forward, not quite looking at her, waiting.

'It's Brian,' she said, and stopped.

'I know,' he said. 'It's a small island.'

What did he mean? That everyone knew? Or that it happened often, when people were thrown so closely together?

'It didn't begin here.' She told him how they had worked together, first the pastoral visits that had developed into poetry readings. He seemed to understand that, the delicacy of a personal affair that began with love of the same words and thoughts, the shared imagery, and grew into love of each other. And he nodded vigorously as she described how Brian had drawn her into such unlikely work at church, the young people like an exotic culture to her staid academic lifestyle.

He twisted the mug in his hands. 'I'm divorced, you know? My wife went off with one of our church elders.'

He saw her shocked face and misinterpreted it. With a brisk laugh he said, 'Not a good advertisement, is it? For a Church of Scotland minister? I can't keep my own family together and I preach to others.'

'I wasn't thinking about that. But here am I, unloading my silly little quarrel on you. And you've got far bigger problems of your own. This may never come to that. It was nothing, really.'

Ian held up his hand. 'Quieten down, lassie. It's old news now. Two years ago. And I can listen to other folks' troubles with more humility because I've been through it. You'll not get glib answers from me. But I'll listen.'

He was watching her now. He had dark intent eyes, which did not dance like Brian's. They disturbed her in a different way. Where Brian would tease her, skipping away from the hard questions, this man would not avoid them, nor allow her to do so. He was beginning to frighten her. Layers of academic rationality might not be enough to prevent him probing to the turmoil of personal feelings she hid from the world.

'I met him at Columba's hermitage. I didn't mean to. I didn't know he was anywhere near.' She remembered Ruth's accusation. 'I don't know if *he* knew,' she added honestly.

'And?'

'He said he loved me.'

'He never said that before?'

'No! It wasn't like that. It was the poetry, and the youth club, and writing *The Exile* together. There was nothing between us. Well, nothing explicit.'

'Did you want him to say it?'

'No!'

'But when he had?' The eyes would not let her go, like a lifeline of truth she must hold on to.

'Then I knew. Yes, I suppose I had been wanting it. I'd never admitted it to myself until then. Suddenly we couldn't help it.'

'I warned you. It's a thin place.'

She raised her chin defiantly. 'But I knew it had to stop. If only he hadn't said it, we could have gone on.'

'With metaphors of poetry.'

'Yes.' The acknowledgement surprised her.

'But the naked truth will not go away, now you've spoken it.'

'No. But we can do something about it, physically. Not see each other alone. Not touch each other, even in public.'

'No more poetry readings in the afternoon. That will be hard for him, to take that innocent joy away, that secret nourishment of his soul, when everyone else feeds off him.' She must have looked startled that he saw so deeply. 'I'm a minister, too. It's an occupational

123

hazard. We all end up eaten, if we're any good at the job.'

She struggled to work out what he meant. 'Then . . . you think I should go on with it, as if this had never happened?'

'You dropped a stone in the basket on Wednesday evening. Was that stone Brian?' He laughed a little ruefully. 'You've made me your spiritual director. I have a right to ask that.'

'Yes. I was . . . giving him away. The most precious thing I had. To Ruth and . . . Maurice.'

'And Maurice is. . . ?'

'My husband.'

'You haven't mentioned him till now.'

'There isn't much to say. Maurice is just . . . there.'

Ian seemed to be reading her face for a long time.

'And did you think that Brian is not a *thing*, to be given away? He's a man, with a hard job to do, with personal needs.'

'He's got a wife.' Too quick, too sharp. Ian raised his eyebrows. 'This is the bit I find difficult to talk about. Ruth knows,' she explained with a sigh. 'Or thinks she does. She's got it all wrong.' It was painful to tell of the scene on the beach, the bitter words.

'Maybe it's Ruth should be sitting in that chair, not you. I could heal her better. I know where she's been.'

Someone took Ian's wife from him, and Ruth thinks I'm taking Brian.

'I don't want Brian. Not like that. I wouldn't.'

Again that lift of the thick black eyebrows, ironic.

'You would like to, in your heart of hearts, wouldn't you? Only you've been too well brought up, a good Christian wife. It's not just that you don't want to hurt other people: Maurice, Ruth, your children. It would shatter your image of yourself, wouldn't it? The upright churchwoman, the respectable academic.'

She burst out laughing. 'Almost everyone I know at the university is separated, or never bothered to get married in the first place. It's positively subversive to be a monogamous Methodist. I'm the cause of much hilarity.'

'Poor Margaret.' The eyebrows twitched this time with revelation. 'Few resting places for you, either. The sympathetic shoulder,

124

metaphorically, of course. Or perhaps the cool spaces of understanding, where nothing needs to be spoken. An inward hermitage.'

'Yes . . . it was like that.'

'You were receiving, as well as giving, those teatimes in the
window by the fishpond?' The smile was gently teasing now, but
with more sympathy, more concern for her as a person with her
own needs than, she realized, Brian had ever shown. She had really
believed that he was the one who needed help.

'You make it sound worse than I thought. I was feeding on him
too, when I thought I was helping him. He's better rid of me.'

'I didn't say that. I just want you to see what it is you're giving
up.'

'I know that already. Only I kidded myself that it only started
when he said he loved me.'

'I'm not talking about lust, physical attraction. The need in your
soul for what he gave you.'

'It looks like lust to Ruth . . .' Her voice dropped to a whisper.
'And it is, partly, anyway.'

'The body trips us up. Like the half-fairy Strephon in *Iolanthe*.
He could squeeze his top half through a keyhole, but his legs were
left dangling behind and no way could he get them to follow where
his head wanted to go.'

'I gave Brian up. I dropped the stone.'

'And Brian didn't.'

The blush mounted. 'He says he needs me. But he mustn't. Even
without Ruth . . .'

'Ruth has always been there for him.'

'Exactly.'

'And you'll still be there. Part of his poem.'

'What are you saying? That Brian's right, and Ruth and I are
wrong? That *his* need is more important?' Even as she spoke, she
was surprised to realize that Ruth and she were not truly enemies,
that they had a common cause.

'You need a spiritual support. Brian needs a refuge, real friends.
Ruth needs faith, the security of love.'

'And Maurice?'

'Tranquillity?'

She laughed shortly. 'Yes! Ruth won't feel secure now, while I'm around. I don't feel like a *femme fatale*, but she thinks I am.'

'Poetry can be very seductive.'

'But he writes love poems about *her*.'

'I wish I could talk to Ruth. Brian could go away, of course. Your Methodist system makes it easy for ministers to move on.'

'It's a two-year process, unless there's a scandal or someone breaks down.'

This time, the eyebrows appreciated the dramatic potential. 'A lot can happen in two years. People make adjustments. Even to the unthinkable, the insupportable.' His voice fell, quiet, retreating into his own loneliness. She ached to move towards him, maternally, but dared not. 'If Brian moves on,' he continued with an effort, 'you both lose what gives you strength. Of course, there are other possibilities. Another minister for you, new friends for Brian. But maybe not. The personal chemistry isn't always there. One doesn't often strike lucky twice running.'

'So . . . we could go back to Boulton and carry on as before?'

'To some extent you'll have to. What else can you do immediately?'

'And forget Hy?'

'No one ever forgets Hy.'

'I'm not sure that I understand what you're saying. That I shouldn't have dropped my stone? And it was so hard to let go. I couldn't throw it into the sea.'

'Was it so very special?'

'Tim gave it to me. That boy who hurt his leg? He picked it up at Columba's Landing. It had a cross on it. He gave it to me.'

'He loves you, too.' A startled look must have passed over her face. 'Didn't you know that?' She mumbled something incoherent. 'And that was Brian's doing, bringing you together here. The stone had a cross marked on it, did it? And you dropped it.'

'I didn't mean to give up *that*, the youth club, anything I can do to help him at church. I *said* that.'

'Only the personal contact? Can the Gospel of incarnate love be

126

spread by words alone?'

'You're making it harder, not easier.'

'Who said the Gospel was easy?'

'But Ruth?'

'She loves him. And she loves the same Christ as you.'

'I don't want to hurt her.'

'You might help her.'

'She doesn't see that.'

'Not now.'

'I don't know if I'm strong enough.'

'You won't until you try. And not in your own strength.'

'Do I have to tell her she's nothing to be afraid of? She won't believe me. Or Brian.'

'Maybe I should find a way to talk to her . . . Would you like to pray with me?'

It was mostly silence. After a few moments, she found it was Ian opposite her she was praying for, and was caught by surprise when he voiced other names lovingly. 'Brian. Ruth. Maurice. Margaret.' Names in the cast of a play she had temporarily forgotten. She did not have the courage to voice his own name aloud in prayer.

'Go to the beach here,' he said, standing up. 'Pick up your own stone. Maybe not so pretty as the one Tim gave you. Hard, plain, cool. Hold on to it. It'll grow warm in your hand.' The brown eyes flashed a smile, under the dark brows.

20

There was a stone under her hand again. Margaret did not need to take it out in the leaping firelight on the beach to look at it. The very feel of it conveyed its image to her mind's eye. She had gone to a nearby beach just south of the village. Not the far stony cove of Columba's Landing. Not the silver sweep of the northern coast with the great ocean beyond. This was a homelier shore, looking across the narrow strait to the big dark hills of Mull. There was flotsam, bits of cork and polystyrene, plastic bottles, sodden food wrappers, but amongst this everyday detritus, the pristine beauty of rock-pools, with sea anemones opening to the kiss of salt water. She had chosen her stone. No symbolic cross upon this one. Nothing out of the ordinary. It was an unremarkable pale brown, speckled with white. That was the way it must be from now on. A plain ordinary life, lived out like others, expecting nothing soul-shaking, doing her duty. Like Ruth.

Only, when Margaret washed her stone in the sea, it had sparkled.

This last night was not ordinary. They had lit a fire on the beach with the logs they had each brought from the English Midlands at Brian's insistence, mindful of the lack of trees on a Hebridean island. They had also had a riotous afternoon on the beach, gleaning whatever driftwood the sea afforded them, bleached grey by salt and sun. But there had not been enough to find for so many people. The practical search had collapsed into chases across the sand, Tim pursuing Ceri at a hobbling run with a skein of dripping kelp, gull's feathers tickling the back of unsuspecting necks.

Then Brian had got them building a whole Celtic monastery out of damp sand, which Pete, Zak and others had invaded with Viking longships. It had ended in a sand fight, everyone spattered, sand in hair and eyes and even mouths, the teenagers laughing and complaining in the same breath. Ruth had stood aside from this, faintly disapproving. Margaret, uncharacteristically, had joined in, somewhat wildly.

Now, supper was over and the flames leaped clear and true. Michelle was leading them all in song.

'You've got the warmest place tonight.' Ian crouched beside Margaret, rubbing his hands.

She turned to him gratefully. Across the fire, the light danced on Brian's face, Ruth's in shadow beside him. Margaret had carefully separated herself from them by the fire stack. She found it comforting to have Ian beside her, though there was nothing more personal between them than a brief friendship, the word of the resident chaplain to a troubled visitor, a professional relationship. She would never see him again.

Ian's value tonight was that he was another man, a solid useful presence. He was her security badge, someone to lessen Ruth's pain and suspicion.

His body shut out the wind. The night was warmer, now he had come.

He surprised her. Michelle called his name across the circle and as Ian rose from beside Margaret, he took up from the darkness behind him a set of bagpipes she had not noticed. The notes keened on the night air, away up to the shimmering April stars. The laughter and shouted choruses were stilled.

In the hush that followed, the crackle of the firewood startled them. Ian reached out his hand across the circle. 'Ruth?'

Ruth stood. Faces turned to her in the half-light, curious.

'I don't know why I let myself be talked into this,' she murmured, making her way round the outside of the ring to join Ian. He smiled at her warmly.

They stood together, two short square-set adults, barely silhouetted against the dark as the flames died down. Ian began to pipe 'The Flowers of the Forest'. Ruth's voice soared to the plaintive notes.

Margaret realized she had never heard Ruth sing a solo before. She sang in the church choir, dutiful but unremarkable as always. How had Ian known that she could sing like this, how had he persuaded her to have the confidence? He must have found a reason to be alone with her, a way to talk to her. What else had he said?

Their duet was met with generous applause and cries of 'Encore!' Then, just when the sadness of Celtic laments might have reached sentimentality, Ian swung into a reel. Hands were clapping, feet were tapping with the itch to dance. Everyone was on their feet, with a total disregard for the precision of steps or the pattern of the dance, madly whirling about the beach to the skirl of his pipes.

They had hardly collapsed out of breath before Michelle was urging Brian's party to sing them the songs of *The Exile*. They chose the roistering ones, the boat song, rhythmic over the heaving waves, and shouts of the Druids calling up a storm.

'Be careful!' cried Ian. 'You're taking the boat back to Oban tomorrow, remember.'

Margaret felt a sudden drop into emptiness. It was over so soon. A bittersweet week. Those few moments she would always remember, and ones she wanted desperately to forget and never could. This island itself, all it held of story and song. A sacred stillness, a place of prayer, that would not let go of her heart. The shadowed cathedral in candlelight. This leaping fire. Stirring the porridge for breakfast for a score of hungry teenagers. Sitting chatting with Tim.

'Margaret!' Brian's voice commanded her out of her reverie. She looked up, genuinely surprised. She couldn't sing. No one could expect that of her, in public.

'What about a story?' he said. 'A camp fire tale before we go to bed.'

Panic tightened her throat. Again? Yes, long ago, it seemed now, he had beguiled her into this, when they were sitting far away in a suburban sitting-room. She should never have agreed. She should have imagined then what it would feel like to be here, surrounded by a group of curious faces, this time not just teenagers, who still had scant interest in Celtic history, but strangers staying at the monastery too, Ian, unseen beside her. She might have Welsh blood, but could it really be true that she had the magic of the bardic storyteller, the *hwyl*?

For a moment, her mind was a blank. What had he thought she could tell them?

From the other side of the fire she heard Brian announce, 'Prepare to be amazed by the earliest tale of the Loch Ness Monster!'

Of course! Their own group knew the connection with Columba already. It was in the script. Brian was not going to miss an opportunity like that. There was a heaving, coiling, menacing dance, in which half the cast wove themselves into a monstrous serpent. But they had never listened to the story told in words like this.

Those four words, 'the Loch Ness Monster', had magic in themselves. Pete, who made no disguise of his contempt for the limitations of life on a Hebridean island, leaned his face forward into the firelight with a shine of eagerness.

'From Hy to Inverness, the Great Glen cuts through the heart of Scotland. It's a long dark journey from this western shore to the east.' Margaret surprised herself. It was as though this week of Celtic cadences had sunk into her soul. From the first sentence now, she heard herself speaking with bardic authority.

'There was a quarrel over who owned the sacred island of Hy. So Columba set out for the court of Bruide, King of the Picts. They were an ancient people, who carved stones with signs of their gods and painted the symbols on their skin with war paint, to terrify their enemies.

'With a handful of monks he sailed round Mull and up to Loch Leven under Ben Nevis. But there they must leave their coracle and set out on foot, into the heart of the dark hills.'

Tim was leaning close to her, his face rapt.

'They journeyed from loch to loch. The deeper they went into the land of the Picts, the narrower the glen got, and the steeper the mountains. When they came at last to Loch Ness, the screes seemed to be rushing down and plunging deep, deep under the black water as though there was no bottom to it. Mountains brooded over it on either side. It was the longest, deepest, darkest loch of them all.

'At the foot of it a river ran out, down to the king's fort at Inverness. But before they reached it, they met a mournful procession carrying a dead man. The monks said a prayer for the heathen Pict, then they asked one of the mourners, "Is this the right road to Inverness?"

' "You'll need to cross this end of the loch," said the man, with a shudder, "but rather you than me. That's how this poor soul met his end. He was swimming there when this huge beast reared up out of the depths, grabbed hold of him and dived. We put out in a boat to try and save him, and we threw out a hook. But when we hauled it in, all we got on the end of it was half his mangled body, with the teeth-marks of the monster right down to his bones." '

This went down well. Margaret warmed to their ghoulish cries.

'The monks turned pale, but Columba declared, "The power of Christ will see us through. Is there a ferry?"

'The Picts shook their heads. "There's no one would dare to row you across today."

'The monks stood at the water's edge. The loch was very still and dark and silent. There was a little boat on the far side, moored to the bank.

' "Lugne," said Columba to one of his young men, "swim across and fetch us that boat, will you?"

'Lugne met the saint's eyes. He took a deep breath, pulled off his clothes down to his tunic, and dived in. They watched him swim out from the shore, the white foam splashing from his arms, and his head getting smaller.

'All at once, it was as if there was a volcano under the loch. There was a colossal roar, and up through the black surface of the water burst a huge, horrible head. Fanged jaws sprang open. The monster came tearing down on Lugne, with a great wake boiling behind it.

'Lugne screamed for help. The other monks stood frozen in terror. When there was not the length of a spear between the monster and the monk, Columba raised his hand and made the sign of the cross. In a voice of thunder he shouted, "In the name of Christ, don't you dare touch him! Get back where you came from."

132

'The monster rushed on, faster and huger and closer, till its head began to curve high over the swimming monk, like a snake poised to strike. Then, a second later, a great wave shot up as it pulled up short. Next moment the monster was moving backwards, just as if it was being towed away by a rope. Little by little, they watched it sink under the surface, until only the horns on its horrible head were showing. Then it was gone and there was only a whirlpool in the water.

'Brave Lugne swam on and fetched the boat. A great cheer went up as he brought it to shore. Even the funeral party were praising Christ and Columba. The monks sat very quiet as they rowed across and they looked around them pretty keenly, but they saw not so much as a tooth or a tail of the monster. Columba had sent it to the bottom of Loch Ness. And for all I know, it may be there now.'

There was a flattering silence, then the release of enjoyable shudders.

'It isn't true though, is it?' said Zak.

'It was written down within a hundred years of Columba's death, and the author had spoken to people who knew him.'

'Is that yes or no?'

'I'm sure that story tells us something true.'

'But you're not saying.'

'Like all the best stories, you must work out what it means for yourself.'

'All the same,' Ian supported her, 'it's pretty weird, isn't it? They were telling tales about the Loch Ness Monster fourteen hundred years ago. It makes you think.'

Margaret's panic subsided. She had done it for him. Amazingly, she had worked her own magic. She must not turn her face to Brian for approval. Like the monks, they had come close to disaster, but they had survived. They must carry on to the end of the road.

Around the dying fire they sang a last round. The final notes died away over the lapping waves.

'Home tomorrow. And I'm cooking your breakfast. Time for bed,' said Brian.

They all rose with him and straggled up the path, past the darkened monastery, towards the hostel.

21

Saturday morning was like coming down off a mountain top. The young staff of the Fellowship massed on the slipway, doing a Mexican wave in farewell. Michelle's black hair was streaming sideways in the wind, Ian stood a little to one side.

Margaret turned her head to look around the deck of the little ferry. She was startled to find that some of the teenagers waving back had tears on their faces. What did Hy mean to them now? What would they always remember?

Ian had spoken to her in a low voice, before she boarded. 'Have you got your wee stone safe?' The smile in his eyes had been warm under the dark brows. She had taken it out, silently, and showed him. So very plain and brown, this one, yet, as he had suggested, warm from her holding it. His hand had closed over hers, briefly. A stubbier hand than Brian's, but hard and strong. His grip was reassuring. It was a little disturbing, too, yet that was because it challenged her to be stronger, not weaker. Ian did not expect her to let him down. In their own way, both men wanted the same thing from her, a painful faithfulness. Brian wanted her loyalty for his own need, Ian for someone else's.

She watched his stocky form dwindle, with the island and its sturdy grey monastery, as the workaday ferry chugged across to the shore of Mull. The bus was waiting on the village road, equally spartan. It was a hard place they were leaving, a spirit of rock. There was no place for sentimentality about Celtic Christianity, once you understood it. It had become easier for her to imagine saints who strode into cold water up to their waists and prayed for hours with goose-pimpled arms upraised to heaven. And if sea otters had once dried Saint Cuthbert's feet and warmed them, Margaret, too, had found comfort from one of Hy's creatures. Ian was small, shaggy, at home in this element. She found herself smiling at the thought.

She stared out of the bus. Perhaps coming down from the peak of Everest was like this. Too much pain, blindness, struggle, even loss, to feel an unalloyed triumph. Could you realize the achievement of where you had stood, what you had done? Wouldn't the body, which you had pushed to the limits, cloud the spirit which had wanted to do this?

What had it been like for her on the summit? Would she remember? Should it have needed a silver beach in the Hebrides, a romantic history of saints, to achieve that moment of oneness?

There had been such a moment, hadn't there? It was hard to define. She did not want to analyse it.

She squinted upwards. Hard to see the sky now she was in amongst the looming hills of Mull. Other hermits had gone to their meeting with God in a windowless cell, never seeing the sky for years on end.

Would she remember the sky over the ocean? Or those soiled, trampled minutes when everything had gone wrong, which her mind continually played over again, desperately trying to make it come out differently, to say the right words, to do wiser things, to justify herself to Ruth?

She was like a climber who had both won and failed, coming down past the frozen body of a companion she had not been able to save.

Brian had so longed to share Hy with her as, years before, he had wanted to share it with Ruth. How would Ruth remember Hy now? Margaret had tarnished it for her. She felt a little sick.

The sun did not shine as they crossed Mull, but it came out to sparkle on the big white Caledonian MacBrayne ferry that would take them over deeper water to Oban and the mainland railway. Margaret sat on the quay in sight of the station, eating prawn sandwiches and joking with Tim and Ceri, as if nothing had happened.

135

'I don't want to go home,' said Tim.

'Go on. Your mum will be missing you.'

'Doubt it. 'S better if I'm not there. She'll have had her boyfriend in every night.'

She hugged his thin shoulders. A cautious part of her brain wondered if she should do this, or whether it would count nowadays as sexual harassment. She decided Tim's need mattered more.

The ride through the Highlands had an elegiac feel. The evocative names of Ben Cruachan, Crianlarich, Loch Lomond fell behind her, probably for ever. Glasgow was built-up, bustling, noisy, already nearer to Boulton.

The low green fields of the Midlands met them, closed round them subtly, like an open prison. They sped past small backyards, which once had been miniature industrial centres, turning out chains, or sprockets, or washers, for the Industrial Revolution. Now weed-grown, unwanted.

At last the little local train. Maurice was in the car park to meet her, with a seemingly warm embrace, a shy kiss.

'Have you missed me?' she laughed.

'Let's say I've exhausted the possibilities of the Chinese takeaway menu.'

'*I've* learned to make real porridge.'

'Thanks! Just what I was looking forward to.'

'And I've copied down a very good recipe for home-made bread.'

'You don't think you're taking this a bit far? I've never seen you as the Aga type.'

She settled herself into the passenger seat, wondering how Maurice had filled his week. Did he regret staying behind? Or had he enjoyed his week of freedom, like Tim's mother? Margaret started against the restraint of the seatbelt. It wouldn't be for the same reason, of course. She couldn't imagine that.

But could Maurice have imagined what had happened to her on Hy?

Nothing did happen, she argued. A few uncensored words. A brief hug. Some tears. There was nothing to confess, nothing Maurice need ever know. Ruth had got it wrong.

136

'Wakey, wakey. They're trying to say goodbye to you.'

Maurice zipped down the window on her side. As though from a great distance, she was aware of Brian and Ruth slamming the car boot on their rucksacks, turning to her in an awkward leave-taking. Brian's hands stretched out briefly, and then withdrew. Ruth stood with her shoulders hunched, her hands in her pockets.

'Goodbye, and thanks. It's been a terrific week.' Someone else seemed to be in charge of Margaret's face, stretching it into a smile.

'We couldn't have done it without you. You did a great job with the kids.'

'Rubbish.'

'See you tomorrow morning. I think we should tell the whole church about it. You could say something about Celtic pilgrimage.'

'I've told you before, that was a one-way journey. We had return tickets.'

'After you've been to Hy, you never come back to the same place.'

Brian smiled, sadly. It was too intimate, in front of Ruth and Maurice.

Laurie looked up as they entered the sitting-room. He was slouched on the sofa in front of the television screen, watching football. He had, Margaret noted with distaste, a can of lager in his hand. This was a new development. She wasn't sure how to react. Maurice had presumably sanctioned it in her absence, if only tacitly.

Laurie's face brightened with rather more eagerness than she was expecting. He threw a lock of hair off his eyes. 'Thank goodness you're back!'

'Why?' She dropped a kiss on his forehead, over the back of the sofa.

'Sanity.' He nodded at Maurice. 'You can't reason with *him*.'

'Since when did we give you permission to turn this house into a beer garden?' Maurice asked.

'See what I mean?'

So, the lager can *was* new. She had misjudged the situation. Did that mean she was going to have to act as referee?

'I hadn't noticed that reasoned argument was your preferred approach,' she tried cautiously.

'Yeah, well. I'm seventeen.'

'What's that supposed to mean?' Maurice demanded.

'Work it out for yourself.' Laurie got to his feet. He hugged Margaret briefly. 'Had a good time? How did the band do?'

'Terrific. You should have been there.'

'Yeah, well,' he shrugged again, 'guess so. Might have been a laugh.'

'Most people seemed to have a good time, though I'm not too sure about Pete.'

'He always likes to make out he's cooler than the rest of us. Got to see Zak. Get debriefed there. See you.'

He was gone.

Margaret sat down slowly. Into her mind came those dark nights in the dormitory, the whispers of girls gossiping, Lucy's insinuating voice one night. 'I didn't know you fancied Brian, miss. Looks like he's not past it, either. I'll say this, you've got bigger boobs than Mrs Hargreaves. Is that 'cause you've had kids?'

Margaret's cheeks had burned in the darkness. She had had to answer, to prevent the final humiliation of hearing Annie defend her privacy, yet not deny the reality of what Lucy had seen.

Did they all know? Were the teenagers talking about it even now, offloading the week's gossip on to eager friends? Was this all that Hy really meant to them, the progress made between boy and girl, between woman and man, in a week away? Would anyone tell Laurie what the gossip was saying about his mother?

She came back from the kitchen. 'Not much in the fridge, is there? I could do you a lentil and bacon casserole, if I nipped down to the corner shop.' She tried to smile naturally at Maurice.

'No need,' he said grandly. 'I knew you'd be tired. I've booked us a table at the Taj Mahal.'

Sunday morning came too soon. She was not ready for this test. To everyone else, most of all to Maurice, it must seem as though she was picking up the threads of her normal life. She had had a refreshing week's holiday. Some useful work had been accomplished with the youth club. All over now.

Yet walking from the car across the church forecourt, she felt she had never seen this place before. Boulton Methodist Church, not Hy, was the strange shore. Everything looked altered. A red and white sign on the wall leaped out at her: PERMIT PARKING ONLY. A gravestone against the wall, salvaged from the old chapel, read, *Louise, beloved wife of Arthur Tomkins. "Her price is far above rubies."* There was an empty beer can in the corner of the church porch.

It was harder to fix her mind on such minutiae inside the church. The glass-fronted foyer was full of people. At the Traidcraft stall, Don and his wife were setting out packets of fairly traded coffee and nuts and muesli. Committee members were checking their pigeon-holes for notification of meetings. Everyone was so very sensible and worthy.

And here, like a blow to her chest, was Brian, theatrical in a hooded white cassock and a yellow stole, greeting his congregation warmly as each arrived. Ruth, Margaret was relieved to see, was not beside him. She must have gone ahead to the choir vestry.

Margaret hung back, letting Maurice go ahead of her to get the warm handshake and a breezy 'hello'. Then she could not put off the moment any longer. Brian turned to her. There was a moment of heart-stopping awkwardness. She had half put out her hand before she realized, a reflex action. She checked, uncertain. She couldn't make this sacrifice, could she? Besides, there were practical reasons to take his hand. If she did not, the oddness of that would surely scream out to anyone watching. But if she and Brian touched . . .

The decision was snatched from her. Brian's long fingers closed round hers. A brief, warm pressure, yet as forcible a contact as if he had punched her across the foyer. He released her swiftly, turned to the people crowding in behind her. It was over. At least he hadn't offered a pastoral kiss.

She was still dizzy. The feel of his hand lingered round hers. She wanted to wrap it in her scarf, seal it safe, preserve it.

The brown stone was in her pocket. She did not reach for it, but felt its weight dragging down her skirt.

She would have liked to slip quietly into a row near the back, but Brian's enthusiasm was relentless. The returned party had to stand out at the front, smiling a slightly smug greeting to the stay-at-homes, singing them one of the songs from Hy, telling their memories of the week. Ridiculous tears pricked Margaret's eyes when Tim spoke in his reedy voice about cleaning the toilets, about hurting his leg, about the final bonfire.

'And Margaret told us this story about Columba and the Loch Ness Monster, and it was, like, re-ally weird.' He turned to grin up at her.

'Well, Margaret, I think that's your cue,' Brian laughed. 'What are you going to tell us about Columba today, to sum it all up?'

The beast. He hadn't warned her, well, not explicitly. He knew she hated to be thrown into things unprepared. No time to research the details, pen careful notes, choose the most apt quotation.

The words came to her unbidden.

'Columba's Church held that there were three types of martyrdom. There was red martyrdom, where you shed your life-blood. There was green martyrdom, where you stayed where you were, but gave up your earthly desires for God. And there was white martyrdom, leaving all that you loved and going wherever the Spirit of God took you. Columba chose white martyrdom, and his exile on Hy was joy and grief together. Celtic pilgrimage is not like ours. We're back with you this morning. But for Columba, this was a one-way voyage. In pilgrimage, you are seeking the place of your resurrection. Where you land, there you will live out the Gospel. There you will die and be buried, and, at the end of time, that is where you will rise to eternal life.'

The church was quiet. Then there was a shuffling of service sheets and Brian steered them into 'St Patrick's Breastplate'. The Hy party trooped back to their seats, embarrassed yet oddly proud.

> I bind unto myself today
> The strong name of the Trinity.

By invocation of the same,
The Three in One, and One in Three.

'Well done,' murmured Maurice, as she squeezed in beside him. She smiled affectionately at him.

Christ in quiet, Christ in danger,
Christ in hearts of all that love me.

After the service, so many people came up to ask her more about the week, to wish the musical well and offer help, to get her to write something about Columba for the church magazine. She was settling back into the friendly arms of the church.

Maurice brought her a mug of coffee and for a few moments she was marooned by the crowd in the sunshine from the rear windows. No richness of stained glass here, no centuries-old carvings. A modern, functional Methodist chapel, probably designed by a committee.

'Hello, Mrs Jenkins. I hope you are well.'

The rather formal politeness, the slight accent, alerted her. Margaret arranged a suitably warm smile.

'Faith! Hello. How are you?'

'I am well.' Faith's own smile seemed a little strained. Margaret noted with surprise that she had abandoned the slim-fitting suit Naomi had talked her into. She was back in the voluminous folds of her African dress. She looked well enough, her face a little fuller under the turban. Strange, that you could be away only for a week and yet things struck you freshly.

The strain, Margaret suspected, must be due to the looming deadline for her dissertation.

'How's it going?' she asked. 'Do you want to come and see me this week?'

'Yes.' Faith seemed to hesitate. 'Yes, I should like to talk to you very much, Mrs Jenkins.'

22

It was one of those rare sweet days at the end of April. Cherry blossom hung in drifts like dawn clouds and grape hyacinths spread blue around the roots, making the daffodils sing a brighter gold. Margaret had set two chairs and a table out on the patio at the edge of the fish-pond. It seemed a pleasanter meeting place than the rather dark and formal dining-room where they usually worked. She was hovering inside the open French windows, not wanting to lose the kiss of the sunshine, yet anxious that she might miss the doorbell. Faith's touch was sometimes too hesitant, apologetic, to set the chimes pealing. It was not really warm enough to leave the windows open today. Only the sunshine outside was warm. In the shade, the air had not yet lost its chill.

The bell pealed briefly. It could not really be any softer than usual, but it seemed so. Margaret went to answer it. Faith stood on the doorstep, her head a little bowed, so that she seemed to glance anxiously up at Margaret, though she was taller. She was dressed neither in her peacock bright African dress nor in the smart tailoring of Naomi's choice. The shapeless navy blue coat might have come from the back rail of a charity shop. Margaret offered to take it from her, but Faith resisted with a little shiver.

'Please, I think I will keep it on.'

'Oh, dear. Does it strike cold to you? And here was I hoping we could sit out in the sun. But if not . . . Would you like me to turn the heating up?' It was not yet time to switch the central heating off, but she had set it, frugally, to come on only in the morning and evening.

'No, please. We will sit where you like. I'm all right.'

Margaret led her through into the sitting room and hesitated. If she sat Faith down in the cane chairs inside the French windows, it would duplicate too exactly the way she sat – had sat – with Brian. It would be Faith's dissertation between them, not Brian's poems. Nit-picking over English grammar would replace the play of syllables and metaphor which delighted the ear and fired the imagination. She had thought it would cheer Faith to sit in the sunshine, be more like home. Faith looked as though she needed comfort.

Margaret slid the French windows shut and led Faith instead to the velvet sofa in front of the fireplace. This view was less welcoming, the grate swept and empty, barred off by a spark-guard. She could have arranged a bowl of flowers there.

She sat down in an armchair, where she could look past Faith out on to the garden. It seemed a pity to waste the sunshine. Faith had set her capacious bag down on the carpet, but seemed in no hurry to draw her dissertation out. She was perched rather uncomfortably on the edge of the seat. For all the smallness of her face, without its turban today, her hips spread generously, tilting the cushions sharply towards the floor. Margaret wondered if she should offer her tea straight away and not wait until the session was over. Changing the room and their seating seemed to have altered the relationship. It required a fresh set of rules.

'I'll put the kettle on and make us a hot drink, while you get your papers out,' she said, making a decision and rising to her feet. She was at the same time changing the conventions and steering them both back to normality. It was strange how unsettled she still felt, as though she had come back to a place that was and was not familiar. She was like the human in a Celtic fairy-tale, who has been to the Land of Eternal Youth for a day and finds on returning that the known world is now a century into the future.

When she came back with the tea, Faith was still sitting on the edge of the sofa, her fingers pleating the wool of her skirt, where the coat fell open. The bag remained closed. She hardly seemed to notice when Margaret set the mug on the coffee-table beside her and took her own back to the armchair. She murmured something incoherent that might have been thanks, but she did not lift her head or pick up the mug.

Margaret waited, her hands cupped round the warm earthenware. It was not just her own perception that was different. Something had changed Faith, too. The silence lengthened. Only Faith's busy fingers seemed to scream aloud.

'Is something wrong?' Margaret asked gently, at last.

Faith raised astonishingly large luminous brown eyes, shining with tears.

'Yes, Mrs Jenkins. I am going to have a baby.'

Margaret felt an almost physical blow to her stomach. It was distress for Faith. She grasped instantly the shattering implication for her culture, the husband at home, the moralistic Christian community in an even stricter Muslim society. At the same time she experienced a personal panic, an instinct of denial. This isn't my responsibility. I'm not her personal tutor.

But she saw all too well the impossibility that Faith could take this problem to the casual young man whom the university had assigned to watch over her. Margaret had little more respect for his interpersonal skills than she had for his academic rigour.

'Have you been to the university counselling service?' she asked, biting back the more childish, 'Are you sure?' It betrayed how desperate she felt to distance herself, to hand this problem over to professionals. 'I mean, these things happen. They get problems like this all the time. I'm sure they could help you.'

'No one can help me.' Faith hung her head. 'I have sinned.'

Margaret had to make a conscious effort to reach forward and take Faith's hand. She was not a naturally demonstrative person. It was an act of will, not a spontaneous gesture, to offer physical comfort.

'So have we all,' she said, 'but only some of us get found out. Who was it?'

Faith shook her head. 'I forget his name. I was drunk. Naomi took me to this party, where there was dancing. At home, I was a very good dancer, but the dancing we do in church, it is not the same.'

It was easy to imagine Faith in her traditional robes, dancing up the aisle to the beat of drums, expressing her joy. Now, Margaret had seen her light shapely body in more revealing clothes. Most of the time, as now, Faith seemed to be presenting herself as older and more matronly than she really was. On a dance floor, in a tight skirt of Naomi's choosing . . .

Faith shook her head again and said no more. Tears squeezed down her cheeks. Margaret pushed a box of tissues towards her, guiltily aware that she was substituting these physical moves for the help that was really wanted.

'Would you like me to go to the counselling service with you? Help to explain, about your background?'

'What could they do? It is too late now.'

'They'll give you advice, what to do next. Have you seen a doctor?'

Faith's head signalled a hopeless negative. Margaret moved across to the sofa and put an arm round the woman's shoulders.

'Look, I know it seems terrible now, but it happens to lots of women. Life goes on. Do you think your husband will be very angry?' It seemed a feeble question to a woman whose life had been torn apart.

'He will kill me. Or divorce me. I will never see my children again.'

This baby is not yet a child to her, Margaret thought. Just a personal disaster.

'Perhaps you could stay in this country a bit longer. We could get your dissertation deferred, on medical grounds. Then you can have the baby and get it adopted. There are loads of couples in this country who can't have children. They're crying out for newborn babies.'

Faith stared at her with surprising directness, almost contempt. 'I am a married woman. Do you think they will let me give my baby away without my husband's consent?'

Margaret blushed. Faith was an intelligent woman. Of course she had thought of all the implications of her situation. Between them lay one unspoken possibility. Margaret did not want either of them to name it.

'I do not want this baby,' Faith said, her voice hardening.

'No, of course not. But it's a fact. We have to start from where we are.'

'You must help me.'

'How? I've said I'll come to the counselling service with you. It's up to you whether I sit in on the session or not. If you want me to help explain things, make sure they understand what it means back home, and you understand the possibilities open to you . . . Or I'll go to the doctor with you.'

'Naomi says that you can stop this baby.'

Margaret tested each word carefully before she let it out. 'I . . . The law says that you can have . . . an abortion . . . if you satisfy certain conditions. I don't know what they are. I'm not . . . I don't approve of abortion. I think it's taking human life. I know it's only a few cells, it's not the same as a full-term baby, but, scientifically, it's got DNA that's distinct from the DNA of the father and mother. I think that makes it a separate human being.'

Faith looked at her blankly. 'I cannot have this baby. I will die.'

'Oh, now, let's not get melodramatic.' She hated herself for the way she was distancing herself from Faith's need, taking refuge behind moral argument and offering nothing in its place.

'I think there are doctors who would do this without so much trouble. Quickly, so nobody will find out.'

'You mean a private clinic, that specializes in that sort of thing? Yes, I suppose there are. But you'd have to pay. And NHS data is confidential, you know. If you're really determined to do this, a doctor at the university health centre could arrange it for free.'

Faith looked shocked. 'I cannot tell them at the university. What would they think of me? I have money. My husband is generous to me and I have my government grant. I have spent very little.'

That's true, thought Margaret. Until Naomi revamped Faith's wardrobe, she had lived a life of almost monastic frugality.

'Well, then. You've got the choice. Whatever I think, it's not against the law.'

'You have to help me.'

'But I just said . . .'

146

'Please. You are my only friend.'

'Couldn't you ask Naomi?'

Faith shook her head vigorously. 'It is her fault. She is a bad woman. I should not have gone with her. She made me drunk. She introduced me to that man. She is not my friend.'

'You can't expect *me* to arrange an abortion.'

'You are my friend. You are my only friend. Please, I ask you.'

In a treacherous shift of focus, Margaret longed for Brian to be sitting beside her, so that she could unload this crisis of conscience on him, between laughter and tears. How could she find herself in this situation? A sober medievalist with a rather old-fashioned morality. What did love for Faith demand?

Brian would never be in this sitting room again. There was no way now she could share with him these intimate questions of birth and death. Couldn't she phone him? But what if Ruth answered?

She grasped at the slender plank of her academic discipline, her notions of fairness. She had a duty of care to present the options to Faith, then leave the decision to her.

'Look,' she said, 'I don't know the ins and outs of the law. This isn't my scene. But I'm sure the university counsellors meet this problem all the time. I'll come with you. We'll see what they say, and you can tell them what you want to do. And whatever you decide, I'll stay your friend. You can count on that.'

'Please,' said Faith, turning her tragic, tear-washed face very close to Margaret's, 'don't tell anyone else. Nobody at the university, nobody at the church. You will promise me this?'

'Of course, if that's what you want,' said Margaret, almost surprised. 'I wouldn't gossip about it. I just want you to get the best advice. I suppose it's all right to tell Maurice, isn't it? He's your friend, too. We'll both stand by you.'

Faith shook her head vigorously, panic in her eyes. It was hard to say that her dark face blushed, but it seemed to swell with the heat of emotion. 'No! Not Mr Maurice. Please! I could not bear it if a man knew this about me.'

Margaret patted her hand. 'It's OK. I won't say a word if you don't want me to. It'll be our secret.'

147

'And you will help me find a clinic?'

Margaret was surprised to find she was trembling. She took a deep breath. 'I suppose so.'

23

How did I let this happen to me? Why do I keep finding myself in situations I'm completely unsuitable for?

Margaret leaned against the back wall of the church hall, fighting off a headache. This was their last complete run-through before the dress rehearsal, the last chance to check if the words could be heard from the back, if the pattern of the dances made the best use of the stage, if the balance of voices and instruments was right.

Notes of Brian's music flew through the air. They seemed to be coloured: jade green, purple, scarlet. She no longer thought of the noisier passages as a cacophony. She could distinguish themes now, sense changes of mood. In that way, he had educated her. He was musician as well as poet.

But even after Hy, she was out of her depth in the racy chatter of the girls, the football obsession of the boys. She didn't have Brian's easy camaraderie or Ruth's dogged motherliness. She still felt the polite stranger, out of place, not knowing the language.

Tim nudged at her elbow. 'Brought you an orange squash, miss. That all right?'

She smiled down at him, suddenly moved. Tim was like a stray dog who had adopted her. She could almost see his tail wagging. She pushed away the thought that she might have had some success here. It was nothing she had done. She just happened to be the one on duty when he cut his knee. Tim was lonely and frightened about other things in his life, too. She was a convenient rock to whom he could cling.

She didn't feel like a rock. She felt like helpless flotsam being rushed towards a weir, unable to turn back. Had she really agreed to go with Faith to an abortion clinic? She was revolted by the whole idea. But the printout from the website was in her top desk drawer, along with her postage stamps and paper clips. It was a delicate green and white, with a tasteful logo of a snowdrop, chastely virginal. She had taken it out, almost furtively, when Maurice was out of the house, and rung the number. Wednesday, three o'clock. If she felt this terrified of the appointment, what must Faith be undergoing?

All she was really fit for was quiet teatimes at home, watching the flicker of orange fish-tails under the water-lily leaves, hearing Brian read his poetry to her. That was what she was good at, what she was naturally made for. She could really help him with perception and encouragement, the critical friend.

An aching emptiness stretched out in front of her. She had shut the door on that absolutely. She had denied the only thing which gave loveliness and meaning to her life.

The music rose into Columba's keening for his lost Ireland. Oh, come on, she scolded herself wryly, as tears pricked behind her eyelids. Don't be falsely melodramatic, like the lightning bolt which rips the night apart as the murder is committed in the Gothic castle. This is not how real life is. You're more likely to hear the television playing *Who Wants to Be a Millionaire?* when your heart breaks.

She hadn't wanted to come this evening. She had argued with herself that her role was over. Far too late to change the script now. When, with some truth, she had pleaded a headache, Laurie, surprisingly, had expressed dismay.

'You can't back out now, Mum. The show's on Saturday. Everybody's got to turn up tonight.'

'You don't need me any more. You know it backwards by now. Or, if you don't, it's too late.'

'But we . . . the guys . . . sort of depend on you. It's more than just knowing the words. You can tell if everybody's . . . well . . . doing it right. Like, if it comes across or what.'

She gave him a twisted smile. 'You mean if it sounds OK to an old fuddy-duddy like me, it should keep the rest of the audience happy?'

'No. It's like . . . Well, Brian's got this sort of vision thing, but you can tell him if it's working.'

Margaret stared at him. Had her sloppy, alienated, seventeen-year-old son seen this so clearly? Did everyone else know it?

Then, in the car, he had asked her, looking straight ahead through the windscreen down the dappled avenue. 'You and Brian, on Hy. They're saying you were an item. That right?'

'No,' she said, unable to prevent the catch in her voice, the slight jerk on the steering-wheel. 'That's just a silly rumour. I got lost one day. When you're on Hy, you find parts of it are a lot bigger and wilder than they look on the map. I ran across Brian and he showed me the way back. That's all.'

It was not completely true, but it had been true in intention. What had happened at the hermitage had been an accident, something neither of them should have let escape from a lifetime's moral discipline. It was back in the box now, the lid secured, whatever Ruth thought.

Then why could Margaret not let go of it? Why was every moment of stillness invaded by the insistent memory of the feel of his arms, the shock of Ruth's anger? Why must she incessantly rehearse speeches of explanation, self-justification she wished she had spoken, but had not?

'Yeah, yeah, only they're saying it was the way you looked at him, and him at you, when you weren't watching. That's all they can think about, those girls, who's got the hots for who. *Boring.* But they can read the signs, trust me.' He flashed a quick grin sideways. 'I wouldn't blame you. Dad's an asshole.'

'Laurie!'

'It's true, isn't it?'

'No, it's not. You've not the slightest idea what you're talking about. Just because Dad and I don't kiss in front of you any more, doesn't mean we've stopped being fond of each other. Love's . . . a more private thing when you get older. And you should have more respect for your father. Goodness knows, he finds it a hard enough job being a parent to you.'

'Doesn't seem to bother you.'

'Mothers are different. Mother goddesses are supposed to be all-embracing. With Father gods, you have to keep the rules.'

'I reckon Brian's a Mother goddess, then.'

She laughed. 'Yes! He's got room for everyone, even you.'

They had pulled into the church car park. Laurie leaped out and slammed his door. He leaned his elbows on the roof of the car and grinned at her over the top of it. 'Don't worry about me. If you want to have a bit on the side, good luck to you. I wish Brian was my dad.'

'If you say anything remotely like that again, I'll put my foot through your bass drum.'

Yet why had his words given a lift to her spirits? She should have been horrified, once she dared to unpack the meaning of that exchange. Her own son was encouraging her to commit adultery with a Methodist minister. Watching Laurie now, throwing all his energy into a last roll of the drums, the suggestion was so ludicrous she almost burst out laughing.

Only the sight of Ruth, coming down the side steps from the stage, sobered her.

'Going out.'

The terseness of Laurie's communications was not, Margaret realized, because they were monosyllabic; rather, it was that they lacked a subject. Looking at her son, ready for a night out, her perception shifted. At home, he kept the door to his mind almost shut, allowing his parents only the narrowest of glimpses into its brightly lit interior. But outside, it was different. As soon as he met his mates, words danced. In the car last night, he had been quite shatteringly fluent.

Was the problem only Maurice? She sighed. It was such a stereo-typed relationship, old-fashioned father, teenage son. The literary critic in her longed for a less predictable characterization.

Life is not a novel, she scolded herself. Laurie and Maurice are real. They hurt each other, and I love them both.

She looked Laurie over fondly, surprised at how much warmer

152

her relationship with her son had become since she returned from Hy. They had already been growing closer since rehearsals began. This, at last, was something they could share. He didn't even resent the fact that she might be trespassing on his territory. He seemed almost proud of her involvement.

Laurie might not be a character in a novel, but he was a work of art tonight. The narrow black trousers flattered his hips. She did not remember having seen the magenta shirt before, with its sharply buttoned collar. The jacket was older, though, the leather kneaded by use into buttery softness. She wanted to stroke it. He had inserted three silver rings in the lobe of his left ear, which would have to be removed for school tomorrow. Did she remember hearing somewhere that the choice of ear had coded significance? She still felt in his culture like an inefficient anthropologist.

'You look nice.'

He grinned, a little embarrassed. 'Really think so?'

'Like the shirt.' Her own subjects were slipping out of sentences now.

She found herself imagining him removing that jacket, slipping off the silky shirt. It was surprisingly easy for her to picture, on the pale thin elbows of her adolescent son, a vivid sinewy tattoo. Would he do that one day? Would he come home and provocatively display the Loch Ness Monster indelibly rearing in front of Maurice's disapproving eyes? Or an image more shocking?

Laurie kissed her forehead, a thing he did not often do. He seemed to have become rather sweetly protective of her lately. In an odd way, the rumours about her and Brian seemed to have pleased, rather than shocked him.

'See you.'

'Have a good time. Don't be too late back.'

'Trust me.'

A conventional exchange and he was gone. Margaret sat, hugging a warmth she had rarely felt over Laurie until recently. It scared her. It was too sweet to last. She was swept by a sudden horror that this would be the last time she saw him. There would be a ring at the doorbell late at night, two police officers shadowy on the doorstep, a gruff suggestion that she should sit down.

Or the illusion would shatter another way, with the plate glass of a shop front, a mugging in the street, a stolen car, a pregnant girl. How well did any mother know her child?

The most dangerous thing she knew about Laurie was his possession of the rumours, about Hy, Brian and her. She should be scared for herself, as much as for Laurie. And, in a way, she was. Yet, still filled with the buzz of anxious excitement she had felt watching her glamorous son stride into the night, she became aware of her own ambivalent feelings about the fear of revelation.

She had discovered that she was not just a conventional middle-aged Methodist woman. An attractive man loved her. Treacherous though it was to her friend, even Ruth's anger was a kind of flattery, acknowledging Margaret's attraction. She possessed unrealized glamour. She felt the glow of that affirmation, warm as firelight, even while her stomach screwed with the imminent possibility of its revelation to Maurice.

It was over, and yet it was not. The waves were still spreading, like the wash of the Caledonian MacBrayne steamer that had carried them away from the Hebrides. The sense of danger was scary. It was not unattractive.

24

'I've got to go into town this afternoon. Might be late back. Have you got your key?'

The words had a ring of cheery falseness that made Margaret feel guilty. She had left it until the last minute, getting out of the car at the university's history building, before Maurice drove on to a further car park by the administration block.

Maurice checked his pocket. 'Affirmative. Shopping for something nice?'

'Nothing exciting. It's really an errand for someone else. I'll get the bus back.' She kissed him quickly and shut the door. He drove off, lifting his hand slightly in an absent-minded wave.

That was a downright lie, not just an evasion, she told herself. *Exciting* was perhaps not the word she would have chosen to use, but her errand this afternoon was certainly neither as boring nor as ordinary as she had made it sound. She already felt sick with apprehension. A week ago, she could never have imagined herself telephoning an abortion clinic to make an appointment. It hardly mattered that it was not for herself, but for Faith.

She watched the blue car dwindling past the tennis courts with a pang of belated regret. She wished she could have told Maurice. She had needed to talk to someone, to share her confusion. She had no great confidence that Maurice would have been able to give her any better advice, but simply talking to him would have helped her clarify her own mind. And it would have been comforting to share with him the guilt she felt. Maurice would, she thought, have absolved her, given her moral support. But she had promised Faith she would keep silent, and so she must struggle with the burden alone.

Had the fact that she would have made a different decision for herself given her the right to refuse Faith's plea to make this appointment? Was she going to be responsible for killing Faith's unborn child? What if she had refused? Surely Faith would have turned to someone else?

But Margaret knew she would not have. It had been such a huge thing for Faith to bring herself to confess it, even to Margaret, a married woman and a mother, like herself. There was no one else she trusted, not here in England. Naomi might have helped, but Faith was too bitter to speak to her. What might Faith have done, alone and friendless? Margaret swallowed hard. No. It was Faith's decision. Margaret had promised she would stand by her, whatever she chose. Yet she knew she was going to be haunted by that lost child for the rest of her life.

Don't get melodramatic, she scolded herself. It's really not a child yet, is it? Just a cluster of cells on their way to becoming one. Thousands of foetuses are aborted spontaneously all the time. There's a huge waste in nature, a careless generosity of creation.

But for others, dearth. The pain of people like Ruth, who could never have a child. There must be pain for Brian, too.

She walked up the tall flight of steps from the quadrangle, hardly acknowledging the students overtaking her. Allowing herself to say Brian's name, even in her mind, brought an aching pain. If only she could . . .

There was no one she would rather share this with than Brian. She dismissed him too lightly sometimes as a little boy needing her maternal indulgence. Yet Brian had been into areas of other people's pain which she could not begin to imagine. The blue eyes, which danced with mischief for her, had ached for griefs he could not stem. He would know shocking things about people and keep them secret. The loneliness and uncertainty she felt over Faith were his, in his role as minister, multiplied a hundredfold.

All the same, a reasonable part of her argued, ministers have a system of pastoral support. There's always someone they can go to who will share the load. But who can I go to, if not Brian?

She wanted very much to be with him now.

As she climbed the stone stairs past the overfull noticeboards, she thought suddenly, refreshingly, of Ian on Hy. Could she write to him? After all, it would have been impossible to tell Brian about this, even if she had not cut off private talk with him. He would soon guess she was talking about Faith, and she had promised to tell no one, especially not a man.

But Ian didn't know Faith. Margaret could put the problem in general terms and ask his advice. Where would he stand on abortion? He had the tough kind of personality that might accept the necessity. Death was always close in a fishing community. Or did that make life more precious?

The appointment was already made for this afternoon.

'I shoved my essay under your door. Did you read it?' Jonathan, from her first-year tutorial group, was hovering anxiously as she struggled to unlock her study door.

'Yes, I think so. I mean, no. I've got it, but I haven't read it yet. It was two days late, you know.'

'Yeah, but this one's good. Better than the last one, anyway. Do you know what this guy Reginald of Darlington or Durham or something said . . .'

'Let me read it first. OK?'

'He said if you were writing about a saint, it didn't matter what miracles you said he did.'

'Because if your man didn't do it, some other saint did.'

'You knew about that?' Jonathan's face looked crestfallen. 'And I thought you'd be chuffed with it.'

She could have kicked herself. She hadn't needed to trample over his rare flash of enthusiasm so brutally. The excitement of discovering something is not less because others have enjoyed the same moment of discovery before you.

'It's an interesting theory,' she said, trying to make amends. 'Have you discussed the implications? The communion of saints. That we're all part of the body of the Church. When someone triumphs over evil, we all feel lifted up. When one of us falls, we're all diminished.'

He was looking less certain. 'Well, I'm not really into that stuff myself. Like, we're responsible for ourselves, aren't we? Not anybody else.'

She looked at him wearily, the pimpled chin, the unwashed hair. Probably living on baked beans and beer. 'You may feel differently when you're older. Married, maybe. If your lot are still getting married by then. No man is an island. All that. Look, I'm not going to hold a tutorial in the corridor. You're seeing me on Friday.'

'Yeah. Sure. But it's not all rubbish this time. Honest.'

He gave her an anxious grin as she shut the door on him. He seemed younger than Laurie.

Now that she was on her own, the fears crowded back. She ran her fingers through her hair in despair. The room was hardly bigger than a broom cupboard. The stacks of shelves towered over her desk, yet were still inadequate for all her books and files. There was hardly room for anything else besides the computer. The battered chair where a student could sit was too close to her own.

She had to get through this morning. She didn't think she was going to feel like lunch.

The waiting room was oppressively pink, the blond coffee tables scattered with white and green leaflets, like her printout from the website, with their inappropriate purity of a snowdrop. Margaret tried to calm her nerves by analysing what effect the designer had hoped to achieve. It clearly aimed to be feminine, like those rails of children's clothes depressingly stereotyped in their gendered colour coding. This pink was so vivid and sugary that it, too, spoke more of childhood than adulthood. Was that the message? Become a child again, return to innocence, before all this happened.

Faith looked like a child, lost and bewildered. Margaret wondered about taking her hand, but felt embarrassed in public. There were three other people waiting. On the couch opposite, the young man nervously accompanying his partner looked as though he wished himself anywhere but here. The nursery pink would do nothing to comfort him. It was, after all, Margaret decided, a mistake to steer the client's thoughts towards babyhood. Here, of all places. The impersonal elegance of chrome and off-white might have been less disturbing.

Still, the young man had come. He was standing by his girlfriend. She would be his girlfriend, wouldn't she, not his wife? She sat stiller than he did, sad but stoic. Her long straight hair looked as if she had not washed it for days, her sallow skin like uncooked pastry. She seemed in a stupor, as though her life had frozen. Someone needed to break through the ice and set her free. Only the white of her tightly clasped knuckles showed her emotion.

The other woman, seated to one side under the window, was older, perhaps thirtyish. She was unaccompanied. She looked sveltely groomed and poised, her legs crossed, flipping slowly through a *Country Living* magazine, as if she might actually be reading its contents. Could she really be here for the same purpose as Faith and the unhappy couple? Perhaps it was not her first time, a minor inconvenience, soon put right.

Margaret found such detachment hard to imagine. She had discovered that she was less objective, more easily shocked, than she had thought. Maybe this stranger's poise was a front to the world, like her carefully groomed cap of hair and skilful make-up.

Faith started, almost jumping from her seat, as the inner door opened. But the receptionist came across the room to the couple opposite.

'Would you come this way? Mr Wilkinson will see you now.'

She did not, as most medical receptionists do, summon them by name. How very tactful, Margaret thought. A professional code of anonymity. But what if you were to meet someone you knew in this waiting-room? For a bizarre moment, she imagined a mother and daughter confronting each other across the thick beige carpet. Somebody could probably make a sitcom out of this, she thought wildly, turning tragedy into hilarity. Or a black comedy, perhaps, that made you laugh to stop you weeping.

'How are the children?' she said to Faith, to fill the emptiness.

It was a bad question. Tears started to roll down Faith's cheeks.

To cover her mistake, Margaret started to chatter haphazardly about her own children. About Ros and Jake at college, Ros's plans for a year in France, Jake's expedition to Iceland, Laurie's drumming.

The tears slowed. Faith's head was bent deeply over her lap. She looked not so much like a child now, but an old woman. The fullness that pregnancy had brought to her face seemed to have collapsed into dry furrows.

A couple Margaret had not seen before came out of the consulting room and crossed silently to the outer door. The other woman was summoned in their place. There was a long wait.

The receptionist came so softly over the thick carpet that Margaret had not heard her approach from behind.

'Follow me, please.'

Faith rose obediently. In that startled moment, Margaret realized she herself did not know what to do.

'Do you want me to come in with you?'

'Please!'

'Is that all right?' Margaret appealed to the receptionist. 'I'm just a friend.'

'Of course. Many of our clients like to have emotional support.'

Another room, smaller, but identically coloured. Two low armchairs before a desk with MRS ANGELA ROSS, COUNSELLOR, helpfully spelt out on a display card. She had a quantity of red-gold hair, permed and lacquered into a sphere around her head. Margaret found herself wondering how it stayed in place.

After some courtesies, which failed to put Faith at her ease, the counsellor began to take her, stumblingly, through her medical history, the details of which she entered on the form in front of her. Faith's pregnancies, the living children, two miscarriages. Mrs Ross skated carefully around the issue of the father's consent. There were exceptional circumstances, she seemed to suggest, continents apart, the need for prompt treatment. Was 'treatment' the right word, Margaret wondered, for what was going to happen? But more probing questions were clearly designed to provide evidence of the stress Faith was under. Her ready tears confirmed this. The counsellor offered a box of pink tissues. Did Faith understand the options? She did.

The paperwork was completed. Mrs Ross murmured into a telephone, then smiled at them.

'The doctor is ready for you. Second door on the left.'

Mr Wilkinson looked more like a solicitor than a surgeon. A well cut suit, with striped waistcoat, thinning black hair. His eyebrows were greyer.

'Come in, come in.' He was motioning them to comfortable seats with a reassuring warmth. The décor here was snowdrop green and white. A little more clinical. There was, Margaret noted, an adjustable chair upholstered in synthetic leather, such as you found in a dentist's surgery.

Examining the counsellor's notes, Mr Wilkinson went over again Faith's reasons for wanting an abortion, her gynaecological record, the choice of method.

'Would you mind removing your tights and pants and getting on the couch for me?'

Margaret was startled. She had been expecting only a preliminary interview. Could he really be planning to do the procedure now? No, of course it couldn't be that. Faith hadn't even signed a consent form yet. She should have realized there would need to be a physical examination.

She took Faith's undergarments, poor scraps of human dignity, and watched the African woman tremble as she mounted the couch. Margaret really would have held her hand now, but there was no room. Would Faith want her to watch this or not?

Margaret had, of course, undergone many such examinations herself. It seemed more intrusive, watching Faith stiffen, sensing her resist. It seemed almost a manual rape. Too late, she wondered if she should have insisted on a female doctor. Perhaps it made a difference that this examination was not intended to lead to a happy outcome, unlike Margaret's own three pregnancies. She felt soiled by it, in a way the expensive carpet and the chaste green and white décor could not change.

She watched him wash his hands and sign the form.

When Faith was dressed again, and had given a blood sample, they returned to the counsellor and the fundamental moment of

161

decision Margaret had been dreading. Was Faith quite sure she wanted to go through with this? She had considered the alternatives? By now, Faith had found her voice. Clearly, and with more force than Margaret expected, she made her will known.

'I do not want this child. You must take it away.'

It had become inevitable now. There was a brief consultation about the method she would prefer. Vacuum extraction, under local anaesthetic. More forms were passed across the desk, Faith bending forward to sign. Margaret realized how much she had been hoping, even praying, that it would not come to this, that Faith would weaken at the last moment – or did she mean find her courage? – and decide she could not go through with this. She would stand by her baby.

As Margaret would stand by her.

It had not happened. It was over now.

'Tuesday morning?'

Margaret knew with a sinking heart that she would have to accompany Faith again. This time it would not be for a discussion of the options. It would be the real thing. Unless Faith changed her mind.

Somehow the two of them got out into the fresh air. There were pink tulips framed by fresh green leaves. Margaret felt sure that when the roses in the flower-beds came into bloom, they would be pink too.

'I should have brought the car.'

Faith was shaking. They would need two bus journeys to get home. It had been cowardice which had held Margaret back from asking Maurice if she could have the car. She would have had to invent a story, a more convincing set of lies than the casually evasive phrases she had dropped at their parting. She went in fear of betraying herself, meshed in deceit, though she had meant this as a kindness.

'We'll take a taxi,' she said, smiling decisively at Faith. She rarely carried a mobile phone, but she had seen a payphone in the foyer of the clinic. There must have been many women before Faith who had collapsed in tears, whether of grief or relief, unable to get themselves home unaided. All things considered, Faith looked surprisingly strong now it was all over.

Except that it was not. Faith had signed a consent form and a cheque. Margaret did not know the amount. But these were only pieces of paper. She still did not have to bring her body here. She could change her mind.

Margaret paid the taxi off at Faith's lodgings, and walked the few streets home. There were swathes of daffodils down the grass reservations between the carriageways, and the cherry trees on the pavement were in blossom. It was so attractive, so orderly, this mellow 1930s estate, each house styled differently, but built in the same unifying warm Midlands brick, each set in a well-tended garden. Maurice was a diligent and knowledgeable gardener. Their own front plot welcomed her, with its curved beds massed with spring colour, yellow, blue, white.

Maurice looked up from his newspaper as she kissed him. 'Did you get what you wanted?'

'It wasn't what I wanted. It was for somebody else.'

163

25

It was amazing. Even Margaret could feel that, sitting in the wings just behind the curtain, with the prompt script open in front of her. She was tapping her feet to music which, a year ago, she would have pulled a face at. The hall was packed, the atmosphere contagious. As the band worked themselves into a frenzy, most of all Laurie on the drums, the audience rose to meet them. This was far different from the few rows of faithfuls who loyally supported any church event. Scores had come from the comprehensive school, where most of the cast were pupils, or had been. There was a sizeable representation from the High School, too. This was their music, their generation.

Yet the story was fourteen hundred years old, and it was still a good story. Deceit and war, heartbreak and exile, sinister magicians and a savage monster, love and loss. The purity of Annie's voice, rising with the exiles' grief, moved her to tears; the whirling dances of sea and storm were a feast for the eyes. Even the older people in the audience were enjoying themselves, generously starting to sway to these new rhythms, as they did to old music hall songs. In the front row, eighty-year-old Mrs Wardle dropped an audible and satisfying 'Aah!' of emotion at Columba's encounter with the old horse.

Brian knows how to do it, Margaret thought. He has his finger on the pulse of humanity. All my scholarship is meaningless beside this.

The applause was ecstatic when the final curtain rose again on the assembled cast. The lights were bright on the rows of glistening faces, astonished themselves at what they had achieved. Margaret's eyes were for Tim, three rows back, but looking more delighted with himself than she had ever seen him. Her hands hurt from clapping.

The kids in the audience were on their feet, stamping and cheering. It seemed as though Laurie's drumsticks were unable to stop. They whirled and rolled out another riff, a clash on the cymbals.

Everyone was shouting for Brian. He was dragged out from the wings, grinning with enjoyment, his wave trying to give their praise to everyone else. But he was loving the applause. Margaret could see Ruth still in the shadows he had left. She had been acting as dresser behind the scenes. No one would pull her on to the stage.

Margaret hardly listened as Brian tried to voice his thanks to the whole team over the shouting. She was aware of him looking around, his hand reaching out. Another roll on Laurie's drums. She didn't understand what Brian wanted. It wasn't until Don strode into the wings, lifted her under the elbow and hauled her out into the light, that she realized. Brian was telling them she was his co-author, that the story had come from her. Without her, none of this could have happened.

She was centre-stage. She felt dazed by the light in her face. She hadn't realized how difficult it was to see the audience, but she didn't want to look at them, anyway. She was grinning with that same mixture of embarrassment and pleasure she had seen on the rest of their faces. There was no stage make-up to hide her blushes. Brian's hand was still grasping hers. He squeezed it hard. He shouldn't do this. It wasn't fair to hold her so publicly that she daren't reject him. She must stand here, knowing that Ruth was watching her husband and Margaret, hand in hand, receiving tumultuous applause.

Maurice was watching too, seated at the card table at the back, where he had been taking the tickets. Dazzled by the stage lights, she could not make out his face.

At the end of the run there was a party at the manse. Margaret squeezed into the narrow kitchen, carrying a boxful of sausage rolls, past women coming in and out with more contributions. Ruth was masterminding the flow of food and drink. The minister's wife seemed the only one not flushed with excitement, the buzz of success. She was, as usual, being stolidly cheerful and efficient, in a contained sort of way. Offerings were swiftly unwrapped, platters found, food passed through the hatch to be added to the buffet on the dining-table. She had detailed some helpers to provide cold and hot drinks. Everything was under control.

Margaret hovered. 'Can I help?' Her voice had the nervousness of a little girl. It was hard to explain to people that she would be less fearful of standing in the pulpit and delivering a sermon than of being asked to make the tea. She had worked out coping strategies to look after her own family, but in the church kitchen she always got things wrong. The tea was too weak, the butter spread too thickly, slices of cake inexpertly reduced to crumbs. No one criticized her to her face, but she would hear the voices of other women behind her, 'I thought we were going to use the white bread for sandwiches, not the brown.'

It was a relief when Ruth gave her a brief glance and said, 'No, thanks. There's no room for anyone else in here. You could go to the dining-room and see that everybody gets a drink.' She gave a quick mechanical smile and bent to put Margaret's sausage rolls in the oven.

Margaret escaped. The big sitting-room was packed with teenagers. They were sprawled over the miscellaneous collection of sofas and easy chairs which Brian and Ruth had accumulated for such occasions. They were lounging against walls and spreading a tangle of limbs across the carpet, like an overgrown forest. Annie sat gracefully cross-legged and upright, almost in a yoga position. How does she manage to carry herself so elegantly, Margaret wondered with envy, even when she's relaxing?

Tim scrambled over several bodies, producing shouts of protest. He had appropriated the horse's white papier mâché head and was wearing it, tipped towards the ceiling so that his thin, eager face peered out from beneath its jaw.

'Miss! Miss! I'm a nightmare!'

'Aaargh!' She clutched her throat and pretended to shudder, though laughing.

'Wasn't it great? I was scared stiff I was going to fall off the stage or forget my words or something. But I never, did I? Did you see me?'

'Of course I saw you, Tim. You were terrific.'

'Was I really?' Conventional praise wasn't enough. He was hungry for affirmation. He was always going to remember this. For once in his life, Tim had done something amazing, that had people on their feet cheering. It had changed the way he thought about himself.

'You were the greatest. I've never seen you dance like that before, even in rehearsals. Was your mother there?'

'Yes.' He glowed with pride. 'And Conrad.'

'Is that her . . . boyfriend?'

Tim nodded. 'He's not so bad. Said it was a great show. Should have been on the London stage.'

'Perhaps you will be,' she laughed. 'Maybe Prince William will get to hear about it, and we'll be summoned to appear at the Royal Variety Show.'

'Do you think so?' He was too naïve, too eager. Tim couldn't appreciate irony.

'Well, I think you probably have to be a bit more famous than that. But it's a start. Maybe if we do this every year, we could make a name for ourselves.'

'Will we? Is there going to be another one?' Tim clearly hadn't thought about this. What he had already was astonishing enough. Joy, success, acceptance. The thought that it could happen again was new, overwhelming.

'I don't know.' She tried to backtrack. 'You'll have to ask Brian. It was a lot of work for everybody. I don't know if we could do it every year.'

'Brian! Brian!' He was already turning away from her, tripping over more protesting bodies as he struggled across the room, the horse's head lurching before him. She heard his high voice above the hubbub. 'Margaret says we ought to do another one. Can we?

167

Can we? Next year?'

Brian swung round. His smile seemed dazzling as a stage light as it searched out her face across the room. His eyes found and held hers. She felt the shock. She could not hear his answer to Tim, but his gaze held hers all the time and his smile told her he was talking about her. She imagined him saying, 'Is that what Margaret wants?'

She didn't want him to go. He mustn't go. He couldn't leave all this, all these people who needed him. Not because of her. She wished she had put Ian's plain brown stone from Hy in her pocket tonight. She needed that hard common sense. There was too much excitement here.

'Lemon or orange. Or would you prefer a coffee?'

Maurice had squeezed into the space behind her, rather inexpertly balancing a tray of disposable plastic beakers.

'A black coffee, I think, please . . . Look, I was supposed to be doing that.' She took the tray from him and started to offer it round the room, glad of an excuse to bend her face away from Brian.

A gong reverberated through the noise. Ruth called, 'Food, everybody. Grab a plate in the dining-room and help yourselves.' There was a general rush.

Margaret stood back, like most of the adults, while the ravenous youngsters swooped into the next room. They were left like rocks when the tide goes out.

'I'll get that coffee,' Maurice volunteered. 'Anyone else? Tea?'

When he had gone, Brian came across the almost empty room. It was dangerous, too intimate. They were not quite alone.

'I think we'll soon have Tim auditioning for RADA. He's really got the bug, hasn't he?'

'It's probably the first time he's ever been a success. And his Mum was there.'

'It went down all right, didn't it?' He needed affirmation as much as Tim.

'It was fabulous.'

'And you think we should do it again?'

'I didn't say that. I said he'd have to ask you.'

'Right now, I'm knackered. I need a month's sabbatical to recuperate. They didn't teach us about directing musicals at theological college.'

'And would you have taken this job if you'd known?' She was trying to keep it light, teasing.

'I wouldn't be anywhere else.' He was not smiling now. Then, as Maurice came back into the room with a tray of hot drinks, he gave a professional laugh. 'Tea? Marvellous. I could drink the pot dry. What do you fancy for the next one, then?' He turned slightly to include the others in the conversation. 'How about a Welsh saint? We could take the cast away to St David's or Bardsey island.'

'I know a wonderful legend about a prince and a runaway girl who turned into a hare to escape him,' Margaret volunteered.

'Pennant Melangell . . .' He swung back to look directly at her. 'Have you been there?'

'No.'

'You would love it. It's another thin place, like Hy, where there's only a wisp of a veil between the world of the spirit and the world of the body. We should go there.'

She knew he meant the two of them. She was terrified that everyone else would see this. The cast were coming back into the room now, plates laden, like a returning tide. Ruth had come out of the kitchen to join them.

'Come on, you lot. I think the gannets have left you a few slices of quiche.'

The older ones picked their way into the emptying dining-room. As they moved around the table, filling their plates with the remnants of the feast still left on the platters, Maurice spoke over Margaret's head to Brian.

'You seem to have had a particularly good time on Hy. Maybe I should have been there.'

26

' I ought to be taking you to church in a chauffeur-driven limousine. You'll have star status this morning. Or maybe I *am* the chauffeur. Would you like me to wait in the car park?'

There was something not quite natural in Maurice's laugh.

'Don't talk rubbish.' She gave his arm an embarrassed punch.

'At least I'm good for one thing. Counting the ticket money. Come to think of it, isn't that what Judas did? Looked after the money bags?'

'Maurice! What is this about?'

He was already getting out of the car. She couldn't possibly conduct this argument with him in the car park. There were people arriving for church all around them. She had to walk at his side, aware of a tension she did not fully understand.

'You're not jealous because of last night?' she tried, when they were momentarily out of earshot of others. 'Because you weren't more involved in it?'

He turned to her with a sad smile. 'I had rather hoped I was more involved with you.'

This was too dangerous. What did he know? She could not stop and confront him here. She could only hope he was not going to carry on with this as they approached the church and the thickening congregation.

Brian was by the door, as always, grinning, if anything, more widely than usual as he shook hands. He was evidently still on a high. The foyer was swarming with teenagers, more than had ever

170

come on a Sunday morning before. There was that same buzz of excitement as last night, which no one wanted to let go. Margaret felt drawn like a magnet towards them. Astonishingly, she was part of this.

But first she had to pass Brian. She attempted only the briefest of handshakes, her hand inert in his. Mercifully, he let her go quickly. She could tell he did not need her today. The sea of admiration was all around him. He had achieved his vision. Everyone had seen it. He was basking in the warm waves of success.

She moved aside to join the cast. Maurice, she realized, had stridden past Brian, ignoring the proffered handshake.

She found herself shaking a little. Could this honestly be jealousy because Margaret had been up on the stage, embarrassed by waves of applause? Or had he seen for himself what the youngsters were saying? Margaret hand in hand with Brian, the spotlights on them as they bowed together. Had he begun to guess? *What* would he guess?

'It's a bit early for a reunion, isn't it? But it's nice to see you all here.' She hardly registered surprise that she could now approach a group of teenagers naturally and join in the conversation. They smiled, accepting her, not quite as one of themselves but as having a right to be with them, a role to play.

It was Lucy who spoke first, with genuine friendliness, devoid of previous malice. 'We're going to sing some of the songs again, miss. Didn't you know?'

Of course. Brian would not miss any opportunity to have his teenagers starring in church. To demonstrate to the congregation what splendid young people they were. To show the youngsters themselves that the Church welcomed them. Simply to give pleasure to people. To revel in his own success.

'That's great, as long as nobody expects me to sing, too.'

'Go on, miss. You could do it.'

Margaret slipped away from them into the church itself. The furniture gleamed honey-gold in shafts of sunshine. People paused at the back, catching up on news. Others were already seated, bowed in silent prayer or listening to the organ and enjoying the sense of a gathering community. She had lost sight of Maurice.

As she moved through the crowd, one face stood out from the rest. One of the welcoming stewards was asking Faith a question, but she stood without turning the intensity of her dark gaze to him, as if she simply hadn't heard. She had seen Margaret, and her eyes were fixed on her friend with the appeal of a drowning woman to her rescuer. Margaret experienced a sudden loss of confidence. This was not a role she wanted. She had to will herself across the space of polished floor, negotiating the bystanders, mechanically responding to their greetings. Faith laid hold of her arm, grasping her with a tenacious grip.

'Mrs Jenkins!'

'I've told you, call me Margaret.'

'I cannot do that. You are higher than me.'

'You make me embarrassed. Perhaps I shouldn't be calling you Faith, but Mrs Dajouba.'

'No, you may call me Faith. I am like a child to you.'

Margaret would have preferred a different relationship. 'You're a married woman with children, the same as me.'

'Yes.' A deeper sadness came into her eyes. 'I wish I could see them.'

Margaret put an arm round her shoulders. She seemed to be making these physical gestures more genuinely now. 'It won't be long. You're nearly through it.'

They both knew it was not only the two months before Faith was due to hand in her dissertation that she meant, but also the days before her next appointment at the clinic. It was easy to take refuge in technical words that avoided emotion – 'appointment', 'procedure', even 'termination'. The death of a baby was what both of them were trying to avoid thinking about.

'Come and sit with us.'

The back of Maurice's head, as he sat in a half-empty row of chairs, was strangely unnerving. There seemed something intentional in his solitude, as though he was aggrieved at the community. What was he grieved about? That was a strange mutation of language. 'Aggrieved' had a negative tone, as though its subject had no right to such feelings, or played unduly on them. 'Grieved' was sympathetic. Had Maurice the right to be indignant with her? She had let nothing happen to betray her loyalty to him. Only her heart knew differently. It did not need a physical unfaithfulness. Maurice had a right to grieve for the loss of the kind of love he once had, the transference of her passion to another man. But she had given him no evidence of that, surely? Or did it shine clear through her eyes for all the world to see?

The little society on Hy had seen. Protestations about getting lost had not fooled the teenagers who had seen them come down from the hills, not quite together, but almost more conspiratorial in their carefully choreographed separation. The light in their faces had not died out soon enough. 'BRIAN LOVES MARGARET.' The words had shone out like a lover's message carved on a tree-trunk.

She and Faith took their places beside Maurice. More conversation was impossible now, to Margaret's relief. Waves of music washed over her, hymns, songs from *The Exile*, hymns again. She watched Brian, the flame of joy clear and tall in him this morning. He was loving them, loving their love, which he could inspire like no one else. She loved him. Ministers of religion have a power, a charisma, an authority to seek out the personal in each individual, at a level which few others feel they have the licence to enter. It is only a short step from making someone feel uniquely known and cared for to igniting another form of love. This must happen to Brian all the time. She had never thought of that before. Ruth was a necessary dragon, guarding him from the attentions of susceptible women, able to satisfy him herself with her companionship and her body. But Margaret had broken through into the forbidden garden.

Had anyone else? Brian and Ruth had moved from one church to another every few years. There must have been many such possibilities. This time Ruth was hurt and jealous. Was what had happened on Hy as unique for Brian and Ruth as it was to Margaret? Had she overdramatized the sacrifice she was forcing him to make?

And what about Maurice?

Brian's eyes found hers from the pulpit and smiled. Ruth sat with the choir, too far to the side for him to turn and share his smile with her. That smile seemed to say it was still Margaret he wanted to share his memories of Hy with.

Maurice stirred uneasily in his seat. Faith sat motionless.

27

'Can I have the car today?' Her mouth felt unexpectedly dry. It was difficult to get the words out steadily.

'What for?'

Both home and university were within easy reach of the main road, with its plentiful bus service. It was not often she needed to ask for the car. There had never seemed any reason for a second one. If she wanted to go home before Maurice, it was no hardship to walk through the university and across the park beyond.

'I've got a hospital check-up. I could take the bus, but it means changing in town. It's quicker round the ring road.'

'You didn't say. Nothing serious?'

'No. I'm sure I'm as right as rain.'

'Something in the women's department, I suppose.'

'Yes.'

She was forced into lying again. Some of that was true, but not all of it. Margaret was appalled at the extent to which she was compromising her conscience to support Faith. First betraying the scrap of human life that was going to end today, and now Maurice's trust. She had promised Faith more than she should.

Almost immediately, she regretted having asked for the car. She might be too nervous to drive safely. She should have used a taxi again.

Still, she was committed now. Maurice drove them both to the administration block and handed over the wheel to her.

'You're sure they don't want you in for anything worrying?'

175

His concern made her feel worse.

'Of course not. I'm one of this Thousand Women Project. They're monitoring us all for breast cancer, but it's not because they think we've got it.' That much was true. But her next appointment was two months off.

'You'd tell me if there was something?' He stood bent over the open car door, to where she had slipped into the driver's seat. He still looked worried. Impulsively, she put her face up and kissed his.

'Of course I'd tell you. That's a promise.'

'All right, then. Take care.' He stepped back, raising his hand in farewell.

She drove to the other side of the campus.

The fine spring weather had lingered. It would have seemed better if it had been a dismal day of rain. The sky would not weep for what was happening. Instead, soft sunshine made a haze between the oak trees, slowed the steps of students below her window with its inviting warmth, made Margaret feel all should be right with the world, lulled her into a sense of unreality. She hardly believed the clock when it told her the time had come to pack up the marking on her desk, close her briefcase, put on her coat. She had had to cancel this morning's lecture, to add to her guilt.

She could not find the reassuring chatter she had intended for Faith in the car. She must concentrate on her driving. She was aware of levels of nervousness below the surface, to which she was not admitting. She would be exhausted tonight when it was all over.

The selfishness of this observation hit her. She turned a brief glance sideways. Faith sat stonily looking ahead. What would it have been like if this had happened back home? Were there women's networks there which would have helped her end it secretly? What would be the penalty if her husband found out?

The criteria on which Margaret would have decided for herself could not be the same as the ones Faith had to live by. She should not judge. But she did, and grieved for the baby.

She got them both to the clinic safely and parked the car. They had been directed to a different entrance this time. As she shepherded Faith into the reception area, she realized there were questions she should have asked. She could not accompany Faith into the operating-room, certainly, but after it was over? How long would Faith need to recover? Could Margaret be with her then? How much did Faith still want from her?

'I'll stay here, shall I, while you go in?' she said, as Faith turned away from the receptionist's desk.

'Thank you.' It had been impossible to get more than monosyllables out of her this morning. Was she mourning, too?

'You know you don't have to go through with this,' Margaret whispered as they settled on another pink couch. 'It's your choice. You can change your mind.'

'I do not have a choice,' Faith said. 'My husband would kill me.'

It was the kind of thing wives said casually. Did Faith mean it literally?

The sunlight dazzled on the glossy white pages of the magazine as Margaret turned them. She saw nothing.

'Mrs Dajouba.' The name, spoken so directly, had the shock of gunfire. There was nobody else in the waiting-room. There was no need for discretion. Margaret had half risen to her feet before she remembered that she could go no further. She clasped Faith's hand. 'Good luck. I'll be thinking of you.'

It was not the right word for what she meant. Faith knew it.

'I need all your prayers. You are very kind to me.' The tears sprang into the corners of Faith's eyes, but she held them back. Her head was proudly high with that carriage Margaret envied. This was her decision. She had a nobility of courage as she passed through the door into a passage beyond.

Margaret was left alone, uncertain. The receptionist came back and took her seat behind a blond counter inlaid with snowdrop green-leather.

'How long does it take?' asked Margaret. 'Should I come back later?'

The receptionist looked surprised. 'That's up to you. The procedure itself is quite quick, ten minutes or so. But we like our clients to wait in the recovery room for an hour or two, just to make sure

177

there are no complications. There hardly ever are, of course. Vacuum extraction is very safe.'

'Would I be allowed to stay with her in the recovery-room?'

'Of course.'

It was all so low-key, so efficiently everyday. If this had been a spontaneous abortion, there would have been grief and heartbreak, floods of tears, bereavement. Perhaps there still would be. But the sun shone unconcernedly through the unfurling rose bushes outside the window. The atmosphere in the waiting room was one of inappropriate peace.

The view from the recovery-room had not been so carefully stage-managed. Only a few paces beyond the window, a brick wall climbed towards a strip of sky. It was not a prospect to lift the spirits.

Faith lay, inert, seemingly shocked, under a white sheet. The young nurse who tiptoed away gave a friendly smile. 'I'll bring you both a cup of tea. Sugar?'

Margaret moved across to take Faith's hand. 'Are you all right?'

The head rolled towards her. The moist brown eyes glittered with the contempt the question deserved. Faith made no other answer. Her face had a yellowish tinge, though it was hard to tell how drained of blood her skin was. It seemed too much of an effort to lift her head.

'I had to do it,' she said at last, as if the words were dredged up from a great depth.

'Of course you did. It's all right. It's over now.' None of those three statements. Margaret realized, was true.

'You look a bit peaky,' Maurice said at supper. 'Are you sure it was just a check-up?'

'Of course it was. Only I hate mammograms. All that squeezing your boobs between cold plates. If you get a heavy-handed radiographer, it's quite painful.'

'As long as they didn't find anything nasty.'

'No. *I'm* all right.' Margaret forced herself to concentrate on the scenario she had substituted for him. 'But you look at the waiting-room. Most of those women in the breast-care unit come in with somebody. Their husband, their mum, sometimes their daughter, even. And you wonder what's going through their minds. The ones with them, I mean. I had a cousin who was diagnosed with breast cancer. Next morning, her husband walked out and never came back. He couldn't handle it.'

'Well, you've no need to worry in that department.' He smiled as he reached across and poured her a glass of wine. 'You needn't be afraid to tell me. I promise I won't cut and run, whatever it is.'

'There's nothing to tell.'

28

Margaret woke with a shock. The massive dark shadow of a man was looming over her bed, shouting at her. She could not take in the words, only the barrage of noise, the threat. The bedroom was in near darkness. Maurice's bedside lamp, carefully shaded so as not to disturb her, threw distorting shadows everywhere else. The light was on in the passage beyond the bedroom door.

'*Maurice!*' She reached out a terrified hand and found emptiness beside her.

Slowly she realized that the thundering figure towering over her in striped pyjamas was Maurice.

'What's the matter? Are you ill?' She grasped at the idea of an inflammation of the brain, the onset of Alzheimer's. What could suddenly turn her husband into an aggressive stranger?

She sat up, drawing the sheet protectively up to her chin, as though he had indeed been a predatory intruder. 'Shall I make us both a cup of tea?'

'Whore!'

She flinched. Little by little, the words of his tirade were sinking into her waking brain. He ripped the sheet and duvet off her, leaving her in her brushed cotton nightdress, and he looked as though he would like to have torn that off, too.

'Where did you do it? On Hy? A romp in the heather, was it, when the rest of us have had all this stuff about a holy island thrust down our throats? I suppose the two of you had it set up from the start, to get a week away from me on your own. You didn't bargain on this.'

'What? I don't know what you're talking about.'

'Or was it going on under my nose before? You'd have had to be pretty quick to get the tests done after you got back from Hy and then scrub out the evidence to make sure I'd never know.'

'Know *what*?'

He turned away in disgust. She could see one of his fists clenched at his side and sensed the effort he was making not to grip her round the throat. She swung her bare feet out of bed and tried to touch him soothingly. But Maurice threw her off. He addressed the bedroom wall with a bitterness that made his frame shake.

'Do you think I haven't seen the two of you? I should think everyone at church must have seen it by now. The way you two hold hands, the smiles you give each other, as though there was no one else but you in the room. You used to smile at me like that once.'

It was pointless to ask whom he was talking about. She was guilty. But of *what*, exactly? What could have provoked this onslaught in the middle of the night? It had to be more than a smile.

He turned back on her. The hurt in his face twisted into contempt. 'Was it here? In this bed? You had plenty of opportunity, didn't you? Pastoral visits, while I was safely in the office. Nothing to make the neighbours talk. Just the minister on his bicycle, calling on one of his congregation. But I never thought it had gone this far.'

'Maurice. What exactly are you getting at?' She was trying to keep her voice level and logical, to stop it shaking.

'This!' He thrust a sheet of paper towards her. It was difficult to make it out clearly, with her body between the lamp and him. The white edges of the paper gleamed softly, enclosing a deeper background. She reached to switch on her own reading-lamp and pick up her glasses. The printout from the website came into focus, green and white, the too-innocent logo of a snowdrop.

Margaret stared at it, her mind racing. She was enmeshed in so much secrecy, multiple possibilities of betrayal. How much should she confess?

'You thought that was for *me*?'

The paper wavered. 'What else would the details of an abortion clinic be doing in your desk?'

She rubbed her eyes. 'Maurice. It's the middle of the night. What were you doing in my study?'

'Couldn't sleep. Went down to the kitchen to make some cocoa. I remembered I'd put a letter out to post, only I'd run out of stamps. Thought you'd have some in your desk. That's where I found *this*.'

She chose her words carefully. 'I told you the other day I had to go into town on an errand for someone else. That bit was true. I was taking her to the clinic. And when I said I was going to the hospital, well, it was the same place. But not for me. I went to hold her hand.'

'Who?'

'I can't tell you. I promised.'

Maurice stared down at her. She could not tell whether he believed her or not. But it hardly mattered now. The suspicions he had voiced could not be unsaid.

A tousled, sleepy head pushed its way round the bedroom door. Margaret saw Laurie start, as she had done, when she found Maurice towering over her. His eyebrows rose. 'You guys OK? I thought I heard shouting.'

'Did you think to pick up a cricket bat? Or were you planning to ask the burglar to excuse you while you dialled 999?' Margaret gabbled maternal jokes to give Maurice time. Neither of them had any answer they could give their son.

Laurie was intelligent enough to draw his own conclusions. 'Yeah, well. No sweat, then.' They watched the bedroom door close.

'Now look what you've done.' It was only half a jest. Laurie already knew far more than his father realized.

'What *I've* done?' The paper trembled in his hand, only part of its accusation allayed.

'Brian's a happily married man and I've got you. There's nothing for you to worry about.'

'If I felt it was reasonable to guess that this was for you, then there is.'

'If we were as close as we used to be, you'd know that I've just had my period.'

182

'Whose fault is that?'

'It's nobody's fault. Just middle age. It doesn't mean we don't love each other.'

'Like you'd love a pet dog. That's not the way you look at Brian, is it?'

'Sometimes. He needs more looking after than you do. I do mother him. Lots of people do.'

'Lots of women do.'

'It goes with the job. He has to be charismatic, to attract people.'

'He's certainly succeeded with you.'

She was too honest to deny it. 'Look, Ruth was on Hy, too. She was the one who went for walks through the heather with him, not me.' Something there remained unsaid. 'You weren't there.'

'Exactly.'

'That's not fair. It was your choice. You could have come.' You should have, a voice was shouting inside her. It would never have happened if you had.

Something *had* happened, even if it was not all that Maurice imagined. And in a sense, it had been. The penetration of Brian into a secret part of herself, which he had never entered before. He had quickened the seed of love, and it was growing. She could not tear it out. She must live with the shame of it, if shame it was, as well as with the delight.

'I'm sorry if I accused you falsely,' he said stiffly, going back to his own side of the bed and laying the paper on the bedside table. He climbed on to the empty half of the mattress. There was something comical in this scene, a part of Margaret's brain told her. Two middle-aged people, their youthful beauty long gone, squabbling about physical attraction. Maurice, a noticeable paunch filling out above the waistband of his pyjama trousers. Her own stick-like legs, beginning to swell with varicose veins.

Yet Brian made her feel as if she was seventeen again. He had never grown up. He seemed to carry a fairy-tale within him wherever he went. Strange that a man who must know far more of the shocking realities of life and death than either of them should seem so whole, so joyful. Perhaps these were the marks of hours of prayer, a love affair with God, which became a love affair with everyone he met.

But Margaret was special. He had told her so.

She hesitated. She could make an act of will, reach out to put an arm round Maurice's neck, kiss him. Hadn't John Wesley said, 'Preach faith until you have it'? Probably it worked for love, too. Each conscious act deepened the reality. But at the first movement of her hand, he twitched away. For all her scruples, she had wronged him, and she did not know how to heal it.

29

'I've got a call to make,' she said, staring at the cereal she had poured into her bowl and realizing she did not want it. 'I'll walk across the park.'

It was difficult. They had avoided speaking to each other in the bedroom, not knowing where to begin. Now Laurie's head, which normally drooped, semi-conscious, over the breakfast table, was lifted, his dark eyes moving warily from one to the other.

It sounded too much like the treacherous evasions she had made in the past few days. Maurice must wonder if she was cheating him again. He could not possibly believe this was an assignation with Brian, could he? She did not know how jealousy might distort common sense. She had never had reason to be jealous on his account.

It hurt her that Maurice was ignoring Faith. Even if he did not know who the woman was, surely he could admit her reality, understand that Margaret had only been trying to help her, that her evasions stemmed from her promise to her friend? Or did he condemn her even for helping? If she had been able to talk it over with him, would he have counselled her against getting involved, convinced her that her own conscience was at odds with Faith's, and that she must stay true to that?

Would it have made any difference, except to leave Faith lonelier and more frightened than ever? Might it have made a difference if Margaret had hardened her heart to say no?

It was too late now. The chance was over. Past, too, the nightmare possibility that Faith might just have killed herself. Enough harm had been done. She must simply do what she could to heal it.

She walked across the dew-wet grass of the park towards Faith's lodgings. The gardeners were lifting the spring bedding, turning the soil, preparing for the next flowering. Paths radiated from the abandoned bandstand. She took one sloping down to the streets that clustered round the university. These were older houses than her own leafy estate. Steps led up, almost from the pavement, to front doors with ranks of bell-pushes. PVC dormer windows jutted from loft conversions. This was bedsit land, teeming with a constantly changing population of students.

She had almost reached the gate in the railings at the lower edge of the park. There, another path converged on hers. A cyclist was bowling down it, blue bobble-cap jauntily on the back of his head to protect the balding scalp from the cool morning air. Bicycle clips made his trousers balloon like a scarecrow's. With a smile of merriment, whose confidence showed a careless disregard for his looks, Brian skidded to a halt in front of her.

'Lovely morning.'

Margaret was shocked into disbelief. She looked swiftly, guiltily, behind her. She had no more meant this than she had intended to meet him at Columba's hermitage, but Maurice would never accept that. Why here, why now? Yet she could not deny the rush of gladness at seeing him. That smile, as always, seemed to crinkle exclusively for her. It probably seemed like that to many other women. She must cling to that.

'What are you doing here? I thought you usually worked in your study in the mornings.'

'Aren't spring and forget-me-nots enough excuse? And shouldn't you be expounding the consequences of the Black Death to somebody?'

'All in good time. I've got some pastoral visiting to do.'

His blue eyes followed the line of the street just below them. 'I wonder if we could have had the same idea. Faith?'

Margaret hesitated, colouring with uncertainty. It would be so easy to be beguiled into saying more than she should. Sharing it with Brian would not be like telling anyone else. Methodist ministers, just like Catholics, understand the secrecy of the confessional. And Margaret herself wanted to confess. There was too much confusion, too much guilt.

She could not. Only Faith could tell him. And the stain that had spread from it into her relationship with Maurice she could not confess to Brian, of all people.

'She's been a bit under the weather lately.' It was on the tip of her tongue to say Faith had had a hospital appointment. But even that was too risky. He might relay it to Faith, in all innocence, ask if there was anything he could do to help. She bit it back.

'I thought so, too.' He pushed his bike beside her through the gate. 'More than that. She's sick at heart, too, isn't she?' His keen gaze into her face was purely professional, nothing personal. 'I see. You know, but you're not allowed to tell me. Fair enough. I'm glad there's somebody she can trust.'

'I'm a woman.'

'Very true.'

The laugh for her now was very personal. She reddened more deeply.

The feeling of guilt and protest was dissipating. It seemed so natural to be walking beside him, delicately discussing a shared responsibility, reading the subtext of each other's conversation.

'So, which of us would do more good this morning? We can hardly arrive on the doorstep as a deputation.'

'I told her I'd look in. She's expecting me.'

He bowed. 'I yield to you, madam. I've got a Circuit meeting this afternoon, which is why I thought I'd fit in a visit now. Do you think she'll be in for the rest of the morning?'

'I've no idea. Either at home or in the library, I should think. She's writing up, so she should have done most of her research by now.'

He checked his watch. Already one foot was on the pedal. 'Maybe I'll come back around twelve. Give me a ring if you think she won't be there.'

'Before eleven, and only if I have to.' Her eyes tried to warn him. She should not be ringing him, for any reason.

He studied her face, and this time it was for her sake alone. 'Something's wrong, isn't it? You didn't look happy when you were coming across the park. And it's such a beautiful morning.'

It wasn't fair. She longed to throw herself into his arms and burst into tears. 'It's Maurice,' she said, staring down at the pavement. 'We haven't been careful enough. He can read my face.'

'And read that you love me.' His voice was soft, but he almost crowed. He shouldn't do that.

'Yes. He thought . . .' Caught up in her own anguish, she had almost betrayed Faith.

'Thought what?'

'Never mind about that bit. It's not mine to tell.'

Brian had spent his working life with people in trouble. She could not deceive him. He did not voice Faith's name, but she was sure that he knew, in part at least.

'Hmm. Would it help if I talked to Maurice?'

'No!'

'Oh.' The little-boy disappointment again. 'Perhaps you're right. I never was a favourite with the Property Committee. And protestations of innocence aren't enough when the other person's in a certain state of mind.'

'We're not innocent.'

'Isn't loving innocent? To do nothing about it, just love.'

'It ought to be, but I don't believe it is. Not if it hurts other people.'

'Was God hurt when Adam and Eve grew up and discovered each other?'

'That was original sin, wasn't it? The tree of knowledge. And they didn't have other partners.'

'Would you have wanted them to stay in Eden as children? Never to know childbearing and work, the two things which give meaning to most people's lives?'

'I thought you were the theologian. What we had was Eden, wasn't it? Reading poetry at teatime.'

'And now we know that we were naked all the time.' So gently, so tenderly.

188

'Yes,' she whispered to the pavement.

'I wish I could kiss you.'

'But we can't.'

'No.'

'We're hurting Ruth and Maurice just by standing here.'

'I am rebuked.' He mounted and wobbled away. 'I love you.'

The morning sun was climbing over the chimneypots.

The curtains of Faith's room were almost drawn. They were an oppressive orange pattern on heavy black material. Only a finger of light separated the folds. The furniture was dingy, ill matched, thrown together by a landlord for the careless use of students to whom it was a temporary pad, not a home.

What was Faith's home like in West Africa? Her husband, from all accounts, was not short of money.

Faith was wearing her overcoat. The room struck chill, though she surely had no reason to worry about feeding the gas meter. Margaret hesitated about suggesting that she light the fire, but decided not. This was Faith's room, Faith's life. She must not try to take over.

She kissed the other woman. She had never done this before. There had always been a touch of formality in the relationship, on Faith's side, at least.

'How are you?'

'It hurts,' Faith said. 'I think he was not a kind man.'

Margaret did not know how to interpret that. Was there physical pain after the suction of the womb? Or did Faith mean something else?

'You're bound to feel bad for a few days,' she said, covering either eventuality. 'Anyone would. I should take the day off and put your feet up, and then get down to work again tomorrow. The more you throw yourself into that, the less time you'll have to think about it. And you've still got a lot to do on your dissertation.'

'I know.' Faith's fingers plucked the fringe of a cushion. 'I think I shall fail. It is no good.'

'Rubbish! Don't say that. You've done so much work. We're not

189

going to let you fail. You're a very intelligent woman.' She refrained from saying that Faith's tutor seemed to have done little to train her in the rigours of academic discipline. 'And what about the children? They're dying to see you come home with your diploma.'

A half-smile twitched Faith's lips. 'Yes. They would be very proud of me.'

'Well, then. We'll see that it happens.'

Faith stared at her knees. 'Do you think I should tell my husband?'

A long silence. Margaret was alarmed at the possible conse-quences of her answer. How could she know? 'It's not for me to say. I don't know your husband. Or the customs of your country.'

'Would you tell Mr Jenkins, if it were you?'

It was hard to bite back the words: 'Maurice already knows.'

Margaret sat down on a hard chair. She explored her words care-fully, thinking as she went. 'I feel if you were going to tell him, it should have been before the abortion. It should have been his deci-sion, too. You never know, he might have forgiven you and decided to adopt the child. On the other hand, he might have thrown you out. I can't tell. But if you tell him now, he may still throw you out. And you don't have the baby. From what you say, you could lose your other children as well. I don't see what good that would do to anybody. To your children, your husband, to you.' She did not say 'to the baby'. 'It's over now. You have to put it behind you.'

'Yes.' There was a sad lack of conviction in Faith's voice.

'Would you like to talk to somebody else about it? I met Brian on the way over here. Don't worry, I didn't tell him anything. But he's got eyes in his head. He's worried about you. He'd listen.'

'Perhaps I should have asked him before.'

'Are you feeling . . . you might have made a mistake?'

Faith stood up and shrugged her shoulders. Though she was not a tall woman, her upright poise made her appear unexpectedly commanding. 'We never know, do we, how we are going to feel until we do something. If I had not done it, I would be sick with fear now, as I was feeling before. But I have done it. It is like a hurricane. You have to pick up the pieces of your house and build it again.'

'I was worried . . .'

Faith even smiled. 'I am a strong woman, Dr Jenkins. It is difficult sometimes, in a foreign country. I do not always make myself
understood. But you have been very kind.'

She could have done this without me, Margaret thought. She has
the courage. What I did wasn't really necessary, only kind. To Faith,
if not to her baby. Yesterday I didn't know that. Would I have acted
differently if I had?

The printout with its pristine snowdrop would not have been
lying in her drawer for Maurice to find. But had that really changed
anything? For the two of them, love and jealousy were already facts,
waiting to be spoken.

Margaret sat with the telephone on her desk, her hand feeling an
almost physical compulsion to reach out and lift the receiver. It was
such a small desk, in the narrow study the university provided. She
could not move the telephone out of her line of vision. There was
no need to lift the handset and phone Brian. Faith would be in when
he called. The mere thought of his visit made her want to turn her
neck and look between the trees of the campus to the slope of the
distant park. In an hour's time, would he come cycling across it, too
far away for her to recognize his slight boyish figure? Yet she would
know it was him, she was sure of that.

She must not phone. It saddened her to think of Ruth now as a
dark dragon, guarding her lair. They had been friends. Brian would
have swept Margaret along to rehearsals and then left her to sink or
swim in the terrifying milieu of a youth club; it was Ruth who had
held her hand, taught her by example the simple questions you
could ask to get a conversation going, made her more truly human;
it was to Ruth she owed her changed relationship with Laurie. It had
needed more than Brian's music to connect her to her son.

She thought of Laurie's alert eyes at breakfast-time, his diplo-
matic awareness when he closed the bedroom door on them last
night. Laurie understood almost everything. He did not condemn
her.

What of Ros and Jake? The older children had flitted in and out

191

briefly at Easter, as student offspring do. What would they see when they came home in the summer? Would Laurie tell them? Would it be written plain on Maurice and Margaret's faces for them to read? Would they, more conventional than Laurie, judge her differently?

She had no doubt now that there was something to be judged. She was in love with Brian. It was as simple as that. She had stopped carrying Ian's hard brown stone around with her. It hadn't changed anything. She could not give Brian up, nor he her. They simply could not pretend that Hy had never happened and take up the work they had left off. It did not matter that he no longer came to read poetry to her in the window-seats. That he had once was a delicious fact she would hug for ever. Every time she saw him, it was as though he had just walked out of her presence for a moment and returned unchanged. Since he had held her in his arms in Columba's hermitage, she knew what those afternoons had meant to them, what they had always meant. She floated in a dream between the times when she could see him. Maurice was right to be jealous.

Feeling so helpless was a kind of joy. She had surrendered. She couldn't stop it, and nor could Brian. There was no way to kill love. Was this how drugs made you feel, floating above the ground on a haze of sunshine, seeing the possible ruin of your own and other people's lives and scarcely caring?

Her fingers tightened momentarily about her pen, as she blocked out the sickening dread of Maurice's anger. Amazingly, she felt reckless and happy.

She laughed out loud. Reckless, her? Almost all her colleagues would assume that if she and Brian were in love, they would go to bed together. What a coy phrase. In biblical language they would 'know' each other. Know each other's bodies, intimately. She was immediately aroused, imagining them naked, caressing each other. She had never allowed herself to do this before. She wanted him, she could not deny it. It was more than poetry and teacups. But there had been nothing more than his arms around her on a Hebridean hillside, her tearful face against his shoulder. There never would be. Just once, to remember. It must not happen again. She would not let it.

Her hand crept towards the phone. She drew it back again. Then she gathered up her lecture notes, snapped her briefcase shut and walked briskly down the corridor, disciplining her thoughts to the Peasants' Revolt.

She was coming down from the high of this morning, approaching her own front door with sick apprehension. Brian had not gone away, but nor had Maurice. Her head tightened with the shocked realization that she was close to wishing he would.

No. It was this conventional home, on a conventional estate, her conventional husband, that she still wanted. Ian was right. It was the picking up of that other, far less glamorous stone that counted. Carrying its weight every day. Never letting go of it. That was the hard test she had failed today, the daily renunciation. She had let Brian enchant her all over again. She had no right to skip like a little girl to the laughter in another man's eyes and still want to come home to this ordered life.

But her home would never be so safe again.

On Wednesday afternoons she worked at home. Brian knew he could always find her alone at teatime, ready to talk, to listen.

He would not come today, or any other day. She must work through the long tense afternoon, waiting for Maurice to come home, wondering what she could say to him.

The key in the lock made her jump. She had not expected him so early. She came nervously down the stairs and checked on the half-landing. Laurie grinned up at her. The sight of him was disorientating.

'Oh! It's you.'

'Who were you expecting? Or is that an indelicate question?'

To her horror, she felt herself blushing. 'Only your father.'

'I'm always home before he is. Hadn't you noticed?' He was staring at her with renewed interest. 'You've changed since Hy. You look ten years younger. But nervous as a kitten. What was all that with Dad last night?'

'Just a misunderstanding. One o'clock in the morning isn't the best time for processing new information.'

'Information about what? Or aren't I allowed to ask?'

'You're seventeen. You can ask whatever you feel you need to. I'll make my own mind up whether I answer.'

'Does that mean you're not telling?'

'There's nothing to tell. We cleared it up. It wasn't what he thought it was.'

'This has got to be to do with Brian. Dad's found out.' It was hardly a question.

The blush would not go away. 'Brian and I have a working relationship in the church. That's all.'

'And I'm a Teletubby.'

'Laurie!'

'You don't fool anyone. I told you, the guys all know. It comes of having an honest face. Me, I could have a future with MI6.'

She came down the last stairs slowly. 'I like Brian. I don't deny that. He's the best thing that's happened to this church. But I like Ruth, too.'

'And Dad?'

'Of course I love him!' Too loud, too defiant.

'Is Brian leaving?'

'*Why?*' The question was swift, urgent.

Laurie shrugged. 'We were asking him about doing another musical. He seemed a bit evasive. I mean, he's had a ball with this last one, hasn't he? It wasn't just us. He loved it. There's got to be a reason he put us off.'

She must not let herself talk about this. It was strange, this was one of the longest conversations she had had with her son for a long while. And, this time, she was not the one dragging information out of him. Yet the subject was too dangerous. The fear of what he was suggesting was struggling to make itself heard.

'He's only been here two and a half years. They usually stay seven.'

'Not if Dad and his lot have their way. They're always complaining about the way we mess up the premises since Brian took over.'

'That's just because there are far more of you teenagers than there used to be, and you *do* more. It's what we have church premises for.'

'I know that. But Dad's Property Committee don't seem to share your enthusiasm.'

'I know.' They grinned at each other. 'Put the kettle on, there's a love. I missed teatime.'

His voice rose above the rushing of the tap. 'What will you do if Brian goes?'

'What will *I* do?' Long colourless days stretched out ahead of her. 'What I've always done.'

'You wouldn't. . . ? No, I guess not. You call it your Christian duty, don't you? Stand by your husband. Keep the home fires burning. Don't cause a scandal. I'm nearly grown up, you know.'

'That'll be the day.'

'And you wouldn't ever leave, because it would hurt Dad? He's pretty hurt now.'

'I couldn't help that. He has no reason to be.'

'Just because he's never going to catch you two bonking?'

'Laurie!'

He handed her a mug of tea. 'What would you like me to do when he comes home? Referee? Make myself scarce?'

'You know, you're not as completely devoid of sensitivity as I've sometimes thought.'

'I have my moments.'

'I think . . . maybe he and I need to talk, though I haven't a clue what we can say.'

'Not "I love you", apparently.'

'But that's the point, about last night. We do. It wouldn't have happened if he hadn't loved me.'

'You just remembered it a bit too late.'

'I hope it's never too late.'

Laurie put his mug down, as tyres crunched on the gravel.

'Good luck.' He bent and kissed her swiftly, then sprang away upstairs as Maurice's key turned in the lock.

Margaret stood in the kitchen doorway, watching the front door

195

open. Normally on a Wednesday, Brian would have gone and she would have been back in her study upstairs. She could not remember when she had stopped going down again to greet Maurice.

He came in slowly, almost warily, as though he were trying to appear a smaller man than he was. He was holding like a trophy before him something coned in florists' wrapping-paper. Margaret felt a small smile of pity inside herself. He's bought me flowers! When was the last time he did that?

Maurice started when he saw her standing so near him. He looked not only nervous now, but embarrassed. He thrust out the gift to her, as though anxious to be rid of it.

'For you.'

Now she could see over the lip of the patterned paper. It was not a bouquet, but a white cyclamen in a green plastic pot.

'I thought I'd get you something that would last. Cut flowers only end up on the compost heap after a week.'

'You're right. Thank you,' she said.

'If you keep the top of the corm dry, they'll keep blooming for decades.'

She kissed his cheek shyly. Love is not like that, she thought. It doesn't improve by being kept dry.

The gift handed over, Maurice seemed relieved, as though the problem had been settled.

She had been nerving herself to say 'Do you want to talk?', but she saw that he did not. He had seen, probably rightly, that words held the potential for more abrasion. Instead, they would resume a physical proximity, hoping that the severed edges of the wound would heal together, without festering, without too ugly a scar.

Laurie will be disappointed in us, she thought wryly. He's expecting a flaming row or a passionate reconciliation, not a cyclamen in a plastic pot. She weighed it in her hand. It was quite sweet, really. An unpretentious, growing thing. Long-lasting. Brian's love was a stone to be discarded, or a weight she must carry. Love for Maurice was something organic, capable of renewal. A pot plant is not as romantic as a bouquet, but practical, companionable.

She set it on the kitchen windowsill and began to prepare supper.

Is this all? Only hours ago, Maurice accused me of having sex with Brian and aborting his child. Now he gives me a potted plant and he thinks it's back to normal.

She had forgotten to offer him a cup of tea. At the sitting room door, embarrassment overtook her, too. A cup of tea was a smaller restitution than a cyclamen. Maurice looked up from the sofa.

'Sherry?' He reached towards the rosewood cabinet.

Margaret was mildly startled. They shared a sherry before Sunday lunch. It was not a weekday ritual. This, from Maurice, amounted to a celebration, a grand gesture. She smiled as genuinely as she could.

'Please. I'll just turn the gas down under the potatoes while you pour it.'

When she returned, she sat down in the armchair at right angles to him. At once, she wondered if this was a mistake. Should she have settled beside him on the sofa? They were proceeding by small symbols, like the opening moves of a chess game. But perhaps, after all, this was Maurice's prelude to a serious talk.

He lifted his glass to her and smiled. 'I see the dahlias are coming up,' he said. 'I'd better get some slug pellets.'

She sipped her sherry, feeling her life hung suspended. If this was a celebration, she did not know of what. Nothing had been resolved.

30

That Friday evening, Margaret stored the leftovers from supper in the fridge, switched on the dishwasher and found herself untypically wondering if there was anything watchable on television. It was a long time since she had been free to relax like this at the end of the week. It was mostly gardening programmes, she seemed to remember. More interesting to Maurice, but at least she could sit with him, companionably.

Laurie was standing in the hall, hands thrust in the pockets of his leather jacket, looking impatient.

'Have a good time,' she said, and resisted the temptation to add, 'and don't be late back.'

'Aren't you ready?' His voice had an aggressive rise.

'Me?'

'Friday? Youth club?'

'The show's over. The fat lady's sung. Well, Annie has.'

'You mean you're not coming?'

'You can walk. You don't need to take your drumkit now.'

'It wasn't the car I was talking about. *You.*'

Margaret stared at her son, as though he was talking a foreign language. 'The show's finished,' she said again. 'That's all I was there for, to help with the story.'

'It wasn't. You were there because Brian needed you to get everything right. Not just the *facts*. He trusted you.'

Her cheeks flamed. 'Well, that's over. No more rehearsals. Normal service will be resumed.'

He kicked the carpet with his toe. 'I thought you'd still come.'

'Laurie Jenkins, let me get this right. You're saying you *want* your mother to come to your youth club?'

His turn to flush. He glanced shyly up at her through thick, dark eyelashes. 'Yeah, well. It's not as if we do anything we wouldn't want you to see.'

Her heart melted. Perhaps rebellion was only a signal for help. He didn't really want her to cast him loose.

'I was never cut out to be a youth club leader, as such. I only came for *The Exile*.'

'Yeah, but it's different since we did it. Sort of, like, everyone's closer. I wish I had gone to Hy.'

She wanted to hug him and kiss it better, like a little boy who has missed a party.

'I'm glad it was special for the others. I wasn't sure about Lucy and co.'

'Lucy's just a big mouth. You don't want to believe all she says. But she took to you.'

'Me? She made me feel like something the cat's brought in.'

'Yeah, that's Lucy. But you let her say it and you didn't walk out on her.'

'You can hardly walk out on anybody on a small island.'

'You're walking out on us now.'

'I'm not! I'm not even in.'

'You were.'

He turned and fumbled with the door catch. 'What'll I tell Brian?'

'You don't need to tell him anything. He won't be expecting me.'

'Oh, no?'

'No. Definitely not. It's over.'

'Suit yourself.'

The door gave a small slam.

What have I done, she thought; did he really mean they need me? I can't believe I've let him down.

It was ridiculous to think that anybody would miss her. She must not let herself even think that Brian might. He could not possibly be expecting her.

Maurice was watching a wildlife programme in the sitting room. He looked up quickly, like a child eager to please.

'Fancy that! Did you know that foxes would just as soon eat fruit as chickens?'

She looked through the uncurtained windows into the shadowy garden. 'A lot of things aren't what we think they are.'

'That doesn't make sense. If you think they *are*, how do you know they're not?'

'Revelation,' she said, giving a half-smile into the twilight. 'You come to a thin place and the truth steps through from the other side.'

She sat in the armchair and watched the screen with him. Hawks swung across the sky, but the commentary passed her by unheeded. A few streets away, in the church hall, there would be loud music thumping, teenagers dancing, the clatter of table tennis balls. Ruth would be moving efficiently about the kitchen, preparing drinks. Brian would . . . She reached for the small brown stone from Hy she had put back in her pocket. She gripped it tightly and concentrated on the credits scrolling up the screen across the sunset-flecked sky.

'Where were you?' One of his hands warm and strong round hers, the other clasped over both their hands, imprisoning her. He would not let her go. She must stand in the church doorway, feeling the warmth flood through her being, with Maurice just behind her.

'The show's finished. You don't need me.'

'Tim was asking for you.'

She saw that thin pasty face, which the Hebridean winds had whipped into temporary colour. Felt him clinging to her hand in panic as Ian treated his wound. The shine in his face after the lights and the music and the applause. It had astonished her then that Tim gave her any importance. That he still needed her had not been part of her thinking. The young ones' need of Brian had been paramount. She knew she must do nothing to endanger that. She must keep away so that he could stay. It had not occurred to her that anyone would think her own absence was a loss.

She drew her hand away. Ruth was watching. She greeted Margaret with a steady smile.

'We were a bit short-handed. It's easy enough to get volunteers for the crêche, but most people run a mile when you mention teenagers. I can't think why.'

'I can. I was terrified. I never knew what I was supposed to do.'

'Not a lot. It's just being there. That's what makes the difference.'

Margaret was acutely aware of Maurice still behind her. He and Brian seemed to be greeting each other normally. It was incredible, as if that bizarre explosion in the middle of the night had so embarrassed Maurice that he had buried it hastily, was denying the whole thing.

Even Ruth seemed to be inviting her back. Did that mean it was over? All that jealousy, suspicion?

Ruth and Maurice are grown-up people. Life has to go on, no matter how hurt you are, so it's better to pretend the uncomfortable bits of it don't exist. You couldn't cope if you kept on taking them out and examining them.

She looked back at Brian's face as he released Maurice's hand and turned his smile to the next couple. She and Brian were more like children. They wore their hearts naked in their faces. Perhaps this was what poetry did for you. Truthfulness was what made poetry resonate. A handful of words that said what no one else would nerve themselves to.

I love you.

That should have been unsayable. Brian was a poet, so he had said it.

'I suppose I could come this Friday, if you still want me.' She clutched the brown stone in her coat pocket.

'Good. We're playing skittles at The Cat and Fiddle.' A brief, efficient smile, and Ruth went off to the choir vestry.

Margaret went thoughtfully into church. This was not what she had planned. She had meant to keep away from Brian, avoid the occasion for their paths to cross, go back to the unemotional life she had led before he came. But Hy had changed other lives besides hers. She understood now why Ian had directed her to choose this other stone and keep it. There were things that could not be thrown away, that would be with her always now. They were her responsibility.

She closed her eyes and prayed for strength. She must tread a narrow dangerous shore, between the jetsam of the teenagers' needs and the ocean of her love for Brian. This would be a hard walk, the sand giving way under each step, the waves always threatening to turn and rise.

The balls thundered down the bowling alley. Ribald cheers greeted Tim's score of two. But he punched his fist in the air and looked pleased to have achieved that much, bowing to the cheers as if they were genuine. Rick followed and demolished the lot.

Margaret stepped outside to let the evening air cool her cheeks. There were enough adult bodies around for the moment. Maurice had even agreed to fill a place on the coach. It had seemed like a lifebelt on the beach.

'I can just imagine what the last generation would have said about this. Taking a Methodist youth club to a pub!' Brian's voice came warm behind her, thrilling her with its unexpectedness and risk.

'Oh, I don't know,' she said, striving to keep a firm footing in fact. 'When Boulton's first chapel was built in 1835, the women who scrubbed it for the opening got paid with beer.'

'You're extraordinary. How do you know things like that?'

'I've got a jackdaw brain. It picks up any little shiny bits of information and stores them away in its nest.'

'I wish I could get into that nest. It must be very beautiful.'

'Don't!'

He did not apologize, and silence fell between them. Summer was on its way. It was nowhere near dark, yet the first stars were adding their faintly shining magic to the evening. Coloured lights around the eaves of the pub had been switched on. Other customers lingered over the tables and benches out of doors.

'It's not enough,' Brian said. 'I feel soul-starved.'

'It's all there can be. Even this is too much. Ruth or Maurice could come out any moment.'

Brian turned away like a spurned dog, and walked back into the pub barn. She almost saw his ears and tail droop. He was so ridiculously like Tim. He would never grow up.

Yet always that reminder that he must daily come face to face with sorrows she would never have to absorb. He had a right to need solace.

He had Ruth.

He wanted someone to share a delicacy of understanding and delight, to wonder over the poetry of the present and stories from the past.

You're not important.

To some people, astonishingly, it seems I am.

She turned her head to the lit skittle alley in the barn. Laurie was seated at the piano, with a row of Coke bottles on the top, filled to different levels. With his right hand he was playing jazz, with his left he skittered a stick along the bottles in a xylophone accompaniment. How does he do that, she marvelled, do the two halves of his brain work independently? His face was alive with the challenge of performing in front of his mates.

Brian's eyes met hers across the barn. He winked. This was their shared achievement. She laughed back.

31

Margaret moved in a heady scent of lilac. Her arms were full of flowers, white, mauve, purple, freshened by contrast with the tender green of their leaves. Wimbledon colours, she thought. Summer.

Yet crossing the church car park on Saturday morning seemed like a dangerous journey across no man's land. Beyond the privet hedge, the manse stood like a command post. Might Ruth, sentinel at a window, spot her?

That was ungracious. Ruth had been magnanimously accepting of her.

I didn't have to volunteer to do the flowers, just because somebody's ill. I ought not to be here alone.

Brian will be taking Saturday off, won't he, or else at home, writing his sermon? There's no reason for him to be in church today. There's nothing in the diary.

She hardly knew whether fear or desire was winning the argument in her head.

She had Maurice's key to the side door. It was awkward, with her arms full of lilac branches. As she bent to fumble with the lock, her hair tangled in the twigs. When she pulled her head away, there were petals caught in the strands.

She pushed inside, into the dim corridor that led to the little cloakroom. She must pass the door to the minister's vestry. It was closed.

Tension sagged into relief, which she must not acknowledge as disappointment. Brian wasn't here. For all that aura of sacred space he carried around him, he never physically shut himself off from other people. If he was working at the church, his door would always be ajar. It was an invitation to anyone to put their head round, 'Can I just have a word?'

So many hundreds of people wanting him, here or elsewhere: church members and attenders, students at the college, hospital patients and staff, prisoners, anyone with a death in the family, or a wedding to celebrate, stewards reporting a leaking roof or a vandalized window, the catering volunteers wanting to know the date of the harvest supper, someone diagnosed with cancer.

She checked outside his vestry door, staring at the blond, blank wood. So many demands pouring in on him when he opened that door, or lifted the telephone, or answered the manse doorbell. How did one person bear it on such narrow shoulders? Prayer, of course. He couldn't do it alone. But she knew how easy it was to take refuge in a platitude. It was possible to pray and not feel the instant comfort of God's strength.

What about herself now, in middle age? She remembered the golden days of her youth, when the whole world was fresh and heaven newly discovered. She had fallen in love with Christ, as with a bridegroom. New-spun psalms had flowed from her in poetry. She had walked through the countryside, rejoicing in creation. She never wrote poetry now.

And she could no more keep up that level of spiritual ecstasy than she and Maurice could sustain the passion that had brought them to marry. She smiled even now to think of passion and Maurice. We all change. Loyalty is what counts, after the flame dies down. An act of will. You stay faithful to your husband because you made promises to each other when you were on a high of love. You committed yourself. You go to church, though the wonder and the revelation aren't always there.

But how much harder is it to preach conviction to others, when you no longer feel it sharp-edged in your spirit? To go on comforting the bereaved, if your own faith is edged by doubt that this life may be all we have?

She shook herself out of the aching anxiety for him and walked on. It was vain of her to think Brian was no better than she was. If she spent the hours in prayer and Bible reading he did, with that professional discipline, those urgent needs driving him to his knees, maybe her own faith would still be vibrant, deep-felt. She had no right to question his closeness to God.

The cloakroom at the end of the corridor was hardly more than a cupboard. A sink, a small counter, shelves of vases. She picked a deep earthenware jug, filled it with water and began to arrange the sprays. The morning sunlight slanted in through the window and made the white lilac brilliant. The purple retreated into sombre shadow.

Holding it steady, she moved into the corridor. Too late, it occurred to her that it would have been more sensible to do the arranging in the church itself. It was hard to see where she was going, through the fragrant stems, and her carefully set angles could not survive the journey down this narrow passage.

'Persephone rising from the underworld to bring back summer!'

Water splashed the front of Margaret's jumper. It was not just a figure of speech to say that her heart leaped.

'Gwen's got shingles. I had my arm twisted to do the flowers, but I'm not really into all that stuff with Oasis and wired stems.'

'These are lovely. Do you want me to carry them for you?'

'No. I'm trying to preserve what I hope will pass for a reasonably tasteful arrangement.'

'I'm in your way.'

'Yes.'

Brian's hand reached sideways and opened the vestry door. She thought he would step into his room and free the way ahead for her, but he stood in front of the door. She concentrated on the fact that the wrist of his navy blue guernsey was fraying.

'Please. I can't get past.'

'I know.'

'*Brian!*' A whisper that sounded like a cry of defeat.

His arms went round her and the jug and the lilac, gently encircling them all. He bent his face over the top of her head. 'You smell delicious. There are petals like confetti in your hair.'

'I shall have lilac twigs up my nose, if you don't let me go.'

His strong hand took the handle of the jug away from her and lifted it all through the vestry door to set it on the carpet. She could have escaped then, though she would have had to return to rescue the flowers.

His hands circled her waist and drew her to him. As their bodies touched, she clung to him. He lifted her, unresisting, into the vestry and shut the door behind them.

'No, Brian. What if someone comes?'

He strained her to him, stroking her hair. 'What if they don't come? Isn't that what we're asking each other? Margaret. Margaret.'

Her arms were round him. She was trembling. Passion was not dead, with him.

He went on kissing her face, her hair. She pressed herself close to him, knowing she wanted more. It would be so easy for her knees to give way, to pull him with her to the carpet.

A stab of reality pierced her. Was this what she would bring him to? It hardly mattered whether anyone saw them. The fact would exist. The minister and a member of his congregation, locked in lust on the floor. The jug overturned, the lilac crushed. Her unglamorous pants discarded among the broken petals.

He was holding her with a fierce hunger, but his hands had strayed no further than to stroke her hair and shoulders. She did not know which of them might be the stronger.

Wearily, with an enormous effort, she pushed him away. 'I love you,' she said, unable to help herself. 'I love you. It isn't that.'

He slid his hands down her retreating arms and held her fingers. 'I'm glad. I know I shouldn't be, but I am. It's selfish to have the love of two good women, and to hurt both. One of you ought to be enough.'

'It's just our age,' she laughed shakily, aware there were tears on her cheeks. 'A bit early for the physical menopause, but a change of life. Families growing up . .' Too late she realized what he had never had. 'I'm sorry!'

'I've got a bigger family.' He smiled sadly.

She bent to retrieve the disarranged lilac. 'They don't look too bad.'

'They're beautiful.' He held the door wide for her.

As she walked on, into the open golden space of the church, she heard his door close tight behind her. She tried not to think of him seated at his desk, his head bowed, face hidden in his arms.

She walked fast, uphill. Anything to make her body hurt, to outrace the thoughts tumbling through her head. It could not have happened. It *must* not have happened.

But it had. She stopped suddenly, her body shivering with the memory of it.

There was open ground ahead. Not the well-kept park that sloped down to the university and Faith's lodgings; this was a remnant of common land at the top of the hill. Sandy hillocks were covered with gorse and brambles that had snagged windblown litter. Rough grass grew between. It was not beautiful, but it was high, clear, windy.

She climbed the highest mound and stood there, let the breeze tug at her short hair. Her hands were thrust deep in her pockets. She took lungfuls of fast-moving air. The horizon swung around her vision, blurred with tears, and steadied. Her fingers found a stone.

She took it out and laid it on the palm of her left hand. Dry, the colours were nothing. Light brown, marbled with white. She searched it for some speck of quartz that would dazzle in the sunlight. There was none. Plain, ordinary, just a pebble.

It came from Hy. No one looking at it would know that, but she did.

The hard, cool evidence of resolve.

Oh, God, I'm sorry!

She pushed away the thought that it had not been entirely her fault. She had not initiated it. They seemed not to be able to help it, this complicity, the delight in the same things, the shared humour. To be together was to find themselves matched, fitting perfectly into each other, as their bodies . . .

No! She began to walk fast again, stumbling on bri
grass, risking turning her ankle in a rabbit-hole.

It could not go on. If she could not help it, if neither of th
help it, something would have to be done.

Yet they *had* stopped it. Though they could not again disg
desperate longing, they had been strong enough, true eno
break apart before anything happened.

Before anything happened . . . The urge of her body, passi
against his. That had not been nothing. She stirred even now.
would not be able to see each other without knowing the fe
their bodies pressing so close towards union. 'Knowing' each o
in the biblical sense, which should lead to the terror and beauty
childbirth.

But, with them, could not. Must not.

She stopped again, realized she was still gripping the stone.

How could she end it? It would have been simple if she were
single. She could simply move. But it was unthinkable that she could
confess this to Maurice. No amount of contrition could outweigh the
hurt. And what possible reason could she give for him to change his
job, or even for them to move house?

Did that mean Brian would have to go? Because of her?

She thought of Laurie, of Tim, of Lucy, those ranks of eager
faces on the stage. The pride, the memories they were stacking up.
She looked at the plain brown stone. She could be strong enough
for this, couldn't she? But the young ones? Without the glamour, the
attraction, all the things which had drawn her, as well as them, to
him – how would they survive? Would they just drop a plain, brown
stone like this back on the beach and walk on, forgetting in a year
or so that something wonderful had ever happened?

He must not go.

On the way down the hill, a simple thought struck her.

I could just change to another church. The Quakers, maybe?

She went up the front path with a lighter step. Maurice came
round from the back garden, his hands earthy, his face anxious.

'Oh, you're back. I was getting worried. I thought you'd only
gone to arrange a few flowers.'

209

'That didn't take long. You know me. Stick them in a jug and hope for the best. I went for a walk on Barrow Top.'

'It's put roses in your cheeks.'

She took his arm and steered him into the kitchen. 'You know, I've been thinking. Kids leaving home. Fresh start, all that. I'd like to try out a different church for a bit. Get a new perspective. United Reformed, Quakers. I might even sample the Catholics. Would you mind?'

He hugged her shoulders. 'If you're saying what I think you are, it sounds like a good idea.'

She kissed his cheek. 'I think it's best, don't you? I'm glad you don't mind.'

'I'd come with you, but you know how it is. Property steward, all that. Can't just hand over my keys and walk out on them . . . Talking of which, does that mean you won't be going on the youth club ramble tomorrow?'

Margaret's hand flew to her mouth. 'You're right. I promised.'

There were too many ties binding her to him. She could not easily walk away from Brian.

She did not trust herself to be near him.

32

'I wonder why it is that teenage boys don't walk.'

Margaret followed the nod of Ruth's head along the straggling line of figures winding around the side of the dale. Brian was striding far ahead, closely pursued by Tim, who was eager to keep up with him, but still looked hardly more than a child. There were plenty of girls on the ramble, stepping out in their white trainers, scorning the hoof-marked mud. Their cheeks bloomed with health and energy, and the wind teased their hair. Some way behind Margaret and Ruth, Maurice was keeping up an avuncular banter with the slower ones such as Lucy. Ruth was right. A significant element of the club was missing.

'I see what you mean. Laurie turned up his nose. Said hiking wasn't cool. Looks like he's not the only one.'

'Zak and Jon always turn up, whatever. They come from that sort of family. They're a tower of strength to Brian . . . Sorry! I didn't mean your . . .'

'No need to apologize! Maurice's assessment of Laurie is far more colourful, I can assure you. I've sometimes had this odd feeling, wondering if he was a changeling. We're a sort of mirror image of children who can't believe they've got their real parents. Ros and Jake weren't like him They were always half-way civilized.'

'Don't get me wrong. Laurie's great. When he gets on the drums . . .'

'That's Brian's doing. But he's definitely not one for the great outdoors. Still, he's sorry he missed Hy . . .'

The wind seemed to snatch up the name. She found she could say no more. Nor could Ruth. They walked on, picking their way in single file round the grassy contour. Below, the rushing of the river filled the silence.

Why am I walking with her, Margaret wondered. I can't be up in front with Brian, of course. He wouldn't even want me just now. He's happy on his own today. But I could have fallen back with Maurice, or be chatting to the girls.

It was almost as if Ruth had wanted this space to talk with her, as their distance from the others lengthened before and behind.

'We're . . . next year.' Ruth in front did not turn her head and Margaret lost the vital verb. She hurried to close the gap between them on the narrow path.

'Sorry. I missed that.'

Ruth tilted her face sideways, mouthing louder into the wind.

'Next year. We'll be moving on.'

The words were too imprecise. They might not mean what they seemed to.

'What do you mean, "moving on"? And who's "we"?' Margaret even managed to laugh.

Ruth must mean the youth club programme. Some new idea of Brian's. Not . . .

'Brian's told the stationing committee he'd like a transfer to another church. If nothing comes of that, he might even look outside the circuit ministry. There was a prison chaplaincy advertised.'

Margaret stared back, wide-eyed. The narrow sheep track broadened into a stony path. She caught Ruth up. She was still too scared to take in the enormity of what she had just heard. There were too many urgent questions, questions she dared not ask Ruth. This was just what she had decided must not happen.

'We'll miss you,' she managed, with lame understatement. 'The kids'll be heartbroken. Brian's made such a difference to them.' It was incredible that she should be mouthing such conventional politeness. All her careful resolve was crumbling into nothing, faced with the reality. *He can't leave!*

'There'll be other teenagers. Even in a prison. *Especially* in prison.'

It was true. Margaret could not pretend her son, her church, her town, needed Brian more than anyone else. *He is irreplaceable. What will happen to Laurie?*

'When's he going to tell them?' *Does anyone else know? Why couldn't he tell me himself?*

Ruth's usually controlled face looked confused. 'I'm sorry. I may be speaking out of turn. The District Chairman knows, but he hasn't broken it to the stewards yet.' She looked at Margaret in urgent appeal.

'It's all right. I can keep a secret.' *So why did you tell me? Is this your revenge? You can take Brian away from me and there is nothing I can do about it.*

You were going to leave the church yourself.

Maybe Brian had wanted her to find out this way, too afraid to break the news to her himself, yet not wanting her to learn of it from others. Was he taking shelter behind Ruth, his faithful dragon?

But he doesn't need to go. *I'll go.*

The pain of what both of them had now committed themselves to do hit her. Was it already too late?

The sound of water roared in her ears.

They dipped down to the river and spread themselves across the slope under the trees to eat their picnic lunch. The water went churning over boulders, leaping down falls, all rush and power and noise and white foam.

'Look!' called Jon. 'There's a red squirrel!'

They followed its springing progress through the branches. The flame of its tail whisked over the grey boughs and in and out of the yellow-green leaves of early summer.

'That's the first time I've ever seen one of those,' Margaret said, wondering at the steadiness of her voice. 'I thought the greys had won and the reds were only in children's story-books now.'

'Don't give up on magic. You can still find it if you look for it.' Brian's voice came from above her. '*The angels keep their ancient places . . .*'

'Turn but a stone and start a wing.'

I'll always remember this. The last day I was happy. It wasn't much I had, but Brian was there. Beauty, colour, companionship. Before the grey drove out the red.

Annie, Zak and others of the older group were balancing long-legged across the wet boulders mid-stream. The sun glinted on them through the leaves like spotlights.

'Be careful!' shouted Ruth. 'If you fall in there, you'll be half-way down to the Humber before anything stops you.'

Annie waved casually, as elegant as if on a fashion camera-shoot, with the falls leaping behind her.

Maurice rose uneasily, glancing back at Brian. 'Shouldn't some-body stop them?'

Brian doesn't recognize danger. Or he gets a buzz out of it. People could get hurt.

'They're more sure-footed than we are,' Brian laughed down at them. 'Don't you remember what it was like when you were young? The trouble comes when you grow up and start being afraid.'

'It's kids' lives you're playing with. We're responsible.'

Ruth stood up. 'Annie! Zak! That's far enough. Come back.'

Zak reached out his arm across the gap to Annie, who took his hand like a princess. Hearts in mouths, the adults watched her spring across the churning rapids to land on the sloping slippery rock beside him. Obedient but confident, the teenagers came step-ping back the perilous way to the bank. The river raced on behind them, sunlit, unexplored.

It was almost over. Sandwich wrappings were being put away in knapsacks. Brian hoisted himself to his feet and reached for his stick. The line was reforming. Margaret felt an aching need to fall into step beside him. So much hurt. Why? You can't go. You must-n't leave us. If anyone leaves, it should be me.

It was already too late. Brian and Ruth had acted. The machin-ery of Methodist bureaucracy had been set in motion. Once Brian had formally asked the District Chairman for a move, he could not easily take it back. She had no say in that decision. She had no right. He was not her husband.

She caught his eye, across the golden-brown carpet of last year's beech leaves. They might have been the only two people in the wood. He saw from her stricken face that she knew. He grimaced shamefacedly, a little boy's expression of apology.

It must have been an hour later that he dropped back, letting Ruth and the older girls take the lead. It no longer seemed natural when he fell into step beside her.

'You might have told me.'

'I was too scared.'

'You know what you're doing? If you walk out on us . . . the kids . . . all this . . .'

'I'd be doing harm by staying. I couldn't promise not to.' He was checking unhappily before and behind, to see if Ruth or Maurice were in sight round a curve in the leaf-hung path. Why should it grieve her that he was at last behaving like an adult?

'But I was going to move to another church. It'll be my fault if you go.'

'*No!*' He reached across and swiftly kissed her. She shook from the unexpectedness, the unfairness, of it. 'No. Never say that. *I'm* the weak one. You know that. All the time you're here, a few streets away . . . I need you, but I can't have you. And I can't live so close, not having you.'

'So everyone else has to lose you, too? It *is* my fault.'

'Margaret! I'm not committing suicide. Boulton isn't the only church with teenagers.'

'Laurie . . .'

'Laurie leaves school this year. He's nearly grown-up.'

'As if!'

'Margaret, do you think I can still work with Maurice, pretending you don't exist? Knowing your front door is only a few minutes away? I can't stay. Don't ask.'

'I didn't.'

'It sounded like it.'

'I was trying to show you just how much it will hurt. And I only wanted to help you!' Her voice was rising dangerously.

'I didn't want to hurt you, anything but that.' He was walking too

215

close to her. 'But I'd hurt everyone by staying. I can't hide how I feel.'

'Half a loaf would have been better than no bread at all.' She had lowered her voice, but it shook in spite of herself. 'I was willing to live with that.'

'You're stronger than I am. I've fouled it up.' He turned his head. His voice changed, professionally. 'Lucy! How are you doing? Blisters?'

'I've gone and split one of my trainers. Look.'

Brian knelt beside her. Lucy looked from one to the other of them. Her eyes glittered briefly with a smile at Margaret. Her face was knowing, but not entirely unsympathetic.

'I've got sticking plaster, bandages, a prismatic compass and a bar of chocolate in my knapsack. But glue, no. Have some chocolate instead?'

'Bloody countryside. Cost me a bomb, they did.'

Brian coaxed her, limping, along with them. Thus chaperoned, they came in sight of Ruth and her party, waiting for them by a stile at the end of the wood. Margaret fell back behind Lucy and Brian. She was thankful when Maurice appeared, urging the stragglers on to close the gap. There was banter when the group was reunited, discussion of the best route back to the car park.

It was all over. The dull reality of it descended on Margaret like a fog. There was nothing more she would have the chance to say to Brian. The news would soon be broken to the church, to the youth club, to her family. There was nothing she could do to stop it, no one else she could even talk to about it. Too late now for the more persuasive arguments forming in her head. She had had one brief chance. It had not been enough.

33

Her hand hovered over the telephone. Though she had often wanted to, she had never found the courage to ring him before, but now her world was shaken to pieces. She had to talk to someone. Yet she was afraid of him, afraid of his hard, loving clarity. She had placed the brown stone from Hy on the desk in front of her. She cupped her left hand around it now. It felt cool, firm, pounded into smoothness by Atlantic storms and the grinding of its rough edges against other stones thrown upon it. What had emerged, cast up on the beach for her to find, was not notably beautiful, except as each pebble is uniquely textured, coloured, shaped, holding its history for those with insight to read. Margaret herself was not remarkable and yet unique.

She picked up the phone and dialled the number from the leaflet beside her. The lilt of a Scottish voice answered her like distant music. She had to swallow before she found her own voice.

'Can I speak to Ian McGregor, please?'

At once she realized how unlikely it was that he would answer. There were so many places he could be – out and about on the island talking to tourists and fishermen, busy with a session on Celtic spirituality for a visiting party, in the cathedral church, or at work out of doors, in the monastery gardens, the garage. Just so would Columba have been at work in his abbey fourteen hundred years ago, give or take a pick-up truck for the old white mare.

'Yes?'

The sudden decisiveness of his voice startled her. For a moment it drove all thought of what she wanted to say out of her head. She gathered her scattered wits together and stammered, 'It's me, Margaret Jenkins. I was on Hy in April with . . .'

'Margaret! Great to hear from you. How did the musical go? That's some great wee singers you have there. Annie, now. They're still talking about her here.'

'Annie's fine. Yes, the show brought the roof down. You should have seen Tim, he was so proud. Do you remember . . .'

'Of course I remember Tim. Does he still put on a limp to impress his friends?'

'I don't think he needs to now. He impressed them anyway in the show. He really did.'

'I'm glad.' The warmth in his voice was genuine. He let a silence fall, then, 'You weren't ringing me to tell me about Tim, were you? How are things with you, Margaret?' His voice had slowed. She felt the power of it, even through the receiver.

'It is about Tim, really. All of them. I've messed it up.'

Again a pause. 'How?'

She told him. It seemed like a betrayal to talk about the lilac and the vestry. Did she have the right to confess the actions of one minister to another? It was herself she wanted to accuse.

'He didn't *do* anything. Just held me and stroked my hair. I was the one who wanted him to go on. At least I didn't; neither of us did. We stopped ourselves. But we couldn't stop ourselves wanting.'

'And you're thinking, *Whosoever looks on a woman to lust after her has committed adultery with her already in his heart.*'

'Something like that.'

'And was there intention in Brian to commit adultery with you, or you with him?'

'No.'

'Intention is what counts. To long is not the same as to lust. It hurts the one longing a lot more. Lust hurts the other.'

'But we shouldn't even have done what we did.'

218

'No, you shouldn't.'

'I've got your stone in front of me.'

'Hold on to it. It's hard.'

'But now he's going away. He's ripping himself out of the lives of all of those kids. And they *need* him.'

'He's given them something they'll never forget. It's them he's left his seed in.'

'But it's my fault. If it hadn't been for me, he'd stay for seven years.'

'Why are you ringing me, Margaret? What did you think I could change?'

'I needed to talk to somebody. There's nobody else.' She poured out all that had happened with Maurice, with Faith, the abortion.

'Poor Margaret. You've had a rough time. Do you ever wish Brian had never come to you?'

'No. . . ! I suppose I ought to. Maurice wouldn't have been hurt, or Ruth.'

'Ruth will weather it. She's strong. She has Brian still. And maybe it's pride for her that she keeps what another woman wants. She's the winner, not you. And Maurice seems to have hurt himself because he didn't know you as well as he might have done. You didn't deserve that. There was no baby from Brian, and there never could have been. You both decided that, there in the vestry.'

'We decided that on Hy.'

'So what is it you're asking me?'

'I suppose, if there's any way I could keep him here. Make him change his mind. I've already said I could go to a different church.'

'Brian's a grown man, though he honours the child in himself. He knows his strength and his weakness. He's made his decision. He and Ruth. And you've said yourself, he's told his Chairman. It's done, Margaret.'

'I can't go on without him. I couldn't even trust myself to write.'

'You can go on. People do, all the time. Bereavement, exile. Do you remember Columba's song?

'*Isn't it delightful to rest on the breast of an island, on a peak of rock? To gaze out on the calm sea?*

'*To watch the waves roll in over the glittering ocean, chanting music to their Father on the eternal round?*

'*To know the ebb-tide and the flood-tide in their turn?*

'*This is my name, this is the secret I tell you, "I am he who turned his back on Ireland." '*

It was Brian's words he was singing to her. Her own voice took up the strain:

'*It is good to feel repentance break over me as I gaze on God's creation, to give voice to my grief for many sins, so hard to speak.*'

And his answered, '*It is good to bless the Lord who has power over all, Heaven with its host of angels; earth, ebb and flood-tide.*'

The music of the waves was in his voice, pain turned to beauty. Only now she remembered how his wife had left him.

'Ian, I'm sorry! I never thought. You and . . .'

'Jeanie. I've got my own stone, Meg. Sometimes I need to hold on to it.'

'I've been incredibly selfish.'

'No. I'm a chaplain. This is what they pay me for.' There was a smile in his voice.

'How do they teach you to be the sort of person people talk to? To feel they can open up their troubles and pour the whole bag in your lap and expect you to sort it into some sort of order?'

'*They* don't teach us. God does that.'

'Brian has it, too. If he hadn't been like that . . . If they hadn't drained him, so that he needed somebody else to make him whole again . . .'

'You were his soul-friend. A sister-confessor yourself. Now you see why women who did that were often nuns. Shut up in a cell like Julian of Norwich or running an abbey like Hilda of Whitby. The nun's habit is a defence, like a nurse's uniform. You may fall in love with her, but there is a barrier of authority.'

'Being a laywoman is messier. And a wife and a mother. Laurie knows about Brian and he doesn't even seem to mind.'

'Laurie?'

'My son. He plays the drums.'

'I'd like to have heard that,' he laughed. 'You're full of surprises. I took you for a staid academic when I met you in the monastery museum.'

'I've surprised myself.'

'And it was Brian's doing. Would you have been helping to write a rock musical, getting alongside bairns like Tim, giving your son an opportunity to play his drums for God, without Brian?'

'No.'

'He's changed you as much as he's changed the kids. You'll never be the same again. He's left his seed in you, too. And that wasn't adultery. Don't blame him too much.'

'I didn't . . .'

'You wanted to blame somebody, didn't you? Yourself, Brian, fate. You had what you had. Hold the stone, Margaret. It won't go away.'

'Hold yours, too.'

'I will. And if you ever need to talk . . .'

Professionally, he was closing the conversation, just as Brian had always leaped to his feet after half an hour. She had come closer to this chaplain, but not that close.

She gave a little laugh. 'What's Maurice going to say if he finds out I'm phoning another minister, on Hy? He'll think I've got some kind of fetish.'

'Look, since you've made contact again, it's crossed my mind a few times that what you were all doing was too good to keep to yourselves. There's the script of *The Exile*. Other clubs would love that. And then there's the way you told those legends to the kids. Of course, it's all in the sources, but a good story's always worth retelling. I've a publisher in mind and we've got the monastery shop to sell them.'

'I've never thought of myself as a storyteller. I write academic papers, of course, but they don't count.'

'Don't count? Well, maybe they don't sell as well to the tourist trade. Think on it.'

'I need to think on something.'

'God bless you, Meg. I'll pray for you, all of you. Give my love to Tim. And keep in touch.'

She put the phone down. Under her other hand, the plain brown stone had grown warm.